MW01100824

OCEANVIEW
THE BEGINNING

By

Josh Sadovnick

ISBN: 1-4140-2494-0 (e-book)
ISBN: 1-4140-2493-2 (Paperback)

Library of Congress Control Number: 2003098254

This book is printed on acid free paper.

Printed in the United States of America
Bloomington, In

1stBooks – rev. 11/20/03

Dedicated to the people of Hatikvah whose stories changed my life.

CHAPTER 1 – THE BEGINNING

It was an eerie night out in those woods, one where all you could feel was the cold and darkness that surrounded you. Not a sound could be heard from the lush forest, which was usually alive with its vibrant colours and countless animals that called it home. The rich green of the leaves and auburn of the bark were replaced with a slick blackness that reached deep into one's soul. What during the day was a peaceful stretch of nature, which beckoned people into its protective boundaries, had quickly become a dark abyss that housed the worst of nightmares. Once the sun set and the warm flickering rays of orange light made way for the thin night air, the forest transformed into a sinister and deadly place that was dangerous to all who dared enter.

Charles had arrived in the small British colony only a few months ago, but had become very accustomed to his new surroundings. Although he would never consider himself to be an expert on the area or to hold the key to all its secrets, he knew enough to manoeuvre easily through it, at least during the day. Charles was an active boy who had moved grudgingly to the New World, and found his only happiness while searching what, to him, was the great unknown. Most justified his unusual desire for getting lost in the thick of the woods as a way of adjusting to his new life. Had the term been invented in this era, his daring feats would have been summed up as a part of his adolescence. No one quite understood why he loved to swim in the crashing ocean, or tramp off alone through the massive oaks in the forest. While his parents had hoped that upon reaching the age of fifteen he would start focusing more on his chores and obligations than his wanderings, they did very little to deter their son's curiosity.

Several hours ago, Charles had been excused from his lessons in the small one-roomed schoolhouse located on the highest hill in the relatively new colony. While he saw it as being excused, the reality was much different. After he'd dazed off during the day's lesson and caused a few minor disturbances such as verbal fights with the ancient schoolmaster, it was more of a permanent expulsion. Charles, on the other hand, saw this as an opportunity to depart from the stuffy old classroom and venture into the woods that intrigued him so much more than the names of King Arthur and the deeds of great knights who once ruled the British Empire. The thoughts of bizarre native rituals taking place deep within the expansive forest, which he had overheard some of the adults recently speak of, drew him towards his next great adventure. Charles went to his home and grabbed his hunting gun. He was unsure what to expect if he found any of the 'uncivilised' people who gathered deep inside the woods, but he wanted to be ready for anything. If nothing exciting occurred, he would at least be able to shoot some game to be brought home to his parents for supper. This might get him off the hook for his unexpected dismissal, even though he was sure that it was not his fault.

Charles' parents were both hard workers from England who had been out in the fields attempting to cultivate the land; 'their' new home, as Charles constantly stressed. If they had seen their son depart they would have warned him against his foolish desires to explore the woods and force him to take up extra chores to make up for his lack of discipline. Or, at the very least, warn their only child about the dangers that lurked in the darkened corners of the great forest that surrounded them all.

Alone and totally unknowing of what was to come, the boy ventured into a vastly different world.

Charles had explored for some time before stumbling across a small group of natives, who were busily preparing for something. Charles hid himself in some nearby bushes, praying that he would prove to be like his father, built like an ox, who could single-handedly take on a group of these so-called 'savages'. He had heard stories from countless people both here in Oceanview and back in England about the horrendous things these native people were capable of doing. He had heard tales that these people never bathed, that they sacrificed their young, and bit the heads off live animals. But as he looked secretly upon this small group, all of these stories began to melt away to reveal the truth. Charles pushed his long brown hair out of his eyes and stared intently at these unique dark-skinned inhabitants.

Each native wore clothing made from the skins of dead animals, almost like a suede or leather, which was a tanned colour. On some, there were patches of fur that hung close to their skin to offer protective warmth. A few females were wearing a feather or two, tucked snugly in their hair, almost like a natural ending for a braid. A strange grooming technique for a people, who were supposedly uncivilised, thought Charles in fascination at his discovery. All of the natives wore an assortment of wooden and bone jewellery around their arms, ankles, and necks. Each piece was crafted with greater care and skill than the crown jewels of England, which Charles had once seen. As an outside observer, Charles did not understand why this small group was picking up stones and pine-cones, but his attention was fixed as though the careful collection of these objects was the most important thing in the world. It was clear that these people were not savages or uncivilised. Charles quickly understood that they were just different.

Charles felt his leg begin to fall asleep from the strange position he was squatting in; he needed to stretch so he could rid himself of the numbness. While he tried to move silently, he clumsily toppled backwards onto a large pile of dead leaves and twigs. The natives froze in their positions and listened carefully. They understood the dangers of the forest and knew of the things that lurked in the dark gaps between trees. Raising a bow and arrow, poised in the ready position, the eldest of the group looked around his immediate area with a calm that emphasised the seriousness of the situation. Charles felt his heart beat rapidly as a shiver of fear ran through his body.

Within a moment the native caught sight of the awkward boy, who now had all the colour drained from his face. The man said something in a language Charles had never heard before and motioned for him to stand up. All the while the sharpened tip of the arrow was aimed at the heart of the frightened youth. Feeling rather dumb and peculiar, yet full of frightful anticipation, Charles rose from his position on the ground and stepped cautiously towards the five natives standing before him. He could feel his heart racing, and a nervous sweat trickle down his scalp as he stepped from his hiding place. Charles was in such a frightful state of nervousness he completely forgot about the gun strapped over his shoulder.

The native with the arrow pointed at Charles and said something to his companions, which was followed by a round of laughter from all the natives. Charles felt his ears go red as the laughter increased, but then felt great relief as the arrow that could have killed him instantly was lowered. The natives did not know the language of Charles nor Charles the language of the natives, but through the use of hand-signals and the odd familiar sounding word, they managed a basic form of communication. The eldest pointed to the sky and warned of the impending darkness. He insisted that Charles follow them back to their camp, for he knew that if the young boy were left alone in the woods he would surely be lost. Still unsure if he could trust these strange new people, Charles followed the group, whom he later learned called themselves the Wampanoag.

Soon all six arrived at a large clearing that contained many tents arranged in a half circle, made of the same material as the Wampanoags' clothes. In the centre was a large fire with people gathered all around it. It was immediately recognizable as a celebration, yet it was unlike any Charles had ever seen before. As far as he could make out, the eldest male who had led the group was someone of extreme importance, possibly the chief. The celebration was some kind of tribute to a beautiful girl. Judging by the interaction of the man and this exquisite young woman, Charles assumed that she was his daughter. By the pictures in the dirt, illuminated by the fire, Charles discovered that she was named Moon Light Seeker and this celebration was in her honour. Charles smiled at Moon Light Seeker and she smiled warmly back. She had long jet-black hair that complemented her brown complexion. She wore a dress made of the same animal skin as the others, with a bright white necklace made of some strange type of bead that shimmered in the firelight. Her smile sent sparks through Charles, and when she gave him a necklace made of the same beads as she wore, the white boy turned a deep shade of red.

Music was played, dances were danced, and food, unlike anything Charles had eaten, were all a part of this celebration. Charles smiled and enjoyed the festivities more than he had ever enjoyed Christmas, yet as the night carried on he felt a strange type of homesickness for his family. After several hours, the boy realized how late it was. The grandness of the party and the warmth of his hosts had made Charles blind to the darkness and cold that surrounded him and his newfound friends. His parents must have been extremely worried by now and, regardless of the discoveries he had made, they would be very upset and angry. Quickly Charles thanked Moon Light Seeker and her father and stumbled away from the Wampanoag tribe. The elder tried to stop the boy, but he was stubborn, as most fifteen-year-olds are. The man tried to explain that he would arrange for a guide, but the language gap and Charles' determination to get home made this message impossible. The native left to find a guide for Charles, someone who would escort him safely to the limits of their land and the beginning of his, but when he returned the boy had vanished into the darkness.

The night was colder and darker than Charles ever remembered; he felt as though he was trapped in a murky blackness that went on forever. He was beginning to realize that his parents were right in their warnings. The forest was a dangerous place. If Charles had not already known what fear was, he definitely knew now as he sped through the unnaturally crisp night air. Charles had heard stories of people entering the forest at night and never returning, in fact he had known people who had vanished. The fear that this reality might befall him was causing his legs to work even harder as they carried him deeper into the night in the hope of safely reaching his home. Instead of things becoming familiar, Charles found that everything was becoming more twisted and confusing. Soon he could no longer tell if he was getting closer to the town or further away.

Without any sense as to how long he had been running, Charles found himself in a clearing. He looked all around for something familiar, but he could see nothing other than a few dim stars above his head. He paused to catch his breath and smelt something foul. Although he had never smelt it before, he knew instinctively exactly what it was. The stench of death was all around him. The longer he stood, the more he realized that the stars above were fighting a losing battle. A great darkness was overwhelming them and clouding them from sight. The night rapidly grew darker and the air became so cold that his nose was being nipped by frost.

Out of nowhere, a howling wind blew past Charles, sending a shiver up his spine. The animals, which had been making the occasional sound, quickly stopped all noise and movement, as though they anticipated that something evil was about to happen. The scared boy drew his gun from where it rested on his shoulder and prepared it in case of attack by some ferocious unseen animal. The fear he felt was tenfold what he had felt as the eldest native held him at arrow point. Slowly and carefully, he headed across the clearing to find a path on the other side that might take him home.

Suddenly, a large animal leapt in front of the boy. It was much bigger than a dog and showed teeth that shone a majestic white in the darkness. The beast growled and shook its wild mane-like hair. Its shadowy shape paced several feet in front of the terrified boy, as though it was contemplating which part of him would be the juiciest. Charles took a step away from the beast, who responded with a low bark which rose from the depths of its being. Finding an unknown courage, Charles fired his gun at the beast, but missed due to the incredible shaking in his hands. The creature that had looked so terrifying howled towards the unseen moon turned and ran back into the woods from whence it came. Charles gained back some of his lost composure and felt a great sense of pride, for he had scared off the horrific creature that could have easily devoured him.

"I believe that animal was trying to lead you home," a thickly accented voice commented from behind, causing Charles to jump in surprise. Slowly, he turned, and saw an old man standing with his arms crossed. He was wearing a large black hat and a cloak that covered his entire body. In his outstretched skeletal hand he held an old lantern filled with a dim glow. The man looked down at the boy with only his eyes glimmering in the yellow light.

"Lead me home?" Charles asked confused. He could tell by how the man spoke that he was from

England; he had a similar accent to his grandfather's, but for some reason that didn't seem to be comforting. "I'm not sure what you mean, sir. I think he was planning on eating me…Please…Are-are you from Oceanview…sir? I'm lost and I need to get home." As Charles spoke, he could feel deep within that something was not right.

"No, boy, I am not from Oceanview. However, I have been there many times." the man said nonchalantly as he began to move as though in thought. "Home, such a strange idea, don't you think? A place where you curl up underneath a thick warm quilt and feel all safe and cozy. I always find it amusing how you young ones think a four-walled box of timber and the loving naiveties of your precious parents will keep you safe. Perhaps the creature *was* going to rip the meat from your bones. But I think she was trying to protect you, as best as any mother could. Yes, protect you. You see…some friends of yours who live deep in these woods sent her; I believe they call themselves the Wampanoag. They hoped she would save you from the most dangerous being one can find out here."

Charles tried to ask what the most dangerous thing in these woods was, but he had a feeling he already knew. He was staring at it. The boy tried to scream for help. To make a sound, any sound. Yet all that escaped his lips was a feeble whisper that even the man five feet in front of him could barely hear. Frozen, the boy stared at what he knew to be the manifestation of evil.

The man smiled, showing his teeth that seemed to grow jagged and ferocious. "Don't trust what you see child...stupid, stupid boy. Scaring away that that was meant to guide and protect." The man dropped his cloak to reveal himself growing in size. His skin began to glow in the darkness as it changed from a light, fleshy pink to a dark, leathery red. His ears began to point and his long, thick, bright white hair flowed in length until it pushed his hat right off his head. A pale yellow horn began to protrude from the top of the man's scalp and extended until it reached a piercing point.

Charles forced himself to scream as he turned and ran towards the edge of the clearing. It took all he had to move, but it was all in vain. He was only a few feet from safety when he felt a prickling sensation swarm around his body. His feet began to lift off the ground moments before he spun violently to face the demon the old man had become. Orange sparks trailed from the tips of the creature's outstretched fingers until they exploded in an icy eruption around Charles. The large hand began to motion for the boy to be brought closer and sure enough Charles floated towards what he felt was the end. Once the two beings were face to face, the monster's eyes began to flash a brilliant red as Charles was painfully dropped to the ground, where all he could see was the creature's claw-like feet.

With each flash from the eyes of the monster, Charles felt himself grow weaker and weaker. He began to feel a wave of exhaustion rush through his body, and any desire to get up was quickly replaced with fatigue and hopelessness. His mind began to clutter with the final screams of people he had never heard before, while at the same time being wiped of all conscious thought. Charles closed his eyes to try and rid himself of the noise and pain, and he began to float while fighting off the urge to throw up. He slowly opened his heavy eyelids and saw his body slumped on the ground beneath him. His head flopped back as he felt his very soul enter into the icy body of the demon.

Once the soul of the adventurous boy was fully inside the beast, he released a deep, blood-curdling roar. All the once silent animals ran in open fear of this hideous noise. He turned and entered into the darkened forest, as the trees themselves seemed to move out of his way.

Shortly after the demon departed, another boy crawled cautiously into the clearing. He had been sent into the woods with nearly half the colonists to find the missing youth who had disappeared earlier that day. Slowly, he reached out and touched the lifeless body on the ground; it was the body of the boy, the body of his best friend. He had seen everything, but was too scared to help, too frightened to move. He let out a cry, bringing many of the nearby colonists to his aid. A sweeping silence fell upon the crowd as they saw the body of the once vibrant youth.

That was almost two hundred and fifty years ago.

Welcome to Oceanview.

CHAPTER 2 – WHO AM I?

To explain who I am is pretty complicated. It would probably be easier to raise the Titanic. You see, I don't really know. The only thing I am sure of is that I am unique, because there really isn't anyone like me. I've searched. Now seems as good a time as any to tell you what makes me so, well, 'special'. As far as I can figure, I'm not really alive. But at the same time, I am definitely not dead! You could say that I'm somewhere in between, just floating in a type of limbo, trapped in a place that isn't really here, or there. As cool as that might sound, you have no idea how many times I've wished to be on one side or the other.

My life is pretty simple for someone so complex. Obviously I have no family; that much at least I know. Or at least I've never met a family member, and I can't remember having parents. In fact, I can't remember anything other than one day waking up and being like this. I don't have any friends, but I guess that's understandable since no one can see or hear me. I am completely invisible, and I think the word is 'intangible'; that means nothing can touch me. I pass through things, from walls to people, as easily as you walk through air. There is one exception to all this. Although people can't see or hear me, animals can...I think. Whenever I'm near animals, whether they're as shy as a cat or as tough as a bear, they go nuts. They act totally freaked out. I think I give them that feeling. You know, the one that makes the hair on the back of your neck stand up. It would definitely explain the howling and growling I get from even the most docile squirrel.

Let's see, what else...I don't have to sleep and I don't have to eat, which is probably a good thing since I would have a little bit of trouble doing either. Then there are the little things. I have no idea what I look like, because being invisible means I have no reflection. I wish I did, because then I could figure out how old I am, for sure I mean. I have a gut feeling that I might be a teenager because I seem to understand them the best. Only catch is, I've been around for a really long time and I have no idea if I age like a normal human.

I'll be honest. It's not all bad. There are a few things that I can do that most people only dream of. I can fly, and walking through solid objects is pretty cool. At first, I loved just flying in circles and walking through, well, pretty much everything. But after a while, it sort of loses interest.

You can probably imagine by now that my life is pretty lonely.

I try to keep myself busy in this small town where I live, if you can call it living. The name of the place is Oceanview, and it is an amazing little town. You can't ask for a better location, unless you have something against huge forests and a beautiful stretch of ocean. The story says that it started off as a British colony around two hundred and fifty years ago. Then something happened and it almost turned into a ghost town, no pun intended. Fortunately it didn't, and eventually it started to grow until it became what it is today. There are a few buildings, but nothing so big that it destroys the natural beauty of Oceanview. From up high, the town looks like it holds onto the vast forest like a safety blanket, while at the same time using the ocean to stay connected to the rest of the world. Nowadays most people tend to use the highway to get out of town, but I try to ignore that. I once heard a tourist describe the town as a 'semi-isolated paradise with all the warmth of home and the beauty of nature'. How's that for a town slogan? It was adopted a little while later. I only wish the founders of the town had been a little more inspired by their surroundings and had given the town a more deserving name. Instead, since everyone had a great view of the ocean, they called it, rather uncreatively, Oceanview.

The buildings of Oceanview are an eclectic mix of old and new. Some of the houses date way back to when a bunch of rich English settlers decided to make this place home. Others are brand new. There is one section of town where the mish-mash of styles is so noticeable it looks as though you are stuck in a twisted time warp. I mean, there are these huge Victorian style mansions with pillar-like towers standing right next to monster cube homes that look like they belong on a *Monopoly* board.

That brings me to another point about why I'd like to be either alive or dead. I'm not sure if it's a giant cosmic joke, or cruel torture, but houses and I don't mix. I would love to fly through a wall and check out what a real family is like, but that just isn't in the cards. Whenever I try to enter a house where someone lives, I crash into a giant brick wall. Or at least it feels like one. Doesn't seem to matter if I'm flying through an open window or door, but as soon as I'm about to enter, wham. Right into an invisible barrier. At first I thought it was a fluke or something, but after the millionth try, you figure out that you are not welcome.

Bet your wondering what I do all day. Well, even if you're not, I'm going to tell you. Remember the last TV show you watched? Now imagine you were watching it, but it was real life, without any commercial breaks. That's what I do. Like you, I have my favourite channels and shows, only they are real people. I float behind them for a couple of days and watch their lives unfold, like a reality-based soap opera. I pretend that when they talk to themselves to work out their problems or to keep themselves awake, they are actually speaking to me. For a long time I even thought that is what I was here for…some invisible entity that people can talk to and trust with all their secrets, 'cause boy, do I know a lot of them. But if that was true, shouldn't I be able to talk back to them and let them know everything would be okay?

When I get bored with a particular person, I 'switch channels'. I refocus my attention onto another person or group of people. Sometimes I flip channels, I think you call it 'channel surfing', so I can see a couple of my 'shows' all at once. Other times I get so focused on one person I completely forget that anything else exists. Sure, maybe it seems like I'm invading other people's privacy, but it really doesn't feel that way to me. At least I tell myself it doesn't.

Remember that thing I said about avoiding that road out of town? There's a reason for that. There once was a woman named Jessica Hardin whom I'd followed since she was a baby. I have to admit, she was one of my favourites and I felt that, even though she never saw me, she knew I was around. As people do, she grew up, got married and became the mother of three little girls. It was a fairy-tale life if I had ever seen one, and I felt a part of it. Jessica was warm and caring and went out of her way to help people, even complete strangers who had just arrived in town. I can still see her smiling face and hear those sweet lullabies she sang so softly to her daughters. I would float outside the window every night listening to Jessica's angelic voice send her children to sleep. But as I knew from watching so many stories, good things don't always last. After their eldest daughter graduated from the high school, Jessica's husband lost his job at the bank.

The family had to sell a lot of their belongings and use up most of their savings just to stay afloat while Jessica and her husband both looked for work. No one in town would help them, not even those who were supposed to be their best friends; they just said that they wished they could, in superficial sympathy…even though I knew that these so-called friends could do much more. Eventually, the family had to sell their home and move to some big city far away where both Jessica and her husband found jobs.

I was so angry with the people of my town, the people I had seen grow up, that I decided to move with the Hardins. I had been in Oceanview all my life, and although the town had changed, I never even thought of leaving. That day, my delusion of paradise was blown apart. I felt disgusted and let down, like a sheet had been lifted, revealing a gross underbelly.

I watched all day as the Hardins packed their remaining belongings into a rental truck that would take them to their new home. Once they had said their good-byes and pulled away, I floated down and hitched a ride on the roof. It would have felt pretty cool sitting up there with the wind rushing through my hair, assuming I have hair, all the way to a new world. Remember that brick wall I told you about? Well, I hit it again and found another place I wasn't allowed to go or, in this case, leave.

As soon as the dark blue truck passed the border of Oceanview, I slammed into that familiar invisible barrier. The speed at which I hit caused me to go flying in the opposite direction. I landed smack down on the pavement. Well, part of me was on the pavement; most of my body was three feet beneath. As I sat there, watching a family I admired leave their home, I realized that that was another thing I would never be able to do. I can never leave Oceanview, no matter how much I sometimes wished I could. I spent a long time in hiding after that day before I could even look at another Oceanviewer. I just sat in the dark by myself, only entering the town in the early morning. When I finally convinced myself to go back, I realized how long I had been gone. A child I had been watching in kindergarten was now graduating from high school. That was a long time ago, but since then

I've avoided that road out of town at all costs because it hurt too much, but not because of the brick wall.

Well, that's a quick summary of my life so far. You can't imagine how frustrating it is to be able to see and hear everything, without ever being involved. I try to get noticed; I mean there must be someone who can see me. There must be! Too bad there's a better chance of a fly getting struck by lightning.

CHAPTER 3 – HIGH POINT SECONDARY

There is a place is town that I call home. It's the school, 'High Point Secondary,' located on top of the tallest hill. It may not have the most inspirational name, but the building sure has style. It's located in the heart of town, and from any window you can see for miles. I spend most of my time here because there is always something going on. The school also holds my most precious secret, the doorway to my world.

The building stands on the very same spot as the old one-room schoolhouse from the settler days. Since it was finished it has been renovated twice, once because of overcrowding and again when the yellowing walls started to look as though they were on the verge of crumbling. The latest version of the school is state of the art. It mixes the history of the town with the latest in technology. The building is made of the finest material, and no detail, no matter how small has been overlooked. I don't really understand the whole time thing, since it doesn't really apply to me, but the latest upgrade was finished about seventeen or eighteen graduations ago.

The walls of High Point are made of solid white brick. It is a perfectly rectangular, three-storey building, with the basement floor built right into the hill. Facing each direction is one of four towers, giving the school a castle-like appearance. Halfway up each tower is carved the giant initial of the direction it faces, making the school into an oversized compass. Atop each tower is a large crown that holds lighthouse-style beacons, but they are just for decoration. I don't think I have ever seen them lit.

Strung along the outside of the building are richly coloured crests and coats-of-arms. This makes a bright line that runs just above the windows of the top floor, breaking the monotony of the whitewashed walls. Each crest represents a different event in the history of Oceanview. In the north corner, the crest shows the landing of the first settlers, and the subsequent crests work clockwise towards the last one showing the building of the school. Coats-of-arms are in between every second crest, and they represent either an original founding family or a clan from the native tribe that lived in the surrounding forest. Spread out on the south and west sides of the building are two large grass fields that are used for a whole bunch of sports and events. Circling the field on the south side of the building is an eight-lane asphalt track.

Assuming I have counted right, which I am pretty sure I have, for lack of anything better to do, there are thirty-two classrooms, two gymnasiums (one big and one small), an auditorium for assemblies and town meetings, six offices, one cafeteria, and the teachers' lounge.

Through some intuition I know I am a teenager, so I guess it's weird that I *like* to hang around a school, but it's fun. I can pretend to really fit in. Sometimes I float through the halls and join in on the constant gossip and your general teenage fun. I also sit in on classes. I find myself an empty seat and try to sit down, which is difficult when you keep sliding right through the chair. Once I get the hovering just right, I listen to the teacher just like the other students; I also goof around like them when boredom sets in. If there is no seat, I float behind the teacher, pretending to teach the class. I recite the memorised lecture, or make up one about whatever I feel like talking about.

My favourite class is history because I get to hear stories about places outside of Oceanview, places I will apparently never be able to see for myself. Every year the teacher, Ms. Tarnal, a thin woman with wisps of grey hair and thick circular glasses, spends a week on the history of Oceanview. I haven't missed one of these classes since she started them thirty graduations ago. I listen closely, hoping to hear about a boy who became a ghost, or disappeared, or something unusual! So far I haven't found out much. Surprisingly for a town as old as this there are not many stories, just a whole lot of facts about the number of cows shipped over from England and other practical things. The few scattered tales that are interesting are usually ignored and put off as folklore or else are just really dull. No one knows for sure what it was like back at the beginning of the colony, not even the families that have lived here since then. It is almost as though people chose to forget about the really early times. But I have a feeling that one day, if I keep my eyes and ears open, I will learn who and what I am.

This morning, shortly after the bell had rung for lunch, I drifted into Ms. Tarnal's class. It was exam day so I thought that this would be a good time to see if anyone would notice me. I try this whenever there is a major test because I figure that if people are desperate enough, or just really stressed, they might notice a friendly ghost with all the answers. During this Tarnal test, you could smell the fear and apprehension in the room.

I tried my regular routine. I floated down to the person I thought was having the most trouble; I got really close and tried to move his pen to the right multiple choice answer. As usual, my hand slid right through the pen and the student had no idea I was there. Instead he was left freaking out, because he

33

decided to open his textbook for the first time last period.

If at first you don't succeed, try, try again. That's my motto. I moved even closer to the student, a panic-stricken 16-year-old who was failing most of his courses according to, well, pretty much everybody. I looked at the next question he was working on which read:

"These were the names of Columbus's ship(s)..."

An easy question, if you've sat in on a hundred history classes like me. The answer was 'B', the *Nina*, *Pinta* and *Santa Maria*. Apparently, this guy hadn't been awake for a single class and didn't notice the giant Columbus poster at the front of the room that had the answer in big bold letters. After wiping the sweat from his forehead and scratching his scalp with the end of his pen, he guessed the answer was 'C', the *Spanish Explorer*.

I could see the beads of sweat trickle down the side of his face. Just by looking at him I was getting agitated about a test I wasn't even writing. This could be it. The pen, clenched in his blood-drained fist, slowly moved towards the paper and all seemed still. The point scratched the paper as the wrong answer was about to be circled. Without a moment of hesitation I screamed the letter 'B' as though my life depended on it. Nothing. He still put down 'C' without so much as a pause. He was on his own. I truly was what most people feared to become, completely alone for all eternity. Depressed, I sank through the floor of the classroom, through the pipes and wires, and finally through the ceiling of the big gym.

Once inside, I got an aerial view of the grade nines playing basketball. Tayvn Lynch, a tall 15-year-old with short dark hair and light brown eyes, was one of the kids playing, and he was centre as always. I always felt an admiration and hatred for Tayvn. On one hand, he is the nicest person I have ever watched and by far the coolest kid in town, although he never acts like it. Truth is that he is nothing more than a genuine human being who is a friend to everyone.

Josh Sadovnick

Tayvn is also easily the best athlete ever to play for this school.

On his upper right arm, on the outside of his shoulder was a small but dark tattoo that he had had since he was very young. The design was unique and in a strange way matched Tayvn's personality. At the very centre of the tattoo was a simple circle. Points stretched from the circle in dark black, taking on the shape of a mythical exploding star, the North Star, like the ones found on ancient maps, stretching out in every direction. Everyone knew this star as Tayvn's symbol, his mark. But no one knew why he had gotten it.

Tayvn's best characteristic is that he goes out of his way to make people feel special, a trait that seems really rare. I remember once watching him play a pick-up game of basketball after school; he was a lot younger then, but he was still the best ballplayer around. There was this other kid, his name was Jaret, and he was not an athlete; I had a better shot, and I couldn't touch the ball. Jaret was always picked last and made fun of because he handled the ball like it was

36

made of concrete. But that day was different. Tayvn picked Jaret first. There was no reason; Tayvn just felt that it would be a good thing to do. For the entire game, Jaret felt as if he had a role on the court and this was solely because of Tayvn. Just before everyone had to head home, the teams decided to have a shoot-out because the game had been so close. Jaret was the first up. He missed, not much of a surprise, and everyone made fun of him. Tayvn was up later on; he took his shot, and missed. No one noticed, except me, that Tayvn missed on purpose. He didn't care what people thought or said, but he knew it would mean a lot to Jaret.

On the other hand, it was because he could do all these things that I hated Tayvn.

To feel better from the disappointment of being invisible to the kid upstairs, I decided to play a little ghost basketball. I glided over to Tayvn and started to shadow him. Every move he made, I would mimic. I had played this way so many times before that I could move with Tayvn as though we were one person. I blocked open players and shouted to my team-mates. I simulated picks and pretended to dribble, I leapt for the lay-ups and made every one of Tayvn's jump shots as though I was the one shooting.

None of it was real and I knew it. I was just a shadow that had no real purpose. It was fun to play for a while, but I was just pretending to be something I'm not. There was nothing real in it, at least not for me. When the ball was passed, it was to the human, not the ghost. All I would ever be was a cheap imitation. When a time-out was called I remembered what I truly was, and that real people live in a world I am not a part of. People didn't even know or care that I existed. I could only watch from the sidelines as they played their stupid game. Sure I knew everything about each and every player, in fact each and every person in town, but I would never be one of them.

Needing to escape from the cheeriness around me, I floated towards the entrance to my secret world.

A long time ago there was a janitor whom everyone nicknamed 'Creepy Sweepy'. He was an old guy who smelt like stale wet carpet. The stench was bloody awful. You could tell by his mossy teeth and greasy hair that he didn't take good care of himself. He had one glass eye that didn't perfectly match the brown colour of his natural one. People would stare at it, half-expecting the marble sized eye to pop loose and bounce through the halls. Creepy Sweepy never said anything other than his infamous grunt that was echoed through the halls by mocking students and teachers. To be honest, no one really cared that he stuck to himself; in fact because of the way he looked and smelled they preferred it.

Creepy Sweepy, or Alfred as I found out his name was, sparked my interest, since I never saw him leave the school. I followed him around for a few hours and found out his secret. Some time ago, he had discovered a forgotten attic. The wooden door that hid the dark creaking stairs to this space was located in the third floor hall, but matched the wall so perfectly that if you didn't know it was there, you would walk right by it. There was no handle, just a smooth keyhole sunk deep into the door, covered by a wooden latch. Creepy Sweepy somehow found the door and had made the attic into a makeshift apartment. It must have been dark and gloomy when he first found the abandoned attic. Not to mention crowded. There were tons of boxes and crates from all over town, old school equipment, props from plays, and other assorted junk that people were glad be rid of. It was a place for all the misplaced and unwanted things in Oceanview, including lost souls like Alfred and me.

Creepy Sweepy had managed to sneak a yellow couch into a section of the attic he had cleared. He had also dug up a green trunk from the Second World War that he used as a table. Gathered on the trunk were a couple cans of food that had been half eaten, and were now swarming with bugs that trailed their way over the nearby crusted magazines. The darkness had been replaced by a faint buzzing glow of light, thanks to a few odd and misshapen lamps that had been set up. Not that the lamps ever gave off more than a dim orange light, but it made the cold suffocating space into the closest thing to a welcoming home. There was only one way for the sun to get in, and that was through the skylight, but it was so coated with dirt you wouldn't have noticed the glass if you were standing on top of it.

Each night after work, Alfred would explore the contents of one of the mysterious old boxes and find forgotten pieces of history that he would organise. There was a cupboard sagging with old books, surrounded by neatly stacked volumes that would not fit on the shelves. I called this the library. Alfred discovered ancient things, from bows and arrows to old movie projectors that he cleaned and displayed as though they were in a museum. Plopped in the centre of the trunk, beneath a mouldy coffee mug, was the original manifest of the first settler ship ever to arrive in Oceanview. Written inside were the names of every family that had come to this settlement from England.

There was one box which Alfred had marked with a thick black skull and cross-bones. One night during a huge storm that shut down the entire town, I flew up to the attic to check on my friend. When I arrived in the attic, he was sitting on the floor staring at the 'forbidden box' as though it was responsible for the damage the storm was causing. Some nights my curiosity got the best of me and I would stick my head through the stiff cardboard, but it was always too dark inside to see anything.

Other nights I would float up to the rafters and watch spiders as they built intricate webs. When things really got dull I would challenge Oscar to a staring contest.

Hidden behind a broad vertical ceiling support is Oscar, an old stuffed grizzly bear. I don't know if he is real or not, but it doesn't matter. Some rich guy donated him for a play the school put on over forty graduations ago. The bear, which I named after the rich guy, is huge, and bumps his snarling head against the ceiling. He is perched on his hind legs with both arms clawing the air. By the expression on his face I can only imagine the awesomeness of his roar and the power of his gleaming teeth. Beneath the thick coat of dust and his fierce pose I always saw Oscar as a gentle beast who wouldn't hurt a fly. I could see him defending his cubs in the same way I often pictured him protecting me. [Would a male bear defend cubs, or would he be a loner?] Figures a ghost's best friend would be a stuffed old bear, but around him I always feel safe and understood.

Another great thing about the attic is that along the floor are vents that run throughout the school. These vents let you hear conversations being carried on anywhere in the school, one technological step better than those tin-can-and-string phones. This let Alfred know when people were looking for him and what they wanted. I don't know for sure, but I think Alfred used these vents to keep track of everything that went on in this place, kind of like me. Using the vents, he too could hear things he wasn't supposed to, and when he cleaned up around the halls people treated him as though he was invisible.

Creepy Sweepy disappeared about eighteen graduations ago. He was tired and sick and wanted to leave the life he knew on his own terms. One night I followed him into the woods underneath a full moon. With nothing more than an old bag slung over his shoulder holding all of his life possessions, he walked in silence. Eventually he crossed the town boundary and I had to stop. I felt a tear drip down my cheek as I watched the strangest man I had ever known vanish in a tangle of shadows. He had no friends and no one cared what he did or who he was. Except for me. Alfred was just like me and, without ever knowing I existed, he'd been my best friend. No one ever found out what happened to him.

When I returned to the attic, I adopted it for myself. My secret world away from reality. A place where I was a real person.

After arriving in the attic from the gym, I told Oscar about my day. I then floated up to the rafters to check on the silk web my spider friends were working on so diligently. Whenever I am up in the attic during school hours, there is a low rumble of noise sent up through the vents. Usually I ignore it, but this time something caught my attention. I searched for the vent that interested me and concentrated hard to figure out what was going on. The vent near the foot of the dust-covered library had sent up the word 'new girl' and I wanted to hear more.

I twisted my face so I could hear better and soon realized that it was Ms. Tarnal and Principal Kai speaking about a new student coming to High Point. She was moving here from somewhere in Canada, which is North of us, if I remember the map in Tarnal's room. I couldn't make out the name of the new kid, but from the sound of it, Ms. Tarnal was not thrilled about having a new student halfway through the semester.

Most of the conversation was echoed gibberish as the words bounced around inside the tin pipes, but I was able to pick up on most of it. This girl had a reputation for being different. She was really smart and popular, but a year ago something had happened which made her change. There were notes from her previous teachers attached to her academic record about getting into fights, and something about a fire. This intrigued me, so I followed the vent to the teachers' lounge. I was a little hesitant to enter the realm of the teachers, but then I remembered that I'm invisible, I'm a ghost, so there was no reason for me to be scared of being caught. Sometimes I get a little too carried away pretending I'm a real kid.

From my angle I could see the top of Principal Kai's fat, bald head. Kai was a short man with a bald patch that seemed to grow bigger and bigger as the graduations went by. He's pretty funny and a good man, but sometimes it's hard to take him seriously. Especially when he combs hair over his bald spot hoping no one would notice, or when he sprays what looks like black paint he thinks look like hair on the top of his head.

'… they say her grandmother, is a bit, well, off, Anne,' Kai was finishing saying. How did he know about the new girl's grandmother?

'That's an understatement, Peter. The note from her counsellor at her previous school said that her grandmother is a certifiable nut case. She believes that she is a witch, and the counsellor thinks that is the cause of the granddaughter's problems.' Ms. Tarnal was very adamant about this conclusion. '"The note said that the grandmother was seen "prancing around during a thunderstorm chanting in Latin"; no wonder her granddaughter is the way she is.'

'Witches aren't real' I added, forgetting that they couldn't hear me. But then it hit me. Isn't that what they say about ghosts?

Ms. Tarnal and Principal Kai continued to gossip about this new student for several minutes while sipping coffee. There was a rumour that the grandmother was trying some elaborate magical spell that required the bones of human beings. When a boy from the girl's old school went missing, everyone assumed that the grandmother had him. There was some sort of riot; the family's home was vandalised and the grandmother took off into the night never to return. The father decided that night to move to Oceanview; it was their only way out. Both Ms.

Tarnal and Principal Kai agreed that they should keep this story quiet so people around town wouldn't freak out and do something stupid. That was the end of their gossip session, and the two shifted the conversation towards the upcoming staff meeting.

I knew better than most people that the news about this girl and her family would spread through Oceanview like wildfire. Half the town would hear the story by dinner and the rest would hear by breakfast. I felt bad for the girl and her family, moving to a new town and already having a reputation. So much for making a fresh start. I tried to convince myself the rumour was wrong, but I couldn't help wonder if it could possibly be true. Maybe the girl was the granddaughter of a real live witch. Maybe she would be a danger to my town and a threat to the people I cared about. Then again, I'd never met a witch before, or anyone related to one. Who knew what kind of magic she could bring? These thoughts frightened and excited me. I shot straight through the ceiling and made a mad dash to the attic. Soon this new girl, for better or for worse, would be arriving in my town, and I would be waiting.

CHAPTER 4 – THE ARRIVAL

I burst through the floor and into the attic, overwhelmed with excitement. In just a little while a new girl would be arriving in town, and she might be the one to change my life. I rushed over to Oscar and filled him in on the details, and deep within his glass eyes I thought I saw a faint sparkle of hope. I knew that I shouldn't believe everything that I hear, but what if she really was a witch? It was an opportunity that was just too good to ignore. Maybe she would be no different than the countless other people I have followed, but what if she was something more?

I darted around the attic in anticipation of her arrival. I had so much energy after hearing Tarnal and Kai that I felt an uncontrollable restlessness, but all I could do was wait.

I floated past the spiders and up onto the roof. I drifted all night long beneath the clear starlit sky, getting my thoughts in order and trying to keep a level head. It was as if all my hopes and dreams were on the verge of coming true and some new stranger held the key. I didn't even know her name. I was so involved in the moment that I had a hard time remembering or even noticing anything else. All I could focus on was the conversation in the teachers' lounge; nothing else seemed to matter.

The darkness of the night slowly retreated and was replaced by a pale blue sky. I stared from the top of the school out over the ocean and watched the creeping sun rise past the horizon. The warm light painted the sky in pastel oranges and pinks as it slowly beckoned the start of a new day. Once the light had blanketed the town, the first of many lights in the nearby homes came to life. Soon, I thought, I might really be a part of their world. I was still perched on the roof of the school as the first car entered the empty parking lot. In no time each stall was filled with a car and my day officially began.

I slipped through the roof and searched the hallways for a new face, but there was nothing out of the ordinary, with one exception. The word about this new girl must have been the hot topic last night, because everyone was in a buzz over it. Some people dismissed the rumours as just that, while others were terrified by the still-unknown and unseen new kid. I entered into Ms. Tarnal's room and waited. When the girl finally showed up, this was where she would be.

The first bell rang, signalling the start of first period, but there was no new girl.

The bell for lunch rang in no time, and still no new girl.

Finally, the bell announcing the end of the day rang, and I had barely moved from my spot in front of the blackboard. But there was no new girl. Disappointed, I went back up to the roof. She was coming; she had to be. It was now just a matter of when. I watched the sunset, the lights in the homes and shops go out, and the stars poke through the blackness of the night. There was no moon.

The sun was taking its time rising out of the Atlantic the next morning, but soon it shone dimly through the thin clouds that had crawled across the sky. I arrived in Tarnal's classroom a little early. When I had floated down through the ceiling, the lights where still off and the hallway was still dead quiet. I had waited this long, a little while longer wouldn't hurt. It felt as if an entire day had passed before the janitor turned on the lights.

I was overwhelmed with the idea that this girl was coming and that she might have magical powers to make me real. Imagine, me running on the ground instead of hovering just above it. Eating food, feeling the wetness of the rain. Being able to touch something as smooth as silk or as rough as gravel. True, it was her grandmother who had been the witch, but maybe the granddaughter had some tricks of her own.

After an eternity, Ms. Tarnal finally appeared in the room. Her arrival meant that the students would be here soon and the new girl might be among them. Thoughts I had never had started to rush through my mind. Did I look all right? Did I smell okay? Was I having a good hair day? Did I have any hair? I guess I had been watching too many people go out on their first date. I'm not sure what terrified me more, meeting a magical girl who could see me, or the disappointment if she couldn't.

The students began to enter the classroom. I stared at each one from the front of the class, looking for someone new. The last one in the class was Tayvn, who sat in the back of the room near the far window. I recognised every face; the new girl was nowhere to be seen.

I moved to the back of the room and floated in one of the empty seats so I could get a better view if anyone entered the room. As I sat, I overheard a girl in front of me talking about last Halloween when she dressed up like a witch. The students had obviously been talking about the new girl and had heard the rumour. Had anyone in town not heard it? This girl spoke about how she had painted her face grey and wrinkly and stuck on fake warts.

Wait a minute. What if this girl was right? What if the new girl was a witch and looked the part…wrinkles, grey hair, and a hooked nose…just like in the movies or those posters you see on Halloween? If the rumours about her being a witch were true, what if the ones about the fights and the fires were also true? I couldn't tell if these thoughts were just nerves, but I was starting to scare myself. What if she could see me and decided to turn me into a frog or a lizard? Could someone die twice?

It was hard to be optimistic after these thoughts started crowding into my head. Every time I tried to think that everything would work out the way I hoped, I would envision myself locked in a bell jar; medieval torture would be easier to endure. I had to relax. That's what Oscar would tell me. All I needed to do was calm down. I started to chant 'relax' to myself as if it were my mantra.

What if I was wrong and I wasn't a teenager, a 15-year-old-spirit? What if I was two hundred years old and I had no skin? 'RELAX!' I finally yelled at the top of my lungs. For once I was glad people couldn't hear me.

Homeroom dragged on at a snail's pace. As Ms. Tarnal kept blabbing about some big assembly and something about the choir, I kept looking from desk to desk to see if the new girl was here and I had just missed her. But I recognised everyone. What if this girl wasn't going to show? Maybe I had just imagined the whole thing and I was actually beginning to lose my mind after all this time. I was getting impatient waiting. I needed to leave. I was just about to slide through the desk when I heard a knock on the door. Everyone in the class perked up with curiosity. For once everyone in the room — the kids, the ghost, and the teacher — all wanted to know who was on the other side.

Ms. Tarnal walked over to the door, pretending not to be interested in who was knocking. She stopped in front of the door and pushed her glasses up from the tip of her nose, straightened the collar of her blouse and opened the door. Principal Kai said a few words to Tarnal, and then waddled into the room while Ms. Tarnal stood by the door talking to someone.

'Okay, students,' he began as he cleared his throat so he sounded more authoritative. 'We have a new student here at High Point. I hope you will make her feel welcome. Sarah, come on in.'

The entire class turned toward the door where Ms. Tarnal stood, and watched intently as Sarah made her long-awaited appearance. Mr. Kai shook hands with the new girl and grinned at Tarnal, thinking that they were the only two in on the secret. With a little bit of bounce, Kai briskly left the room.

I couldn't believe it! She was here! It seemed like fifty graduations since I had found out about her, and now she was here. As she came into the room, I studied her. She was about average height, and there was this natural glow about her. It could have been nothing more than my imagination, but she seemed to shine with a confidence I had never seen in anyone that young before. Her dark blonde hair, which went down to her shoulders, shimmered under the lights. Her eyes were a magical sea green perfectly complemented by her slight tan, possibly left over from some exotic vacation. Everything about this new girl radiated with the brilliance of life. For someone who filled me with so much wonder, I was surprised when I noticed a nervous grin across her face. One thing I knew for sure was that regardless of whether or not she was a witch, she would be an interesting addition to my town. I was eager to discover the truth about this mysterious new girl whose very presence seemed to change everything. If anyone had the power to see me, it would be she.

Sarah slowly walked to the front of the class as instructed by Ms. Tarnal. She carefully placed her bag over her left shoulder as she moved in front of the blackboard. Self-consciously, Sarah stuck her hands deep into the pockets of her brown corduroy jacket and let out a nervous laugh as she gazed over the many new faces. Sarah knew nothing about any of her new classmates, but by the expressions on some of their faces you could tell that they thought they knew a whole lot about her. I turned toward Tayvn, and was surprised by the look on his face. He didn't seem to have heard any of the rumours, and if he had, he didn't seem to care. He smiled warmly at the new girl while the other kids looked more bewildered.

'Why don't you introduce yourself, Ms. Winters?' Ms. Tarnal said quietly in a tone that barely hid her own interest. 'Please tell everyone about yourself. I'm sure we are all very curious about what brings you to our quaint town.'

All new kids know right away that being asked to introduce themselves wasn't much of a request, more like a first assignment. For some new kids it was the most difficult, because it determined their social standing for life. Sarah glanced around the room and ignored the whispers. Anyone who didn't know about the witch rumours knew now.

'Uh...My name is Sarah Winters,' she stated after a short pause. 'I just moved here from Vancouver, Canada and I guess this is my new home. I've never been to Oceanview before, but so far it seems pretty nice.' The kids in the class continued to whisper about the rumours as Sarah spoke, but they still managed to take in every word, as though they had a hidden fear. Whether the fear was of Ms. Tarnal or Sarah I couldn't tell. 'And, yeah, since everyone already seems to know, yes, my grandmother was a witch and, no, she didn't try to eat some kid from my old school.'

Okay, I wasn't expecting that. Neither was anyone else, because all of the whispering stopped and was replaced with a shocked silence. Even Ms. Tarnal's mouth hung open as the secret was bluntly revealed.

'Well then...Ms. Winters,' Ms. Tarnal chimed in, unsure what her reaction should be. 'There are some empty seats in the back of the room...why don't you make yourself comfortable until the end of the period and then we will get you organised.'

Sarah smiled knowingly at her new classmates. Each one shifted uncomfortably in their seats as Sarah passed on the way to her new desk. The new girl seemed to have enjoyed shutting up all of the whispering students. As for me, I now knew that this girl was special.

OCEANVIEW
THE BEGINNING

Seat in the back of the class? I thought as Sarah walked in my general direction. There were a few seats, but she was aiming right for me. If she sat on me, it meant she couldn't see me; if she sat next to me, there was still a chance. I looked up at the ceiling and shut my eyes tight and prayed that she sat next to me. After not feeling the fuzziness when something solid passed through me, I opened my eyes. With a huge sigh of relief I saw Sarah sitting next to me. Her jacket was draped over the back of her chair and she was smiling at Tayvn, the only one in the room who thought what she said about her grandmother was more funny than shocking. Everyone else in the room still had a look of panic painted across their faces and would turn to glance at the newcomer in the back of the room. Each time a student looked at Sarah she just smiled back, causing the onlooker to spin around towards the front of the class.

'Ahem,' said Ms. Tarnal from the front of the room, trying to get everyone focused on her and the class she was trying to teach. 'Class, let's, uh, continue.   Yes…where were we…?' As the class slowly turned back to Ms. Tarnal, I paid more attention to Sarah.

Now was my chance. I tried to think of the perfect thing to say to test out if I was visible, or at least audible. I knew I should have practised during the last two days, but I thought it would just come to me. How hard could it be to talk to a girl? When you have never spoken to anyone before, it's very hard. I just sat there and stared, trying to think about what the perfect line would be. Maybe a firm 'howdy', or 'so how was your trip over?' or maybe 'so, your grandmother was a witch? Well, I'm a ghost…' No, definitely not that last one. I didn't want to freak her out, although I was starting to get the impression that would be difficult.

There was a faint humming sound. At first it sounded far away, but soon I realised that whatever it was, it was very close. Not like the noise that the lights sometimes make. This humming was softer, like music. I listened carefully to the melody as it became more beautiful with each passing moment. No one else seemed to be aware of the music, as though it was some lullaby that was written just for me being hummed by the sweetest voice, a tune that journeyed to my very centre, filling every thought in my head and every inch of my body as it played. I looked around for the source of the song that I alone heard.

It was coming from Sarah, but she was not singing it.

I felt my attention get pulled towards Sarah's right hand, which was lazily lying on her desk. On her finger was a smooth silver band that was the source of the entrapping song. It was a ring made of pure silver that was slightly thicker than I would have expected to see a girl wear. All around the outside of the ring were strange markings that looked as though they had been finely carved by a talented engraver. It was weird, but as I looked at the ring I had a strange sense of remembrance, as though I had seen this ring before. My eyes were glued to the otherwise simple piece of jewellery; meanwhile the song grew louder and louder.

While I watched, the ring began to change. The markings seemed to come alive in dance and to change. The symbols kept their distance from one another, but the lines that made each intricate shape shifted to make countless new forms. From the depth of each line escaped a bright purple glow that seemed to grow lighter and darker in time with the music. No one else even looked up at the noise or light, including Sarah. The carvings danced to the mystical melody emanating from the ring as though following a strict choreography. Everything was in sync and fit together perfectly like a great masterpiece.

I wasn't even aware that I had left my seat and moved closer to the ring. The entire world around me had disappeared and I was alone with the ring around Sarah's finger. My hand, under its own control, reached for the glimmering object and I felt a rush as the tip of my finger made contact with the smooth surface of the ring. My body filled with warmth as my finger pressed against the coolness of the silver. I had touched something! For the first time ever, I could feel. Slowly I moved my hand away and drifted back to the empty seat.

The music had stopped, but no one else was even aware that it had begun. I looked intently at my fingertip, unsure of what had happened. There was a warm purple mark where I had touched the ring. I watched the mark as it grew. Slowly the purple blotch swarmed and expanded over my entire body. But I didn't feel scared, just warm.

'Are you okay?' I heard Sarah ask, but I was too focused on my hands and arms to respond. They were covered in a dim purple hue. The glow then sunk through my skin, and for a second I felt a chill as the warmth vanished.

'Hey, buddy, everyone else is gone. The bell rang a while ago, so I think it's safe to get out of your seat. I didn't mean to terrify you with all that witch stuff.' I looked up and saw Sarah staring directly at me. She could see me. She was talking to me.

'Umm…uhhh…' I stammered in shock while attempting to say something eloquent. I just couldn't believe it. A moment ago I was covered with a purple glow after touching a ring, and now Sarah could see me and was speaking to me. I had no idea what to do. It was all too much. 'Oh, man,' I stammered, 'I...I...I have...I gotta go.'

I panicked. I didn't know what to do. I completely freaked out. I jumped through the desk and hurled myself through the closest wall. I stopped on the other side and tried to make sense of everything that had just happened. I watched the hustle and bustle of students switching classes and ignoring me completely. Having someone walk through me as though I wasn't there I could deal with. Having someone see and hear me...that was scary. I turned and saw Sarah run out of the classroom in just about as much fright as me. Her jaw was almost hitting the floor and her green eyes were wider than ever. Suddenly, the bell rang loudly and I screamed.

Moving faster than I had ever moved in my life I flew straight through the ceiling and hid in my attic.

Amidst the students in the hall, yet unseen by any of them, was an old lady who stood smiling silently in the corner. She watched Sarah and me and remained unseen until the halls had cleared. The old lady lifted her head towards the sky and spoke softly to the air. 'It has begun!' Quietly she turned down the hall and vanished.

CHAPTER 5 – IT STARTS

I ran away. I finally had a part of my truest dream and instead of seizing it, I freaked out. Rather than grabbing the chance of a lifetime, the only thing I ever wanted, I hid my head in the sand.

The whole disaster kept playing in my mind like a broken record, only instead of being the same each time, it kept getting worse. Whenever I closed my eyes, I saw Sarah sitting there talking to me. I would picture how stupid I must have looked diving through a wall in absolute terror. Then when fate gave me a second chance, I disappeared through the ceiling. I tried to pretend that I hadn't acted as dumb as I remembered, that none of it had really happened. But it had, and there was nothing I could do about it. Even worse, I probably scared the daylights out of Sarah, and that look on her face was frozen in my mind. It was one of complete fear and wonder. Her mouth was wide open and her skin as pale as death. Meanwhile her eyes were soaking up everything before her. Sarah

Winters had never seen anyone like me before, while I've seen thousands of people, yet I was the one who was frightened. I was the one who ran.

The strangest part, though, was that I'm not completely sure why I did it. Was it because I was scared of Sarah and the fact that she might be an evil witch? Or was it because the world I had always known had just been shattered and replaced with something new, a world I could only imagine?

I hid in the attic, the safest place I knew. I was scared that if I left I would be seen by Sarah, a fear I had never experienced before. Somewhere in this school was a girl who could see and hear me, and I had already traumatised her enough. I would just wait in my attic until she left the school or town, whichever came first. Alone again, I fidgeted in the dark corners of the world I knew.

After a long talk with Oscar, which was kind of one-sided, I decided that I was being ridiculous. '*Carpe diem*' Oscar would say. '*Seize the day, and if you screw up, try again. You're already dead and invisible to the rest of the world; what have you got to lose? If you hide up here, you will never find out anything.'*

Before I could try again with Sarah I needed to practice. I could not afford to be speechless. Stretching my imagination to its limit, I pretended that an old yellow lamp beneath the dusty skylight in the attic was really Sarah, and I had a conversation with it. I explained everything in great detail. I told it that I'm a friendly guy who just happens to be invisible to everyone on the planet except for her, and that I'm also a ghost trapped in Oceanview. It sounded totally reasonable and logical when spoken out loud to the plastic lamp I was pretending was a fifteen-year-old girl. After several rehearsals, I had built up my confidence, and it was time to find Sarah and say all this to the one I had always dreamed would show up. I felt a wooziness in my stomach, like a million butterflies were fluttering around, having a party I wasn't invited to. The person who might be able to tell me who I was had arrived, and I had never been more nervous. Determined to talk to her, I headed through the wooden floor and into the halls of High Point.

Everything was dark and empty. I hadn't heard the final bell ring; it must have happened while I was practising my speech of explanations. There was no one around, and an eerie silence hung throughout the halls. I had been alone for as long as I can remember, but knowing that Sarah was out there made it feel worse. I charged through the window of a classroom and circled the school in a frenzy. The sun was sinking slowly away in the distance and the old-fashioned lamps along the streets began to shine as my newest problem took form. I had no idea where Sarah lived and I couldn't exactly ask someone for directions.

Driven by a need to make things right, I took to the streets and started some hard-core investigative work, like a real old-time sleuth. I'd like to say that it took a lot of skill and intuition to find out where Sarah lived, but the truth is no one could keep their mouths shut about this strange new family, making my job easy.

If a family with a witch in it was to move to a new town and you wanted to find them, where would you look? Well, as pointed out by Margaret Cratchord, a plump old busybody who was never content unless she knew all the town's deepest and darkest secrets, the only natural place for a family like this would be the McMiller place. Or should I say, the condemned and possibly haunted McMiller place that very few people had ever stepped foot into since McMiller built it, before even I was around.

The house was the oldest in town and by far the biggest. This house was huge and had a sprawling yard full of trees, bushes, a fountain, and an assortment of balls from years of neighbourhood kids who accidentally kicked them over the encompassing wall and were too scared to collect them. Arthur McMiller, one of the richest founders of Oceanview, built his home only two years after the site of the colony was established. McMiller decided that Oceanview would be the place for his legacy, a place his family would call home for generations. Ms. Tarnal said that he arrived in a fleet of ships, each carrying treasure from his family's lucrative past in Europe. Within days construction started, using only the best possible materials, wood from the forests of North America, marble from Italy, gold from Spain, stones from England. While the rest of the colonists lived in wooden shacks of one room, the McMiller mansion was being created for a family that was yet to arrive. According to the story, McMiller spent more money on the design and building of his house than some castles in England.

Along the perimeter of the mansion stood a sentry stone fence of once sun-bleached stones shipped from Greece and stacked together with artistic grace and skill. The house had vibrantly coloured stained glass in intricate windows along the first floor, which were now covered in thick layers of dust or broken over the years of neglect. A large spherical tower stood proudly against the left-hand corner of the three-storey home and was domed with the remnants of once beautifully polished wood. Around every window and outside banister were finely crafted trims and figurines that had been the work of masters. By the time the house was finished, it was considered a work of art and quickly became the envy of everyone who ever saw it.

But the McMillers never lived in the house. Arthur's immense fortunes were lost in a few too many bad business decisions and, shortly after, his wife became very ill. She died without ever crossed the threshold of the work of art that doubled as a home, leaving it cold and empty. Arthur always thought he would get back on his feet and one day return to the house he had never stepped foot in. But he never came back. Years after Arthur died, the people of Oceanview decided that the building was cursed because of rumours that some of the stones and marbles used were stolen from ancient burial grounds and other sacred places. Ms. Tarnal said that there were once plans to destroy the building, but for some reason that had been long forgotten the house was left untouched.

The City Council of Oceanview eventually tried to sell the house, and they succeeded for a little while. It was sold to one family after another, but no one lived in it for long. It was as though the house was waiting for someone in particular and would not allow anyone else to claim it. Although the glamour of the house had steadily vanished, there was always a magic surrounding it that the entire town could feel. As the house slowly decayed, you couldn't help but feel as though within its hallowed walls was a spirit, a soul. People assumed that there was a ghost who haunted it, but no one knew for sure. The only thing people did know was that there was definitely more to it. According to Cratchord, the Winters got the house on the cheap on the condition that they fix it up. Maybe the Winters were the family that the McMiller house was waiting for.

When I arrived at the house it was already dark, but the stars and the thin sliver of the moon gave enough light to remind me why I had avoided the old mansion. The old iron gates that were once tipped with gold were rusted a reddish-brown and leaned crookedly open on either side of the cracked path leading to the house. The yard was overflowing with yellow weeds that outnumbered the dull green grass. The once impressive stone fence that had been stained with lifetimes worth of rain and grime was coated in a thick moss. Dead leaves filled every nook and cranny of the yard, leaving slimy patches of rotting death where magnificent gardens once thrived.

The house didn't look much better. Its once spotless paint job was slowly peeling away from the wood and flaking to the ground. Green vines splashed wildly along the sides of the house and pressed so hard against the walls that large cracks had formed. Some of the broken windows, and there were a lot of them, had planks of wood nailed down to prevent the cool night air from chilling the house. Where once spectacular coloured windows stood were now splotches of faded grey glass and gaping holes. Along either side of the front door was a porch that had a build-up of dust and cobwebs with signs of only recently being disturbed in an attempt to enter the decrepit house. Several of the posts that made up the railing of the porch had fallen away, leaving gaps that reminded me of an old toothless grin.

As I floated past the stone wall of the outer fence and came closer to the house than I had ever dared, I felt a change in the air. The old magical feeling that the house normally gave off was different. It had a fresh feeling that was full of life and joy, as if a long wait had finally ended. It was waiting for the right family to move into it and make it feel alive and the Winters were that family. I could sense it.

Seeing how I can't knock on the front door and ask for Sarah, I decided to fly around the outside of the old mansion and hopefully get her attention through one of the unblocked windows. The butterflies had returned to my stomach with a vengeance. There were no signs of life as I flew around the first floor of the house, and the second floor was also empty of life.

The whole house looked utterly deserted. If not for the feeling in the air, I would have guessed that this house was still empty.

I flew around the uppermost floor and noticed a light sneaking out from a room into the night like a beacon. The tower had a string of big windows that circled the outer wall, giving each of the upper rooms an almost complete view of the surrounding area. An unsealed window had recently been cleaned and opened, probably to rid the house of its musty smell. I flew up beside a large tree that stood a few feet away from the window and peered inside. Bingo! It was Sarah in what I guess was her room.

She sat quietly at a small wooden desk writing in a leather notebook. The desk looked small in the room that took up the entire floor of the tower. Other than the desk there wasn't much else in the room. There were two large duffel bags slumped near the door and a bare mattress in the middle of the room which had a sleeping bag lying on top of it. Boxes were scattered everywhere, which reminded me of my attic. Randomly thrown about the room were objects that added to my intrigue about this girl. She had a baseball bat, a pair of cleats, an old soccer uniform, sheets of music, a sketchbook that was flipped open on the bed, and a picture album lying open on the floor. The walls had the remains of aged wallpaper that hung droopily in sections of the room. Other than the old wooden desk and chair that were probably left in the house by Arthur McMiller, there was nothing in terms of real furniture.

I floated through the tree and went as close to the open window as I could, stopping just before I would be struck by the invisible force I often encountered when I tried to enter a home or leave town. Sarah was concentrating hard on her writing and didn't notice me hovering inches from the open window. I knew I'd forgotten something when I practised with the lamp…I always assumed she would talk to me first, and I had no idea how to get her attention. I decided to try the subtle 'Hi, how are you?' clearing of throat that I had seen Tayvn use once when he was trying to get a girl named Kate's attention. If all went to plan, Sarah would notice me and hopefully not get freaked by the sight of a kid floating outside her window. Since I had never been sick nor had the need to clear my throat, I wasn't quite sure how to cough, and what came out of my mouth sounded more like a moose who had just stubbed its toe on a slab of concrete than a person. But it did the trick.

Sarah jumped up from her chair and looked directly at me. There was a moment of awkward silence before she let out the most ear-piercing scream I had ever heard. The whole house seemed to shake from the sound, and I was sure that anyone near the house would be crashing down the door any minute to see what the problem was, assuming they could brave coming near a haunted house. I was stunned by her painful shriek, but even more shocked with the speed at which Sarah grabbed a baseball bat and held it over her shoulder like she was ready to knock my head off into the next town. Things were not going as I had planned.

'I'm warning you…' she hissed at me through the window. 'Come one step closer and I'll make you wish you never got near my …window?' It just then seemed to dawn on her that in order to be at her window, I had to be floating in mid-air.

'I…I didn't mean to scare you…I just wanted to, uh…say…well…Hi,' I stammered in what seemed to be the fasted sentence ever spoken. It had sounded a lot better during rehearsal. Sarah did not flinch; she just looked at me with hard eyes and held the bat tightly. Somehow I'd imagined a slightly different reaction.

'I don't know what you are or how you're doing this, but get out of here!' Sarah shouted while keeping her distance. 'My dad and brother will be back any second and will make you sorry you were ever born! They are both black belts and know how to deal with creeps like you!' Okay, so maybe this was heading in the exact opposite direction than what I had imagined.

'I just wanted to say "hi",' I said, sounding weak and defenceless. 'I saw you in school…'

'Yeah,' Sarah cut me off. 'I remember, you were staring at my ring and then flew through a wall and ceiling. Things like that are a little hard to forget.'

'About that…'

'So do you scare people and then follow them home?' I wasn't sure if that was a question or an accusation. 'I don't know what you want or…what you are…but I'm not interested!' I wasn't sure if I should turn, tail tucked between my legs, and stick to my "hide-until-Sarah-graduates plan, or try to save the situation.

'I'm sorry…' I started almost expecting her to cut me off. 'I've been in this town for a really long time and no one has ever seen me before. When you could, I didn't know what to do. I got scared.'

'I scared a ghost? That's definitely a twist.' Sarah's knuckles had turned white around the grip of the bat, but slowly she began to loosen her fists and her eyes became less harsh. 'No one has ever seen you before?'

'You're the first,' I stated flatly.

'I thought that it was my imagination playing tricks on me… I've been a little edgy since we moved here, especially since everyone thinks I'm a witch and ate a kid right before deciding to burn down my old school.'

'You heard the rumour?' I asked dumbly.

'Kind of hard not to when everywhere I go people are whispering, thinking that I'm either stupid or deaf,' Sarah was definitely neither and I knew that for certain.

'No, no trick…I was just scared,' I don't think she was expecting this when she woke up this morning. 'You know how people say to be calm when you see an animal because the animal is probably more frightened of you than you of it?'

'Yeah,' she answered.

'Well, it's true,' I smiled at her. 'And if it makes you feel any better, I only heard that your grandmother was a witch and that you had been in a fight before starting the fire that burnt down your old school.' I'm not sure why, but I could have sworn that Sarah cracked a slight smile as I made fun of the rumour that was sounding more and more ridiculous. There was another awkward silence as Sarah eased up on the bat and walked closer to the open window. I think she was starting to get curious about me.

'Grams said that I was special, but I always figured she had to say stuff like that. I had no idea that this was what she meant,' Sarah said softly as she began to smile. She took a close look at me as she fidgeted nervously with her ring. 'So I'm the first one to see you, huh?'

'Yeah,' I said trying to sound as though I didn't have a thousand burning questions. 'I can't even see myself in a mirror. All I know is what my arms and feet look like from looking down.' There was another awkward silence as Sarah stared at me from inside her room.

'Just out of curiosity,' Sarah said as she continued to check me over as though she had discovered a strange new creature. 'How are you outside my third floor window?'

'Oh, that's easy; I can fly and float through things. But I guess you already figured that part out from school,' I chuckled. 'Can I ask you something now?'

'Depends what it is,' Sarah smiled.

'Well, you see, being invisible means I don't have much of a reflection,' I replied bashfully as I looked down, realising that I might not even resemble a human. 'Can you tell me what I look like?'

'I guess that's fair,' she responded suddenly, causing me to look up instantly with a nervous smile strung across my face. 'I'd guess you're about fourteen or fifteen years old and…maybe a little taller than me; it's hard to tell when you're floating. You've got reddish-brown hair that is a little longer on the top than on the bottom, but still isn't that long. You've got nice brown eyes and a smile that looks a lot like my brother's, one of those smiles that makes me think that there is more to you than meets the eye. It sounds like you have a bit of an English accent, or at least used to have one, but I guess you know about that part.

'You might want to do something about those clothes of yours; I think they went out of style about three centuries ago. You're wearing these old fashioned clothes…brown pants…black boots…and a whitish shirt that kind of flares at the sleeves. They remind me a bit of a picture from an old copy of *Huckleberry Finn* Grams gave me. When I unpack I'll show it to you.' I floated quietly, relieved as I tried to let everything she just said sink in. Sarah had one more thought. 'How old are you, anyway?'

'I'm not sure,' I answered honestly, causing Sarah to look puzzled. 'I've been around for as long as I can remember, but I never really kept track as to how long. Let's see, maybe two hundred graduations.'

'Graduations?' Sarah asked even more confused.

'I never really cared about learning time, because it never mattered. I figured I'd just be around forever, so why keep track?' I'd never really thought about that before.

'But what about when you were alive?' Sarah asked searching for some clue. 'What was the date when you died?'

'I don't know,' I mumbled, embarrassed to admit that I had no memory of ever being alive. I felt ashamed that I couldn't remember any family or friends from my past. I looked down at my feet and grew silent at the question.

'I guess using a bat was a dumb move, since you can walk through things, huh?' Sarah commented as she tried to change the topic. 'Can you touch things if you wanted to?'

I simply shook my head 'no'. Sarah placed the bat gently on the floor and walked right to the window, reaching out towards me. I closed my eyes as the warmth of her hand begin to pass through my shoulder as she tried to comfort me, but suddenly I felt a sharp, cold pinch. I opened my eyes wide as Sarah pulled her hand out of my body.

'Well, there was one exception,' I said as Sarah looked at her hand. 'In class today I heard music coming from your ring, and I touched it.'

'Did the shapes on the ring change and give a purple glow?' Sarah asked, causing me to look up at her sea-green eyes. 'I call it the "Remembrance Song".'

'You heard it!' I exclaimed in an almost uncontrollable excitement. 'You heard the song in class, too?'

'No,' she said quietly. 'I only hear it sometimes when I need to remember someone or something important. The ring was my mom's, and she when she got sick, she gave it to me. After some bad stuff happened, the song started. When I told Grams about it she said that some things were better left a mystery. If the ring needed to sing to me, I should listen to it.

Grams is a witch and is proud of her uniqueness because it lets her understand a different side of the world. She told me that the ring my mom gave me was a special gift that would "let me see what others could only dream". Somehow, I guess she meant you...she knew that I would one day meet you,' Sarah said as her mind drifted a thousand miles away. I could see a thin tear trail down her cheek as she remembered something awful. In a moment she wiped the tear from her face and smiled faintly.

'The ring must be what lets you see me, and that might be why I can touch it,' I said trying to change the topic. I reached out for the ring, unaware that Sarah had brought it back through the window. I bashed my fingers on the invisible brick wall and let out a painful cry.

'What's wrong?' Sarah asked as she heard me wince in pain. She looked worried.

'Part of some great cosmic scheme...or joke. I can't enter into a house or even leave town without running into a really painful invisible wall,' I said bluntly, trying to hold back the tears of pain that were welling in my eyes. 'I'm sorry I made you sad just now, Sarah. I didn't know that the ring was part of a bad memory for you.'

'Don't worry about it...I never did ask what your name was,' Sarah asked suddenly. 'Seems only polite that when you scare a girl at school and then show up floating outside her room, you'd introduce yourself.'

'My name is...uh...it's...' I stammered again; I knew I should have practised this more with the lamp. 'I never really knew anyone before, so there was never a point in having a name.'

'What about your parents...oh, yeah...then as the first person to see you, I guess I have no choice but to name you,' Sarah grinned in a way that kind of scared me. 'I could call you Fred, or Garth, or Constantine...A type of name that you don't hear everyday, one that stands out...or how about Ben. That's kind of like the name of the last person to wear the ring. I think it would suit you very well.'

'Ben,' I said as though trying it on to see if it fit. It felt weird to have a title, a name, but it sounded cool. Even better was the fact that Sarah was naming me after her mom; only someone who wanted to be a friend would do that. I said it a few more times to taste the word in my mouth and to make certain that it was right. 'Done; from now on my name is Ben. Nice to meet you, Sarah.'

'Nice to meet you, Ben,' Sarah said as she reached out the window and pretended to shake my hand, but only the ring made contact. We both smiled at each other in delight; I had found a friend, and Sarah had found a mystery. 'I think I might know how you can come inside if you want to give it a try.'

'What do you mean?' I asked, surprised by her sudden comment.

'Does anything about this house seem odd to you?' she asked. 'As if it was more than just a stack of bricks, wood, and glass?'

'Most people think that it's haunted,' I replied, realising that a ghost had just told a person that her house might have a wandering spirit in it. 'No one knows for sure, but if you ask, I bet everyone would agree that there is a presence around this place.'

'Grams told me once that when you put a lot of love into something, you bring it to life. Like when you look at a painting and get a chill, or read a book that seems to be leading you in its own direction. When she found this place she thought that it might be calling to her, to us, to move in. We heard the stories, and she thought that the house was given a spirit of its own because of the care that was used in making it. If the house invited us in, maybe I can do the same.' I felt as though Sarah was reading my mind about the spirit of the house, and I think we could both feel the house giving off a warmth of happiness as the theory was spoken. 'Ben, I would like you to come inside...I mean, I want you to try and come in, please.'

I was nervous, but what Sarah said made about as much sense as a ghost and a house with a soul. As she invited me in I felt a strange cool sensation rush through my body that was quickly replaced with a warmth similar to what I felt surrounding the house. I stretched out my arms with the palms of my hands facing towards the house. Carefully I moved forward. I closed my eyes, getting ready to bear the brunt of the brick wall as I drifted through the open window.

'Uh…Ben?' Sarah asked. I was concentrating so I hard I didn't realise that she was speaking to me; I guess the name would take a little while to get used to. 'I think you can stop now.' I opened my eyes and looked around. I was floating in her bedroom door, on the opposite wall from the window. I was inside.

'How did you do that?' I was shocked as I began to dart in and out of her room, racing through the floor, out the window, up to the roof. I needed to see every dusty room in her house. I was ecstatic. I rushed through every room, passed through whatever I could as I explored the strange world of the McMiller mansion. After each room had been quickly inspected I flew back to Sarah to fill her in on what I had just seen. A brand-new world of possibilities had just been opened up to me and I needed to take it all in.

CHAPTER 6 – FROM PAST TO PRESENT

My life could not have gotten any better than it was right now! Sarah was turning out to be more than just someone who could see and hear me; she was quickly becoming my friend. The dream that once seemed impossible had now come true, and I wouldn't trade a moment of it. Sarah was taken aback by the whole experience as well; she had never imagined that when she moved to Oceanview her first friend would be a ghost. I wanted to know every detail about her life and she wanted to know everything about mine. While we talked I had a strange desire to fly into the other rooms, a curiosity I couldn't resist. I wanted to see how she lived, what made her the person she was. Sarah told me that I was being pretty obnoxious dashing through walls in the middle of a conversation, but neither of us could keep straight faces as she jokingly lectured me about manners.

'You're like a little kid, Ben,' she announced after I floated through a box, entering her room from below. 'My brother did exactly the same thing when we got here, except he used the doors and stairs. He was determined to find a secret passage or something. He couldn't sit still, and was pretty surprised when he found some junk that was left over by the old owners.'

'Is this the same brother who was going to be coming any second to beat me up?' I asked sarcastically. 'Running around like a little kid?'

'Ben,' Sarah said sheepishly. 'I kind of lied about them being home any minute...and about them being black belts. David's ten years old and about as tough as you are, and my dad, he wouldn't hurt a fly.'

'Hey!' I retorted pretending to be hurt. 'I'm pretty tough!'

'Oh yeah? I must have gotten you confused with the guy who wasn't invisible and could touch things,' Sarah laughed. 'Generally you need to be able to do at least one of those to scare people.'

'I scared you pretty well,' I grinned. 'Or was that bat just part of the normal Canadian greeting?'

'Touché,' Sarah smirked. 'Seeing how you're already a ghost you probably weren't that worried about getting pummelled.'

'Uh, yeah…I wasn't scared of that for a second…at least not of the bat. Now, getting turned into a slug was a different story…' I laughed as I floated on my back near the ceiling of her room. 'Where are they? The way you screamed, I thought your family would be up here in a flash,' I asked innocently as I fought the urge to fly through her closet to see what was on the other side.

'David was a little…will you stop that!' Sarah yelled as I was through her closet door. I quickly returned to her room and tried harder to ignore the urge to check out her home. 'You have no idea how annoying that is.'

'Sorry…as you were saying…about, uh, David?'

'He's still a little bummed about moving here. He finally made it onto a good rugby team two weeks before we had to pack up and ship out. Not to mention having to leave his old school and friends. I don't blame him, though, moving from a big city to this place really wasn't that big of a thrill. No offence.' Sarah answered. 'Dad took him out to explore before you came, to try and get him psyched on Oceanview. I wanted to write some stuff down so I stayed behind.'

'What is that, your diary?' I asked as I pointed to the leather book on her desk. I had seen the insides of girl's diaries a few times at school and they had always been interesting. Sometimes they were filled with love secrets, other times with deep insightful thoughts about life. There were also those filled with incoherent gibberish about nothing. I was very curious, if the book on Sarah's desk was a diary. Who knew what secrets it held inside?

'Sort of,' Sarah responded nonchalantly. 'Grams gave it to me before she left, and told me to write down everything that happened so when she came back she'd be all up-to-date. It's kind of corny, but I'll do it for awhile.'

'Anything about me yet?' I asked.

'Wouldn't you like to know,' Sarah answered sharply. 'You just can't stop sticking your nose into other people's business, can you?'

'I can't really do anything else,' I answered honestly. I never really thought about myself as nosy before, but I guess I was just as bad as old Cratchord. 'Unless you count staring at spiders or talking to stuffed bears.'

Suddenly, out of nowhere, I got a feeling of absolute terror, as though my worst nightmare had been given form and was breathing down my neck. I felt myself sink towards the ground as though an enormous weight had been strapped to my neck. My throat felt swollen and every part of my body seized in pain. My head was throbbing and the world around me was going dark. The words escaping from Sarah's mouth were soundless, as the feeling of extreme fatigue and hopelessness wrapped around me like a cloud of fog, blurring my sight and senses. Then, as quickly as it had begun, all of the feelings of dread vanished and warmth returned to my body. I had no idea what had just come over me, but I was sure that I had felt it before...maybe in some long forgotten dream...or life.

There was an odd look on Sarah's face when things returned to normal; she must not have felt whatever it was that had taken a hold of me. Sarah was confused by the sudden change and seemed scared that she had said something to hurt my feelings. While she thought about what had just happened in my world, I searched desperately for a way to get the memory of what I had felt out of my mind, and out of hers. There was no need to dwell on something bad when everything was going so well. I looked around her room for a cue to a new topic, when I saw a picture in a thin metallic frame lying on top of one of the many boxes piled around the room.

'Is that your family?' I asked as I floated towards the picture, feeling no remnants of the pain from moments ago.

'Yeah,' she said. 'Are you okay? You seemed to blank out a second ago, like something was wrong.' She could read me pretty well for someone who had just met me. I nodded, smiling brightly, which seemed to ease Sarah's fear, allowing her to move towards the picture. She lifted it from the box and held it so I could get a better view. She then introduced me to her family. There were four people in the photograph, standing in front of a large tree that had deep yellow and red leaves bursting from every branch. Sarah had a nice close-up in the bottom-centre of the picture. Behind her were two adults, leaning in so that their chins were beside the forehead of their daughter. The mother, Benita, whom I was named after, had brownish-blonde hair just like her daughter's and deep brown eyes; she reminded me a little of Jessica Hardin.

Sarah's mom looked like the type of mother I would have liked — warm, caring, understanding, but most of all fun. It was weird seeing all of these traits in one picture, but I could tell that I was right. Her dad, Matthew, had a slight shadow of stubble in the picture, but otherwise looked nicely groomed. His hair was dark brown and his grin made me think of a guy I once saw who could make even the worst possible situation seem hopeful.

Just above the parents was a young boy, David, who had both of his arms around his mom and dad's shoulders to help keep him suspended in the air. He had brown hair that was spiky in the front and short along the sides. The look on his face was that of someone who had just conquered the world and was not afraid to show off his accomplishment, while his eyes had a glint of mischief. There was such a happy glow beaming from this picture that I couldn't help being in awe of the people it had captured. Each member of the family had an aura of genuine love and affection as they smiled without a care in the world.

'Your mom is beautiful,' I said quietly. Sarah smiled as a silver tear formed in her eye. 'What's wrong?'

'Nothing,' Sarah said as she wiped the tear away and took a deep breath. I was in such awe of the family in the picture, I almost missed the saddened expression that had replaced Sarah's once happy smile. I floated to her side and tried to put my arm around her shoulder as I had seen people do to comfort friends. 'I just miss her, that's all. She got sick with cancer two years ago and …and …You wouldn't understand.'

'Probably not the way you do, but I think I get it,' I said, trying my best to offer her some comfort. I really did know better than she thought. Young and old, I had seen hundreds of people die, and it hurt every time. The people of Oceanview were more than just entertainment; they were my family, and when one of them died I felt it as deeply as anyone else. I always consoled myself by thinking of whoever died becoming like me and joining others in some far away land. Sometimes I wished I could join them. As I looked at the picture slightly trembling in Sarah's hand, I began to think of Creepy Sweepy and the countless others I had once known.

'Do you remember dying?' Sarah asked suddenly.

'No,' I said, almost disappointed that I couldn't answer her question with something more substantial, but I was betting it had felt a lot like that pain I had felt a little while ago. I couldn't even tell Sarah if there was such thing as heaven or hell. All I knew was that I was a ghost, possibly the only one, certainly the only one in Oceanview. It was about then that headlights flashed in through the window. It was Sarah's dad and brother. Man, was I happy they had come back and ended this part of the conversation!

'I should probably go say "hi",' Sarah said as she wiped one last silvery tear from her eye. 'I tell you what, I'll see you tomorrow at school and we'll hang out, okay?'

'Nice,' I answered as I headed to the window.

'Um…just so you know…I may not talk to you directly at school…' Sarah said after a pause, stopping me in my tracks. 'You know, so people don't start thinking I talk to myself. They already think I'm weird for asking if anyone else saw a ghost and for that whole witch thing.'

I nodded and headed back to the window before stopping again. There was one more question I had to ask before leaving.

'Are you?' I asked, trying to make it sound as innocent as I could. 'Are you a witch?'

'Me? No.' I let out a breath in relief. 'But like I said, Grams was. Although she preferred to be called a Wicca.'

'Did she eat kids like I heard… I mean like all those stupid people at school said… no, I mean…' I think I needed a little more work on being subtle.

'No,' Sarah laughed; I guess she had heard the rumours before. 'She was a retired grade four teacher. She was always interested in magic, and when mom got sick she picked it up as a way to help. Medicine

104

wasn't working and we were all desperate. After...Grams kept up with it...you know collecting crystals and stones and stuff, not eyes of newt or the bones of children.'

'But the missing kid I heard about...what happened to him?'

'Slept over at a friend's house and forgot to call home to tell his parents. Man, this town is Gossip Central!' I was about to open my mouth to ask another question when Sarah cut me off. 'Listen, not to kick you out or anything, but I should talk to my dad sometime tonight so I'll give you the five-second rundown. Dad's a writer and had serious writers' block and blamed the city for it so he decided to move us here. After Grams showed him this house he saw it as a challenge, and since he loves fixing things, this house was perfect. I think it also helped that the town was more than happy to sell it cheap. Grams went to Europe to study with some of her Wicca friends. And as for the infamous fire, it was electrical and started in the middle of the summer while I was out of town.

You see, nothing too creepy or exciting; we're just a regular family.'

'Did you ever…learn magic?'

'I picked up a spell or two from Grams, partly because I didn't believe in the stuff.' I smiled because I'm sure until today she hadn't believed in ghosts. 'I tried some of her simple spells, but nothing happened until…until I started wearing the ring. It's nothing great, but here goes…' Sarah said a couple of words as she extended the palm of her hand towards the ceiling. There was a faint sparkling light that hovered just above her palm, but it fizzled out as quickly as it appeared.

'That was…'

'I know incredible…ooh, the amazing light that resembles a sparkler for about ten seconds,' she said both hurriedly and sarcastically. 'I have to go…I'll see you tomorrow morning. Meet me by the front of school. Now go before my dad or brother walk by; I don't think they'll be able to see you and I don't want them to think I'm losing it.'

'Too late,' came a voice from behind Sarah. David was standing in the doorway looking at his sister. 'I already knew you were losing it. Who are you talking to? Dad said the phones wouldn't be working until Friday.'

'Uh, just talking to myself...' Sarah said defensively while shooting me a nasty look.

'Yeah, cause that's perfectly normal,' David retorted. 'Dad picked up some ice cream on the way back. We looked for an exciting flavour, but this town only has chocolate or vanilla. Guess it's true, boring town, boring ice cream. I'm going to bed. G'night.'

'I don't know, I think this town might have a few surprises,' Sarah said to her brother as he walked down the stairs towards his room. 'Goodnight, Grommet.'

'And say goodnight to your invisible friend for me; wouldn't want him to think I'm rude,' David laughed with a little bit of a twinkle in his eye. 'Oh guess what I heard at the store?'

'What?' Sarah and I both asked.

'Turns out I'm a werewolf…while you're still a pyromaniac witch. Can't wait to get to school tomorrow and hear what they think we did to get sent to this town.' David seemed to be enjoying the rumours being flung around town as he hopped down the stairs towards his room.

'night, Wolf-Boy,' Sarah laughed. 'If you wake up in the middle of the night covered in fur and howling at the moon, I think Dad has his razor in the box in the bathroom.'

'That went well,' I said sarcastically as I floated out the window. 'Hadn't heard the werewolf part before.'

'Shut up,' Sarah replied as she threw a pillow through my head and out the open window.

'I'd pick it up for you and bring it back but, well, I can't,' I laughed. 'See you tomorrow.' With that I flew back towards my attic where I would wait eagerly for the next day.

Meanwhile, deep in the forest that surrounded Oceanview there was another old house that was even more rundown than the one Sarah had moved into. This house, at least what was left of it, had been condemned by the town. No one knew who built the house or where the owners had gone; all that the people of Oceanview knew was that it gave everyone the creeps. The floors had caved in and the roof had fallen under its own weight. The chimney had collapsed and lay in pieces alongside of the ruin. Plants and vines struggled to grow through the cracks, but they died almost as quickly as they could sprout. Some people believed the house to be cursed, and they were probably right.

The area around the house looked like a disaster had once struck from which the land would never recover. The land had no living thing near it, as though the life had been sucked right out of the forest and the animals that dared approach the solitary house. The area was so desolate that the most ferocious animal cringed at the thought of approaching. I had only been out there once and that was not by choice. It was outside this house that I had first appeared. I always thought deep down that this was where I had died.

To say that there was nothing alive on this patch of land was not exactly true. There was one living thing — a large, flourishing oak tree directly across from where the front door of the house had once stood. Its leaves of rich green were the only source of colour in the dry and dreary land around the condemned structure. This single sign of life grew proudly in the midst of all the surrounding death and doom, but even its leaves feared to fall to the ground. That magnificent tree was the only reason this entire area had been left alone.

Unfortunately, at the last town council meeting it was voted unanimously to flatten the area and refertilize it. The day I met Sarah was the day the trucks were scheduled to knock the tree down, and end its struggle to live.

I had planned to see the destruction of the old property; I thought it would act as some form of closure, but because of the unexpected events, I forgot all about it. However, on my way home from Sarah's I saw one of the construction workers who drove the bulldozer that would tear down the tree. I was floating by him when I overheard him say that something odd had happened at the site.

The truck had driven up to the tree and tried to push it over as planned, only it took much more force than expected. It was as though something was pushing against the tree in a desperate attempt to keep it standing. The driver revved the engine to maximum speed and was finally able to rip the tree's roots right out of the ground. The tree tottered for a moment in indecision before crashing down without any resistance.

But that was just the start of the strange happenings.

The driver told his friend that as soon as the tree hit the ground it had completely withered, as though it had been dead for ages. All of the life had been sucked out of it, leaving the once strong branches brittle and weak. Immediately after the worker had destroyed the tree, a strange greyish mist rose from the ground and crept slowly towards the hole where the now-dead tree had once proudly stood. The mist began to swirl around the feet of the workers as it thickened and began to move swiftly down into the depth of the hole, like water down a drain.

Soon after, a funnel of pure darkness, which seemed to scream in a million shrill voices, shot up from the ground and formed threatening clouds in the sky directly above the bald patch of forest. There was no rain, but thunder roared overhead as lighting ripped through the sky. The bolts of lightning were drawn to the hole in the ground and struck it repeatedly. The energy rushed like a serpent through the dirt and decay as it raced towards the metal of the bulldozer and the house.

As the driver jumped out of his vehicle and his fellow workers began to flee, the bulldozer exploded in

112

a blaze of fire and sparks. The workers grabbed whatever equipment they could carry and ran back to Oceanview. Each member of the team was a wreck by the time they entered town. Something evil had been stirred that evening and they could all feel it and, in Sarah's room, so could I. The pain I had felt was connected to what had happened, but I had no interest in rekindling that feeling of dread.

I returned to the attic and let what the driver had said and the fear I felt crawl through my body out of my mind.

CHAPTER 7 – ON THE SECOND DAY…

I really have to work on this time thing. I knew that the students and teachers of High Point show up in the morning…sometime after the sun rises, but I didn't really know when. After my conversation with Sarah the night before, I began to see the world in a new way, and time mattered. But that was just one of the changes. Everything around me, from the grass to the sun, had taken on a new meaning, a new look. For the first time the world seemed real. Life moved in a new way and in colours I had never before noticed. I glanced up at the large clock mounted above the thick wooden doors of the school and stared in awe at the once unnecessary item, looking closely at it for the first time, as though it held an ancient secret.

Moving with an awkward slowness, the big hand stretched towards the nine as Sarah's Dad drove towards the main entrance to the school to drop her off. She said something to her dad before leaving the car and heading my way. Sarah was wearing brown corduroy overalls with a black t-shirt underneath. Her hair was pulled back into a ponytail and her knapsack slumped lazily over her right shoulder. I was completely star-struck, amazed at how she blended in with the other kids hustling about, as though she had been around as long as I have. I flew down and joined her as she rushed inside the building moments before the warning bell announced that the first period was quickly approaching. The school was my territory, yet walking in with Sarah made the old hallways seem new.

Sarah wove her way through the halls expertly and quickly found her locker. Once there she unfastened the lock and opened the thin metallic door, expecting to see an empty space. Instead she found a ghost. I had slipped in without her seeing and was waiting inside to greet her. Sarah jumped when she saw me and then began to laugh at my joke.

'Remember what I said,' she whispered as she threw her bag right through me and into the locker. 'We have things normal at school. People already think I'm strange and I'm really not that interested in helping them prove it by talking to my invisible friend. David was still going on about it at breakfast.'

'Sure, ruin my fun…Yeah, I understand. I've just always wanted to do that. I guess it's part of my ghostly nature to try to scare people.' I laughed as I quickly floated beside her. She didn't have to explain herself to me. No one wants to look like the odd one out, especially when they are new to a strange place. I had seen a lot of kids who were really pretty cool get tormented because they were different.

'Do you hear that?' Sarah whispered out of the corner of her mouth as I dodged the students who kept walking through me on their way to class. I carefully listened and heard the music from the ring. The 'Remembrance Song' was sweetly filling the air, yet only Sarah and I could hear its soft rhythms. We both looked at the ring and saw the dim purple light slipping through the thin scratches of the engraved symbols. Each line danced in a slow and steady manner until they formed one big symbol, a shape I had seen before but couldn't remember from where.

'Look out!!' came a voice, moments before someone crashed into Sarah, causing them to both fall to the ground.

'Thanks; always love getting tackled first thing in the morning!' Sarah muttered with an icy tone as she picked herself up. A boy of about her age had run her over in a futile attempt to catch a football. Sarah grabbed the ball and tossed it lightly into the air as she waited for the receiver to recover. It was Tayvn.

'Hey, Tay,' Kyle laughed from down the hall. 'Watch out for the pedestrians!'

The halls had cleared out as the final bell rang, beginning class. Sarah smiled as she launched the ball towards Kyle in a perfect pass. Kyle caught the ball with a grunt and a winded look.

'Sorry 'bout that,' Tayvn said honestly as Sarah helped him up. 'It's kind of a game Kyle and I play when we have a free period in the morning. We see how obnoxious we can be before getting kicked out of the halls.'

'Sounds intelligent,' Sarah smirked.

'Your name's Sarah, right? The new girl.' He stood up to introduce himself with a slightly nervous smile plastered across his face.

'That's me... You were in history with me yesterday, I think?' Sarah smiled as she faced him.

'My name's Tayvn,' he replied. 'Really, though, I feel bad about knocking you over. It's not my usual method of introducing myself. Usually I'm a little more subtle about making an idiot of myself.'

'I've noticed that so far the people of this town have unique ways of saying "hi",' Sarah remarked. 'I'm almost getting used to the unexpected.' I couldn't help but laugh as Sarah tossed me a quick glance.

'Let me make it up to you,' Tayvn said. 'Where's your first class? I'll give you the grand tour.'

'Mighty neighbourly of you,' Sarah joked. 'I have math, with, uh, Mr. Flannigan?' Tayvn and I both groaned; Flannigan was not only the toughest teacher in school, he was also the dullest. Everything about him was boring, which could explain why his class was better used to catch up on sleep.

'Hope you don't snore,' Tayvn laughed. 'I had Flannigan last year and he's brutal, but you learn a lot if you can stay awake. I better get you to class before we both get in trouble for hanging around in the halls.'

It was here that I felt a spark of jealousy. Sarah was my friend and I was going to show her around, not Tayvn. He could hang out with anyone else in the school, why did he have to go for the one person who was mine? It wasn't fair.

'What about Kyle?' Sarah asked. It was then that we all noticed that Kyle had disappeared. 'Where'd he go?'

'Probably just got bored and took off,' Tayvn answered, turning a little red.

'Thanks for the offer, Tayvn, but I think I'll find it,' Sarah said politely. 'I have a pretty good sense of direction and I don't want to make you lose your game. Just point me in the right direction and I'll get there.'

'It's no problem...' Tayvn started, but Sarah gave him a smile saying that she was fine. 'All right, uh, you go down this hall, turn right, go down the stairs and it is the first door to the left of the stairs.'

'Thanks,' Sarah said as she grabbed a notebook and closed her locker. 'I guess I'll see you later.'

'Definitely,' Tayvn smiled as he ran off in the opposite direction. He turned back at the last minute. 'Hey, a bunch of us meeting up after the basketball game tonight. You should come. We're playing after school and then we'll probably go for food or something.'

'I'll try,' Sarah said as she began to head towards her class. 'Nice to meet you, Tayvn.'

'Same here,' Tayvn said as Sarah hurried to her class.

'I think he ran into you on purpose,' I said to Sarah as I lead her to class. 'I've never seen him play football in the halls before, and he'd never miss a pass like that.'

'I know, it was sort of hard not to pick up on that,' Sarah smiled. 'Sometimes guys try a little too hard to subtly introduce themselves to a girl. You should keep that in mind next time you meet someone who can see you. Who'd have thought that in two days I'd meet two guys, one who says "hi" and jumps through a wall and one who tackles me to do the same? There has to be something in the air.'

'You're not going to let me forget about yesterday, are you?' I asked, pretending to be hurt.

'Probably not,' Sarah giggled.

'By the way,' I grinned. 'Nice pass to Kyle.'

'Thanks,' Sarah replied as she approached the door to her class. 'Dad was on his varsity football team and passed on a few tricks. Well, here goes.' Sarah opened the door and entered.

The morning was pretty straightforward…math, French, and drama. The rumours seemed to have died down a little. People were still talking about Sarah's being a witch and burning things down, but all this was quickly becoming old news. During her classes I gave Sarah the rundown on who everyone was and a brief biography. I didn't go as far as the rumours that preceded Sarah and her family; I just gave information that was more or less common knowledge. Sarah probably wouldn't remember any of the stuff I was telling her anyhow, but I kept the running commentaries going to justify my years of snooping. Sarah listened to everything I told her, and even laughed quietly when I said something funny.

The bell rang, signalling lunch. I was talking to Sarah on her way back to her locker when we turned down a small hallway that cut across the second floor connecting the middle of the square building. I stopped dead in my tracks when I noticed the three teenagers moving towards us.

'Sarah…uh, we should probably go the long way,' I said as the three students began to snicker. 'We really want to avoid those guys.'

'Why?'

'You know how I told you that Tayvn was an awesome guy who was smart, popular, and friendly?'

'Yeah.'

'Now imagine the exact opposite,' I explained as I searched desperately for a way out; if only Sarah could fly through walls. Maybe these three would ignore Sarah, but then again I had never seen them miss the chance to make someone's life miserable. The three students — although I think you need to actually show up to a class to be called a student — were named Axle, Brock, and T. No one knew these three better than me because I was the only one who could get near them without being pummelled.

Axle, or Angela Mahoney as her parents named her, was the leader of this group. She was in grade eleven and was by far one of the toughest people in school. She always wore a black leather jacket and way too much pale make-up, giving her a deathly-zombie look. She had a personal grudge against the entire world and was ready to take it out on anyone who foolishly got in her way. Even teachers were intimidated by her. Axle had no respect for anyone and derived pleasure from proving it in the most extreme ways. The problem was that no one knew the extent of the things she had done. With Axle, you could never prove that she was directly involved in anything, because people were either scared or she had coerced someone else, usually T or Brock, into doing it for her.

Brock was a skinny blond-haired kid who didn't fit in with any other group so he'd joined Axle's. He was a follower, and gravitated toward whoever he thought had the most power. If Axle wanted Brock to do something he would do it without question. I always felt sorry for the guy. I think that if he'd had a different group of friends, any other group of friends, he would have been a great kid instead of a constant jerk. It was too bad, because I knew Brock was a smart kid who for whatever reason had buried his heart long ago.

T, or Taikomoto, was the youngest member of the gang. His parents had moved to Oceanview about two or three graduations ago. He was a short Asian kid whose parents had originally lived in New York. They had started a really successful company, but when they noticed behavioural problems in their son, they decided to move away from the big city to give him a different, less damaging, atmosphere. But small towns can be just as tough as big cities. T was a smart kid, no denying, but was totally under Axle's thumb. She used him for his money and the fact that he would always take the blame for her. She used T's loyalty as a way to get whatever she wanted. He would steal, cheat, lie, and fight for her.

As I said, Axle, T, and Brock were on their way down towards us. Normally I wouldn't care, but Sarah could get hurt and I would not be able to forgive myself if that happened.

'You've got to be joking Ben,' Sarah said catching me off-guard. 'My locker is just down this hall and I plan on getting to it.'

'Sarah,' I said calmly but firmly. 'Turn around and run like hell out of here. Don't just stand around. I hear it only provokes them.' I was hoping she would realize that I was serious and run away, but she just stared at me with a confused look as though I wasn't making sense. 'These three are going to kill you! Now c'mon, let's get out of here!'

'I'm not running away from those losers even if they are bigger than me and outnumber me,' she said sternly. 'I've put up with their type before at my old school, especially when everyone thought my family was a bunch of freaks. Just follow my lead and everything will be fine.' She was serious. She was going to face these three on her second day of school. There were kids who were graduating who wouldn't even dare do such a reckless thing. I knew by the determined look in her eyes that there was no way to convince her to go. Reluctantly I nodded.

'Lookee here,' Axle said excitedly as she faced Sarah. 'It's the new girl we've heard so much about.'

Sarah tried to walk past the three of them, only to find her way blocked.

'I think we should teach her who runs this school, eh, Axle?' T asked as he smiled devilishly at his mentor. 'Or we could just make her cry really bad.'

'I wonder if witches bleed like everyone else? We better be careful or her grandmother might go psycho and try to eat us,' Brock sneered as the trio began to poke at Sarah. Sarah didn't even blink, but I could sense the rage burning beneath her calm demeanour.

'You three must think you are really cool, out-numbering the new kid,' Sarah said. Nobody ever talked back to Axle and her gang. This just proved that Sarah was anything but run-of-the-mill. 'I'll let you in on a secret. People like you may think you're tough, but you really just look pathetically sad, or maybe it's stupid. You think you run the school? The only reason that might happen is because at the rate you're going the three of you will never graduate.'

'Tough talk coming from a freaky girl who had to run away from her old town. Listen, little Miss Canada, I think we should teach you some manners.' Axle was red with anger and started to massage her right fist with her left hand. Sarah just stood in her place silently as the gang was preparing for an all-out attack.

'For your information, Vancouver is a city…this place is a town. If you showed up for social studies at least once you might have figured out the difference,' Sarah said straight-faced. 'You might think you know all of my secrets, but I did my homework on you three and I know all of yours.' That was her plan. It finally made sense to me and it was ingenious, but she would need my help, and she would need it now. Sarah was planning on using the information I had given her to put these bullies in their place. My people-watching was about to pay off big time.

'Hope you're a quick healer,' Axle said as T and Brock laughed in the background, thoroughly entertained by the idea of the upcoming fight. Axle raised her fist and was about to swing when I yelled something quickly to Sarah.

'Hope you don't mind everyone knowing about your ballet recital when you were a kid, Angela,' Sarah said calmly. 'You know, the one when you had to wear a giant rubber ducky costume? Funny, rumour has it that you keep it in your garage. Oh, and I hear that last weekend you snuck into some sappy movie where you left bawling like a little baby. I bet that makes you feel really "hard core".' Sarah was good, real good. As soon as she announced that information, Axle's face went even paler than normal and she dropped her fist as though she herself had been punched in the gut.

By this time a bunch of other students had gathered around to watch the commotion, and on hearing about the costume and movie they all started to laugh.

'We're gonna make you sorry,' T announced in a desperate attempt to protect his fallen leader. He and

Brock got ready to pounce on Sarah and still she did not blink. Sarah just stuck to her plan.

'Get real, T. You think a guy who is still scared of the dark is going to be able to help his girlfriend? I heard that you ran all the way home a few nights ago because a cat jumped out of a bush and scared you. And Brock, what is that name your mom calls you?' T and Brock both recoiled in terror as their long-hidden secrets was blurted for all to hear. 'But if you really want to take your chances, I should warn you, I'm a black belt.'

Realising that they had been humiliated, rather than continue the three bullies decided to turn tail and run away.

'Brock, you mean you don't like being called "my little Pookie Bear"? Oops, did I say that out loud?' Sarah definitely had a mean streak if you forced it out of her.

'You're a dead girl; I don't know how you knew those things, but it doesn't matter 'cause you just signed your own death wish...' Axle cried as she brutally shoved through the surrounding crowd of onlookers. 'One day we're going to get you!' And with that they were gone. Sarah gave me a warm smile and headed down the hall towards her locker. Suddenly there was an eruption of laughter and cheering from behind Sarah. She turned to see more than a dozen students applauding her performance. Sarah turned pink and gave an embarrassed bow to the crowd before turning and, with a slightly quicker pace, headed to her locker.

'Thanks,' she whispered to me.

'That was awesome,' I said as I floated beside her. 'I've never seen anything like that in my whole life. Weren't you scared? That was so incredible!'

'A little scared, I guess,' Sarah replied shyly. 'People back in Vancouver used to give me a hard time about Grams and I just sort of learned how to deal with it. Although having a friend like you is definitely a bonus.' This time it was my turn to blush.

'So again with the black belt thing? Let me guess, your dad use to be a black belt...' I joked remembering the previous night.

'Look, Mr. Can't-Touch-Anything,' Sarah blushed. 'It sounds a whole lot better to say that I'm a black belt than a person who took one karate class when I was eight.'

The rest of the day was pretty uneventful. It was pretty amazing to watch Sarah as she moved around school making friends wherever she went. By the last period, Sarah had been warmly welcomed by about a dozen different people, but what was cool was that no matter how many people congratulated her for making Axle look like an idiot, she always made time for me. The incident before lunch had become the hottest news in the school, and everyone wanted to meet the girl who had single-handedly terrorised the bullies. Sarah kept a really level head about the whole thing and shrugged it off with a genuine modesty.

I think she realized that she had pressed her luck this morning and was in no hurry to do it again.

The last period of the day was gym. Mr. Avers gave Sarah the same introduction as all the other teachers had, asking her to introduce herself and tell about where she was from and what she did. It was pretty funny watching Sarah give the same speech for the twelfth time in front of kids who had it memorised. Once the introductions were done, Avers blew his whistle and divided the class into two teams for a soccer game. After a few minutes of organising the teams, he dropped the ball and the game began. I goofed around for a bit, floating in front of the net when there was an open shot, pretending to body check people as they ran by. I floated over to the sidelines after a while and watched Sarah go. Boy, was she a pro. She was faking people out left, right, and centre and could control the ball as though it was a connected to her foot. She was untouchable. I could see some of the kids trying hard to steal the ball away from her, but she got the best of them every single time.

She was moving towards the net and I was going to have a little fun. I flew down and started to play goalie. I moved back and forth, following her every move and body signal. I was not going to let her score…or at least I would pretend not to let her score. Sarah lined up for the shot and kicked the ball hard. It was flying through the air straight towards me. Deep down I was hoping she would play along and purposely try not to hit me, but I was wrong. The ball sailed right through my head and smacked the back of the net.

'That was awesome,' said Amber, a girl with thick curly hair as she gave Sarah a high-five.

'Thanks,' Sarah said modestly. 'It was nothing; I just picked something to aim at and kicked the ball.' I didn't think it was that funny, since I had been the target. The whistle blew and everyone went to the change-rooms. Avers, a man who was probably thicker than a brick wall, but a really nice guy regardless of his gruff appearance, called Sarah over as she was about to leave with Amber. Sarah motioned for Amber to go on without her and said that she would catch up in a minute; she gave me a look that meant that the same applied to me.

I waited for Sarah outside the girls' change-room for a while, watching the door carefully for my friend. I was tempted to just go in there and tell her to hurry up, but I had a feeling she wouldn't appreciate that too much.

I felt a little left out when I saw Sarah walk out with Amber and a bunch of other girls, laughing and talking. She didn't say a word to me. She didn't even look up. Halfway down the hall, Sarah told the group she was walking with that she had forgotten something in the change room and she would see them tomorrow. She rushed back inside the change room only to come out moments later.

'Sorry,' she said honestly as we walked to her locker. 'I was having some fun and couldn't exactly say that I was ditching them so I could hang out with my invisible friend. I don't think they would have understood.'

'No problem,' I answered. 'What did Avers want?'

'He wanted to know if I was interested in being on the soccer team this year. He said the season had already started but he would love to have me on the team,' Sarah said nonchalantly, as though she didn't realize that this was an honour. Sarah had been hand-picked to play on the school soccer team, the one that had been undefeated for over twelve graduations and was made up of what Avers called his 'elite force'.

'Well?' I asked impatiently.

'I told him I would think about it and let him know tomorrow,' she said. 'I want to make sure it's all right with my dad and stuff...in case he needs me to help out at home or with David. But if he says its okay, I'll...'

'No fan club for you now!' Axle screamed suddenly from behind us as Sarah and I walked down the hall. The three of them had been waiting for her. 'You're toast, witch-girl!!!' The three goons started running full sprint down the lime-green corridor, ready to get even for what had happened this morning.

'RUN!' Sarah and I yelled in unison. As fast as we could, we both ran away from the bullies. We raced down the halls filled with grey lockers and past the old graduation class photos that watched closely from their positions along the walls. The corridors were empty except for the echoing sound of Sarah's racing feet. It always amazed me how quickly people disappeared from High Point at the end of the day, but right now I wished the school was still packed. The entire building seemed deserted except for the five of us.

'Follow me,' I quickly said as I thought of the best place for us hide. I led her up to the third floor of the building. She was breathing heavily after the run, but we had managed to beat our enemies, one of the bonuses of being in shape. Sarah wasn't quite sure where I was leading her, but she trusted me. After all, I knew the school much better than she did and she knew that this time I had the plan.

The door to the attic was on the third floor, across from the French classroom and next to the Lost and Found. The door was still unlocked from when Creepy Sweepy had left, but there was no doorknob, just a flat surface where the knob should have been, and a latch the same colour as the wall that flipped over the keyhole, allowing the door to blend in perfectly. Anyone who might have known about the attic probably assumed that it was locked and empty, assuming anyone other than me even knew that it existed.

Sarah and I reached the door before the bullies had made it up the stairs. I flew through and heard a thud on the other side. Sarah was in such a panic she forgot that I can't open doors and I was in such a panic I forgot she couldn't fly through them. I stuck my head through the door to see if she was okay.

'Are you all right?' I asked quickly.

'Yeah, fine, how do I get in?' We both heard the footsteps of Axle, T, and Brock getting closer.

'Umm…' I thought aloud as I looked for something with which she could pry it open. 'Use your hair clip. Shove it into the crack and push hard.' She did it quickly without even considering the possibility of it not working. With little effort the door swung open. Sarah ran in and closed the entrance behind her, locking it with a loud click by turning the old deadbolt from the inside. She leaned against the dusty door and tried to catch her breath. Soon we heard the muffled voices of Axle and her buddies outside the door. They hadn't seen where Sarah had disappeared, but vowed that she would pay as soon as they found her.

'Up here,' I whispered thinking for some reason that if I spoke too loudly the others might hear me. Carefully I led Sarah up the darkened wooden stairs up into the attic, into my secret place.

CHAPTER 8 – ALIVE

'Where are we?' Sarah whispered as she slowly followed me through the darkness. There were no windows along the steep stairs filling the narrow passage; all she could do was feel her way up through the darkness. She futilely searched the walls on either side of the rickety wooden railing with the palms of her hands for a light switch. There wasn't one. The creaks of each ancient step echoed in the silence as they adjusted to their new burden. It had been a long time since they had been used, causing them to cry out as though they were jolted to attention.

'What's that smell? It's like someone died up here. Ben...this isn't where...'

'No,' I said sharply cutting Sarah off. The place I died had been much darker than this attic could ever be. 'I found this place a while ago, it used to belong to this guy named Creepy Sweepy...uh, never mind...Basically this is where I hang out – my home.'

Once near the top of the stairs, Sarah felt a smooth panel under her right hand. Without much thought she flipped the protruding switch upwards, bringing life to the darkness. The lights flickered like stars being ignited. Two large hanging lights slowly began to buzz as they cast their fluorescent glow. The same switch must have been connected to the lamps, because three out of the five mismatched and scattered lights sparked to life.

Sarah looked around the now illuminated room and saw the various boxes, the couch, the old trunk covered with magazines and cans of decaying food. There were cobwebs and layers of dust covering everything in the crowded space. The dim light from the lamps mixed with the natural light from the skylight created new and wondrous shadows along the dirty wooden floor. I felt a little ashamed that my room was such a mess, but hey, I'm a ghost, what could I do about it?

'I guess no one else comes up here?' Sarah asked as she looked at the thick layer of dust that coated her hands. 'No living people at least. I don't think they could handle that smell. It's rancid, Ben.'

'Sorry,' I muttered. 'I just sort of found the place and took it as is. I followed Creepy Sweepy, and when he left it became mine. Since I can't touch stuff, I never really got a chance to clean it and the cleaning service I hired never showed up. Guess they couldn't find the place.' As I joked, Sarah began to pick up the mouldy food tins and dropped them into a large plastic bag she had dug up from somewhere. As she discarded each rotting item, Sarah grimaced as though she was going to be sick. It's funny, but most of the garbage she was picking up was probably older than her brother. Maybe funny isn't the right word to use; gross would probably be a better fit. Once the trunk was cleared, Sarah tossed the bag down the stairs.

'Now that I can breathe, it's my turn to explore,' Sarah stated as she imitated how I had been in her house last night. It was awesome seeing her wander around as though she had discovered some new world. 'This place is really cool, Ben. Look at all this stuff. David would love it up here. I think he'd be able to occupy himself for weeks digging through these boxes. And my dad would have a field day going through those old books.'

Sarah wandered through the aisles of boxes reading the labels on each one in detail. She gave me a puzzled look when she saw the one with the skull and crossbones on it. I shrugged, not knowing what was inside, but at the same time I was thankful that she didn't open it up to show me. Deep down I was scared of whatever was hidden inside that box with the ominous warning that had scared Creepy Sweepy that night so long ago.

'With a little bit of cleaning this place could be awesome,' Sarah said, then added "Eww, gross!" as she walked into a cobweb.

'Feel free,' I remarked as Sarah began to look inside an old box marked "props". 'While you're at it, I could use a home-cooked meal and possibly a massage.'

'I'm going to pretend I didn't hear that, ghost-boy,' Sarah answered with her back turned to me. 'Do you think Tayvn would have invited me to the game tonight if I had these on?' Sarah spun around and was wearing a pair of bottle-lens glasses. They must have been fifty or even sixty graduations old. They had thick black frames that made perfect circles. The lenses were so thick that they magnified Sarah's eyes so that they looked like they belonged to some sort of cartoon bug. I laughed hysterically as I floated down onto the couch, wondering what else she might discover.

'I think you'd have scared Axle away with those on,' I replied.

'Gee, maybe I should keep them handy,' Sarah laughed. 'With them on I might even be able to locate her brain.' She took a few steps backwards from the box, and then screamed almost as loud as when she had seen me floating by her window. Something cold and furry had grabbed onto her shoulder, something with large sharp claws. Sarah screamed again.

I couldn't help but laugh, louder than I had ever done before in my life. Sarah gave me a shocked look, removed the bottle-lensed glasses, and turned to face her captor. There she stood face to face with a giant stuffed bear that was in the middle of a deep but silent roar.

'Sarah, meet Oscar; Oscar, meet Sarah,' I said. Sarah was staring at me, slightly red, as I introduced her to my friend. 'Oscar, Sarah is my new friend, so I hope you two will play nicely together.'

'Very funny, Ben,' Sarah said sarcastically as she examined the overgrown beast that was standing on its hind legs, arms outstretched.

'What?' I asked, trying desperately to hold back my laughter. 'I can't move it. Stuff has a tendency to slide right through me, remember? Besides, until I met you I needed someone to talk to. You see those cobwebs all over? I've watched most them get spun.'

Sarah looked at the bear and then turned to look at me. There was a saddened expression on her face, as though she was in deep thought. Slowly she moved towards me on the couch. She batted off as much dust as she could and then sat down. She coughed as the dust filled the air as it searched for a new place to settle.

'That's so sad,' Sarah said quietly. 'You must have been really lonely.'

'You get used to it,' I replied. 'There are some things that you just can't change. Besides, it's kind of cool being able to fly and drift through solid objects. Isn't that what most real people dream about?'

'I guess so…But even you can't float through a magic ring,' Sarah said as she began fidgeting with her ring. 'Remember last night when the ring touched you, or you touched it?'

'Yeah, I remember,' I answered. I been hoping she would bring that up; I hadn't stopped thinking about it since it happened. 'When you slid your hand through my face, your ring got caught on something. Why do you think that happened?'

'Maybe it's the same reason the ring lets me see you,' Sarah answered as she continued to fidget with it while looking at me. 'I have an idea. Let's see if I can see you because of the ring or because of, well, me.'

Slowly Sarah twisted the ring around her finger. The ring seemed to resist being removed, but eventually Sarah succeeded. She held the ring in the palm of her hand and stretched it out towards me. It might have been the light, but it looked as though the ring grew while sitting in her hand.

'Ben? Are you still there? I can't see you anymore. Say something,' Sarah asked aloud as she scanned the room. I hadn't moved off the couch, so it must have been the ring that let Sarah see and hear me. I yelled her name as loud as I could, but she didn't hear me.

'Let's try something,' she said then. 'I'm going to put the ring on the trunk and I want you to try to move it.'

Sarah placed the ring down and waited.

Suddenly she let out a gasp as the ring began to slide along the surface of the table. I cautiously picked up the silver piece of metal and began to fly around the room with it. The ring was cool to the touch, but felt somewhat familiar. Was it the sensation of holding a piece of metal, or was it something more? I wanted to make sure I didn't lose this precious piece of jewellery, so I slid it onto my finger. It seemed too small at first, but then the ring magically adjusted until it fit around my finger perfectly.

The 'Remembrance Song' began to play from the ring and the many different engravings began to dance. The intricate carvings along the outside became one solid band of light as they spun faster and faster. Soon the radiant glow began to shine brighter until it encompassed all that I could see. Out of nowhere, a queasy feeling erupted in the pit of my stomach. There were hoards of fluttering butterflies having a wrestling match in my gut. I looked down at my hands, which were now clenching my stomach, and saw a thick purple mist coating my skin. It was almost identical to the mark the ring had made when I first touched it, only thicker. The room began to spin dizzily in circles as my heart jumped into my throat. The glowing mist surrounded my body in an intense warmth and brilliance. I had a sense of protection and safety coupled with utter fear.

The queasiness finally faded and was replaced with a feeling of fullness. I couldn't understand this sudden weighted feeling as I began to sink towards the ground as though I was made of stone. My ability to fly was disappearing with my increased heaviness and eventually I crashed onto the couch, causing a huge cloud of dust to burst into the air. I could feel the softness of the couch and the surge of pain from landing on it.

'What was that?' Sarah exclaimed. 'One minute the ring is flying around the room and then you fizzle into sight and crash…Wait a second…I felt you hit the couch and saw you without the ring…That could only happen if…' Sarah slowly reached out her hand and touched my arm before quickly jerking back her hand as though I was burning hot. She then reached for me again and ruffled my hair.

'Impossible,' I said groggily as my head began to clear and a shearing pain rushed up my body from my less-than-elegant landing. I tried to float up to my feet, but nothing happened. I slowly grabbed hold of the couch and felt the strange soft yet firm furniture for the first time. I looked at my hand and watched the fading residual glow of the ring.

Sarah reached out again with her hand, which was slightly trembling. She pressed against the side of my neck and gasped. 'Ben… I can feel your pulse…'

I placed the palm of my hand smoothly on the shirt that I had worn for as long as I could remember and felt the beating of my heart within my chest. I took a deep breath, and felt the air fill my lungs. 'Sarah, I'm alive… I'm real!'

With all my might I held onto the couch with both hands and pushed myself up to a sitting position, amazed by the dust that fled from my movement. My boots rested heavily on the floor without the slightest indication that they might sink through the wooden boards and into the maze of pipes beneath.

'How did you do that?' Sarah asked, still in awe of what was happening.

'I just put the ring on my finger and then...I became solid.' I grinned as I looked at the dust that was gathering on my fingers. 'Sarah...I'm breathing. I can feel my heart...I can feel my own skin. I'm alive!'

'A real life Pinocchio,' Sarah smiled. 'I knew that ring was magical, but this is unreal. I never would've thought it could bring someone back from the dead.' As Sarah thought about resurrecting the dead, I could see a cloud of sadness hover around her.

'Sarah,' I said without even pausing to think. 'It's your ring and its magic belongs to you. If you want it back, it's no problem...'

'No, Ben,' Sarah smiled, amazed at what I had just said. 'You've wanted to be alive for a long time...longer than I've even been alive. This is your gift. My mom isn't a ghost and she isn't coming back.

The ring was meant to find you and to make you real. I want you to wear it for as long as you want.'

'I don't know what to say,' I stammered pushing back the blurring tears building behind my eyes.

'Mom always said that happiness was the best and only gift in the world,' Sarah said. 'I know that she would want you to have the ring.'

'I promise to give it back,' I replied. 'It's weird, I've known you for only a little while, a speck in my life, but it feels like I have known you for graduations.'

'Same here,' Sarah laughed. 'Now we can sit around here and talk about being alive, or we can figure out how to do it. Let's see if you remember how to walk.'

Slowly I tried to stand. After a few attempts I managed to get up on my feet for a moment. Sarah tried to hold back laughing as I tumbled like a toddler, and then braced me as I tried again. I stood motionless, clutching Sarah for what seemed like an eternity before she forced me to let go. I wobbled awkwardly, but after a few highly uncoordinated steps forward and back, I managed to stand on my own.

'It feels like every part of me is asleep,' I laughed as I numbly felt the floor beneath my feet. Seeking to be a little more adventurous, I tried to take a step forward. After one successful step I toppled to the ground and bounced off the old trunk before hitting the floor. 'Oww!'

'You haven't done this in a long time Ben; it'll take a little getting used to. Remember, baby steps,' Sarah smiled as she helped me up. Sarah helped me walk around the cleared space in the attic. She was doing most of the work, but I was slowly figuring out how to balance on my own.

After a few spins around the attic, I tried to move around by myself. It took a while and a lot more crashing and tumbling, but eventually I managed to cross the room all by myself.

'I...I'm walking,' I said, moments before falling flat on my face. 'One advantage of being a ghost is the lack of pain when you run into something. I'd take the invisible wall over the floor any time. This hurts!'

'Looks like that to me,' Sarah smiled as she helped me up. 'Are you okay? You've had more than your share of landings for the day.'

'Floating is definitely less painful, but this is so much cooler. I can't believe you get to do this every day,' I smiled as I heaved myself off the ground. 'I only hope I don't send myself to the hospital on my first day alive.'

'That makes two of us,' Sarah said as I tried to walk again, this time making it a little further. 'But it looks like you scraped your hand on that last landing. Let me take a look at it and make sure it isn't too bad.'

My hand was stinging in pain, but all I could focus on was the small drop of blood trickling to the ground. I had never seen my own blood before; I hadn't even known I had any.

If I could bleed, then I really was alive, and if I was alive, I must have a reflection.

Half-stumbling and half-walking, I rushed to an old mirror that was tucked away in the back of the attic. With the sleeve of my shirt I rubbed away a thick layer of dust and grime until I uncovered the smooth surface of the glass.

I felt vain looking at myself in the mirror, but at the same time I was amazed. I was exactly as Sarah had described me: red hair that was a little longer on the top, brown eyes, a couple of freckles, and really old-fashioned clothes. *I'm a real boy,* was the only thought in my head. I stared deeply into my own eyes in awe of seeing them focus on their reflection. The ring truly was magical.

From beneath the floor came the tinny noise of a whistle blast, shattering my moment of vanity. The basketball game must have started while I was learning to walk; neither of us had heard the noise that was being sent up to the attic through the pipes of the old school. I turned to Sarah with great anticipation.

'Are you ready for the real world?' she asked as I nodded excitedly like a puppy being told of an upcoming walk. Soon I would make my entrance into a bold new world, the world I yearned to be a part of. With my newest friend, who had given me the greatest gift, I was ready to live. I must have been light-headed from the transformation because I walked headfirst into the door as Sarah and I tried to leave the attic, not the greatest entrance into the world of the living, but it was a start.

'Guess it'll take a little while to get used to, huh?' I chuckled as I felt my throbbing face.

'And since you are now solid, you can take this to the garbage,' Sarah smiled devilishly as she tossed me the foul-smelling garbage bag from the attic. Carefully she opened the door and peered out to see if anyone was in the hall. No one was around, so we crept past the door and closed it silently behind us.

There were only a few minutes left in the basketball game by the time Sarah and I entered the gym. The Oceanview Pioneers were destroying the other team with a twenty-point lead. Sarah and I cheered as our team played. I could only imagine myself one day playing next to Tayvn on centre court. That would be awesome, taking a three-point shot at the buzzer ending the fourth period and winning the final game of the season by one point. True, I was still having trouble standing up let alone walking, but I'd get the hang of it eventually.

Sarah waved to Tayvn from the bleachers as he jogged off towards the change room once the game had ended. The Oceanview Pioneers had managed to remain undefeated for their sixth game and Tayvn, as always, was the M.V.P. Not that you could tell by the way he was acting. He stopped to personally congratulate every other player while continually downplaying his contribution to their win...even though he probably was responsible for over half of the Pioneers' points.

'Hey, Tayvn, nice game!' Sarah shouted as he and Kyle passed by where we were sitting on the bleachers. 'You too, Kyle...guess hallway football just wasn't your sport.'

'Hey!' Kyle laughed. 'I have a great pass; it's the receiver who has no skill at the game.'

'Hands like butter,' Tayvn agreed, showing his palms as though to prove it. 'I'll get changed, and then you want to hang out for a little bit?'

'Sure,' Sarah replied. 'But only if my friend Ben can come.'

'The more the better,' Tayvn said as he and Kyle left the court.

Sarah taught me a little about time as she explained to me that it was fifteen minutes before Tayvn came back to where we had been sitting. He was wearing a different basketball jersey; he said it was his lucky jersey and that he always wore it home after the game.

'Hey, Tayvn,' Sarah smiled. 'This is my, uh, cousin Ben…'

'Nice to meet you,' Tayvn said as he shook my hand. It was incredible to actually shake hands with someone. I could feel the sweat on his palm, the warmth of his skin. I could also hear a faint hum

158

coming from the ring. Why was it singing again? Sarah and I both heard it, but neither of us could tell if Tayvn did.

'Yeah,' I said. 'Nice to meet you, too.' It sounded funny introducing myself to someone I had known for graduations, someone whose parents I had watched when they were babies.

'What happened to Kyle?' Sarah asked. 'I hope I didn't scare him off with that crack about his passes.'

'No,' Tayvn laughed. 'He got a ride home with one of the other guys. I was thinking that maybe I could show you around town a little. Maybe grab something to eat?'

'Sure,' Sarah said, elbowing me in the gut as I laughed about being shown around town. Wow, being poked in the ribs was a lot more painful than I had thought!

'Not to sound rude, Ben,' Tayvn said politely. 'But, uh, what's with the clothes?'

'Huh?' I responded more bewildered by the fact that I was part of a conversation.

'He's in a play,' Sarah lied. 'He's visiting from another town not far from here and had to work in his costume.' I was impressed with the speed of Sarah's explanation, but at the same time a little self-conscious about my clothes. I'm sure that when I was alive they were at the peak of fashion.

Tayvn, Sarah, and I talked for a little while in the gym before leaving the school. I was still shaky on my feet, but Sarah helped out by grabbing onto my arm whenever it looked as if I was going to tumble. I insisted on opening the door leading outside and paused to take in the warmth and multitude of fragrances that were all around me. The world was real and I wanted to savour the feeling of it. The wind as it rustled my hair, the leaves that crunched beneath my feet, even the mere fact that people noticed me as I walked was exhilarating. Even the animals weren't going nuts around me the way they normally did when I had been a ghost. Life was good.

As we walked down Breaker Street, I caught myself looking in every window and mirror. I must have looked vain, but I was more interested in the simple fact that I had a reflection rather than what it looked like.

Eventually the three of us arrived at the local ice-cream shop where we ordered something to snack on. Sarah made some crack about her brother only being able to find the three basic flavours on his quest for ice cream last night. She insisted on ordering for me, seeing that this was going to be my first experience with any type of food. The sweet coolness was a sensation I will never forget. The soft ice cream just melted on my tongue and filled my newly formed taste buds with joy. Unfortunately I also learnt about this other feeling; Tayvn called it 'brain-freeze', a searing pain right between my eyes. I decided to keep this fact tucked away as a mental note, because I was planning on having a whole lot more ice cream. That is, once I mastered eating it without having most of it end up on my face.

After Sarah paid, since I had no money, and I had inhaled my second cone of triple-chocolate-crunch, the three of us wandered towards a nearby park. I felt the damp grass soak through my pants as I sat down. I smiled as I pictured playing soccer in this very park on a warm summer day. The three of us talked about everything and nothing at the same time as the magical ring on my finger sang quietly in the background. I looked at the ring a few times, as did Sarah, as it constantly flashed the same symbol as before when we were by her locker. Tayvn didn't seem to be aware of anything unusual.

Suddenly Sarah gasped as she noticed for the first time the tattoo that was on Tayvn's shoulder. It matched the symbol from the ring perfectly. It was a starburst like the ones used on ancient maps as the compass.

'Ben,' Sarah whispered as she nodded towards the tattoo. 'It's the symbol.' She was right. I looked at the ring, as did Sarah. They were exactly the same. The bursting star that had mysteriously appeared on Tayvn's shoulder was somehow connected to the ring.

I felt like an idiot for not making the connection sooner. Everyone knew this as Tayvn's symbol.

The music began to slow and fade then, as though the ring was losing power. Something weird was about to happen; I could feel it in my bones.

'Some of the guys are coming over to my place to watch TV tonight,' Tayvn said, unaware that his tattoo was of such interest to the two of us. 'If you want to come your more than welcome…both of you.'

I was about to accept when a deep familiar pain returned to my stomach. The butterflies were back.

'Are you okay?' Tayvn asked as I winced in pain.

'Ugh…' was the only response I could make. It felt worse than before, much worse.

'Ben, are you…' Sarah asked as she noticed the carvings on the ring begin to glow in an increasingly brilliant purple. 'He's all right; he's just lactose intolerant — you know, allergic to milk. That ice cream probably wasn't too good for him. C'mon, lets get you home,' Sarah smoothly lied as she helped me up off the grass. The few other people in the park stared as we quickly moved towards a small secluded section of the park.

'Let me help. He's not looking too good,' Tayvn offered.

'No!' Sarah said loudly. 'Sorry, it's just that he's probably going to be embarrassed about this whole thing. I think it'll be better if I just take him. My dad works nearby and he'll have the car.'

'Okay. If you insist,' Tayvn said as he stepped away from Sarah, who had put my arm over her shoulders and was pretty much dragging me along as I struggled to keep up with her. 'If you need me, though, I don't mind.'

'Thanks,' Sarah said without even looking back.

The carvings that were dancing rapidly around the ring were speeding up and Sarah could see my body begin to glow. With each moment the pain in my stomach got worse and my head became lighter. Sarah rushed me out of sight, leaving Tayvn more than a little confused. The world became a blur as it spun quickly around me and my body gave off a spectacular purple hue. The fullness I had felt earlier was now replaced by emptiness, an odd lightness. Sarah slumped me carefully onto the ground as dust and spilt ice cream slid right through me and onto the ground. The glow began to intensify and I could vaguely hear Sarah calling my name.

As quickly as this whole thing started, it finished. I found myself floating high above Sarah. I looked at my finger as the ring dropped through my finger and onto the ground by Sarah's feet.

'Are you okay?' Sarah asked as she placed the ring back onto her finger.

'So much for being alive,' I said as I floated down to Sarah's level.

'The ring probably just needs to recharge or something,' Sarah said optimistically. 'I mean, you were real for almost three hours; that's got to count for something. Besides, I meant what I said about the ring. Whenever you want to be human, I'll let you…no matter what.'

'Thanks,' I said thoughtfully. 'This could be a taste of what could be…or the ultimate cruel joke.'

'At least I can still see you,' Sarah said, looking at the bright side. 'C'mon, let's go back to my place and we'll try to reincarnate you a little later.'

'Sure,' I said a little down. 'Sorry about making you ditch Tayvn.'

'Look at the bright side, maybe we'll be able to figure out what the symbol means,' Sarah said trying to cheer me up. 'At least you won't have to worry about that.' Sarah pointed up into the sky at a large group of dark clouds that was gathering. They seemed to come out of nowhere, covering the bright sun. One thing was for sure, there was going to be a storm tonight, a huge one, and I would rather be invisible with Sarah than solid and trapped in the middle of it with no place to go.

As the storm grew, my memories of life began to fade. It was as though I had awoken from a dream and the longer I remained awake, the less I was able to remember. But the slipping memory of what I had experienced wasn't what I found most frightening; it was the feeling of another type of magic in the air. The wind was carrying something foul which made my spine tingle. Something dark and deadly was coming into town, something that I had faced before in another life, the same thing that I had felt last night that made the whole world seem bleak and cold.

CHAPTER 9 – DAVID

There are some things that should not be forgotten.

He is one of those things.

It took a while for him to gather enough strength to pull himself out of his tomb. It had been far too long since he has felt anything. The taste of life was already wetting his lips, and he was savouring it. First things first, he was reminded as he looked at his dry hands. Until he settled an old score and retrieved what was rightfully his, his cravings would have to wait. He inhaled the fresh air of the forest before exhaling death itself. Yes, he must prepare for his return.

'Pluvia. Tonitrus. Fulgur. Parare ille orbis terrarum pro meus pretium!' he roared into the air as the clouds grew darker and darker. From that one patch of cloud a vast storm was emerged, a vast storm

that was meant to poison the air and frighten the meek, a storm that would announce the return of the demon Omascus.

While Sarah and I were discovering the power of the ring, another person in town who dreamt of discovering some magical heirloom or meeting some strange new friend was feeling lonely and depressed. David, Sarah's brother, was having a very different experience in Oceanview. Like his sister, he had a strong personality and was generally a good-hearted kid. But unlike his older sister, David didn't have a friendly ghost to guide him through his first days at a new school. In fact, he hadn't really made any friends at Willowbrook Elementary, and it wasn't as though he was trying too hard, or not trying enough to make some friends.

The school itself was a pretty boring bungalow with one large field attached to it. It was on the border of a heavily forested section of town and right off the slowest section of Breaker Street. As far as elementary schools went, this one was no better or worse than the countless others anywhere in the country. The kids and teachers were about the same as anywhere else. There were some who were amazing, and others who were not.

The school wasn't what bothered David; it was the fact that he had left his home, the only one he had ever known, and all of his friends, to come to this place, a small town in the middle of nowhere. Sure, it had a cool beach and a forest, but who cared when all the friends you had ever known lived on the other side of the continent? David felt betrayed by his dad, who hadn't even asked if he wanted to move. David tried to put on a brave face like his big sister, but deep down he was miserable. First he had to say good-bye to his mom, then to Grams, and then to all the things that were familiar.

David was slightly small for his age, but a tough kid. He loved swimming and was always working on some new skateboard trick. He had spiky hair, which he styled with a care rarely seen in ten-year-old boys. He had deep brown eyes that sparkled mischievously. It was not as though he had ever been in any serious trouble; rather he had his own brand of mischief-making which made life a little more interesting.

In Oceanview, nobody knew who David was and, to be quite honest, no one really cared. All they knew was that this new kid had moved to town and was from some weird family. That was enough for the kids at Willowbrook. David Winters was nothing but a freaky new kid who would eventually fit in with the other kids, but who really cared when, or how? He was an outsider and that was all they needed to know.

No one said it would be easy for David to go to a new school two months into the school year, and he wasn't expecting it to be. So far no one had given him a chance to prove that he could be a good friend. His sister was going to a school on the other side of town and his dad, although very supportive and understanding, was busy working on the house and trying to get things in order. It seemed as though no one had time for David since the move.

171

David figured that he would be able to find some comfort playing rugby, a sport that he'd always been good at despite his size. He saw rugby as his big chance to shine and at least get noticed. Right before they had moved to Oceanview, David had made it onto his old school's competitive team. At Willowbrook they didn't even offer the sport; in fact some of the coaches only had a vague understanding of that 'European' sport. Instead he had to settle for basketball or soccer which David had always found to be somewhat boring.

All in all, David's second day at school was just as lousy as his first, and he couldn't stand it.

Once the bell had rung, David grabbed all of his things and made his way out of the school. He saw a lot of his classmates being picked up by their parents, hanging out in a group talking, or goofing around near a few wooden swings set up around a large oak tree. He tried to smile at some of them and join in, but they all backed off just enough so that they were not exactly being rude, but were not inviting him into their group, either. Since his dad wasn't going to be able to pick him up today, David began the trek back to his house.

He had the route memorised from the drive the night before when he and his dad had explored the town looking for something interesting. He remembered that he needed to walk down Breaker Street, take a left past the burger place, walk through a small park that led up a hill, take a right, and his new run-down house would be at the end of the street. It was an easy route that was not too long but, to a depressed little boy, it was too long because it gave him enough time to think about how much everything in his new life in his new town stunk. He couldn't wait to get home and e-mail his friends in Vancouver, assuming the phone line had been set up, which he doubted.

That e-mail was never sent, but not because the phone line wasn't ready.

David walked down Breaker Street as he had planned. Halfway up the street he came across a store he hadn't noticed when he'd wandered with his dad in exploration. It was a large store filled with interesting new video games and gadgets, things kids and a lot of adults love. Looking through the window, he eyed one of those electric balls which shot off lines of light that bounced and sparked on the surrounding glass ball. There was also a bunch of lava lamps, and some of the rarest comics he had ever seen. Flickering letters above the thick purple door read 'Welcome to the Fun Shoppe', a fitting name for a store which had toys for all ages.

David was amazed that he hadn't noticed this store earlier. He could have sworn it was a vacant shop with boarded up windows. Maybe it was brand new and today was the first day it was open. Without thinking about it, David ventured into the shop.

A small bell rang as he pulled the door open.

The inside of the store was just as remarkable as the outside. It looked as though millions of different colours covered the walls, creating a surreal atmosphere, like *Alice in Wonderland*. Amazing items lined the walls and cluttered the counters and floor.

David walked over to one of the bright red lava lamps and began to watch the blobs of goo float from the top, all the way to the bottom, and then back up to the top. It was hypnotic to watch. He then noticed out of the side of his eye a metallic top that was continually spinning, almost like magic. David carefully picked up the still-spinning top from the counter, carefully placed it on the palm of his hand and watched as its spin refused to waiver.

'Can I help you, sir?' A scratchy voice with a thick British accent asked from behind the young boy. 'Something of interest? Anything I can do to make your visit more memorable?'

David turned around quickly and saw an older man looking at him. He was thin, with a full head of white hair. His eyes looked old and grey, matching the pale wrinkled skin that wrapped its way around his face. There was also something odd about his teeth...they were unusually jagged and an unnatural white.

Josh Sadovnick

'I was just looking,' David stated, thrown slightly off-guard by the presence of this man who seemed to come out of nowhere. David dropped the top onto the floor, where it continued to spin. 'I'm sorry I was touching it. Honest. I swear I was just looking…'

The man let out a cackle.

'Nonsense, my boy,' he replied like a kind old grandfather. 'Everything here is for you to touch and to have, there is no need to apologize. What fun is there in having a shop full of toys if no one is allowed to play with them? Say, you are the new boy in town, aren't you?'

David shied away for a moment before nodding 'yes' to the old man's question as he picked up the top and carefully placed it back on the counter where he had found it.

'Well then, my name is Mr. Sheffer, but my friends call me Rex. And since you happen to be my first customer, I have something very special for you.'

David's eyes brightened as he heard that he was going to get 'something special', but then he frowned.

'I don't have any money Mr. …uh…Sheffer.' David began to move to the door with his head down. The old man, with a youthful spring in his step, came up behind David and placed a hand on his shoulder.

'Nonsense,' Rex replied. 'I don't remember saying anything about money. Now come with me, my boy, you are sure to love this. That is, if you want to go get it. It is in the back room, right through those curtains.' Rex pointed his pale thin finger towards a set of thick black velvet curtains. David's eyes shone with delight upon hearing the news that the surprise was free, and walked towards the curtains. He was about to enter and then stopped.

'I can't, my dad wants me home right after school,' David said hesitantly, getting a creepy feeling about what was happening. 'Besides, he said I should never talk to strangers. I should go. Thanks anyhow, Mr. Sheffer,' David said as he turned and walked back towards the exit. Rex let him walk past him and almost out of the shop before he replied with a sudden eerie coldness.

'Is this the same dad who made you move to this awful town, away from your friends, and the sport that you love? The same man who has ruined your life? Why, I wouldn't be surprised if he was the one who made your mother sick and chased away your dear old Grandmother.'

David turned around and saw the old man smile wryly. How did he know so perfectly his innermost feelings, no matter how irrational they had been? He had secretly blamed his dad for all those things, even though he knew that for the most part he was being ridiculous.

'My name is Rex and I have a gift that will change your life,' the old man said. 'It is waiting behind that curtain for you. Get it and then you can go home. I promise.'

David could not think of a reason why not, so he shrugged off his bad feeling about Mr. Sheffer and this strange new shop and walked through the curtains in search of his prize. Even though David thought he had made the decision out of his own free will, he could not deny an odd compulsion to go through those curtains, as though even if he'd wanted to refuse, he would be unable.

Rex followed David through the velvet curtains and into the back room. The old man stopped for a moment and stared at the 'Open' sign resting in the shop window. Magically it flipped itself over to the 'Closed' side as the main door locked. The old man's eyes flashed a brilliant red, as thunder and lighting exploded in the grey sky outside. He smiled.

The old man's smile never faded as he followed the unsuspecting boy into the back room. He could sense the power of the ring and was aware of its bearer. All he needed was a tool with which he could claim it. Now he had the one person who could do it.

CHAPTER 10 – THE WARNING

'It lasted for a while,' Sarah said, trying to sound encouraging as she placed her precious ring back on her finger. 'It must still be charging, because a half-hour ago you couldn't even touch the ring.' I knew she was right, but it was discouraging to know that only a little while ago I had been a walking, talking human being. The memories had quickly started to fade once the magic of the ring was lost and I returned to my ghostly state. My experiences with Sarah and Tayvn were slowing etching their way back into some murky darkness to join the lost memories of my life. If I could not remember being alive, how could I possibly miss it? In an odd way I think that was why I could not remember anything before my death. The pain and hurt would have been too much for me to handle. Having to watch my family and friends as they lived a full and happy life without me would have been torture. No matter how much I rationalised that forgetting was a good thing, I didn't really believe it.

'It probably takes time for it to get back to normal,' I said, forcing myself to remember how good it had felt being real.

'You okay, Ben?' Sarah asked with a concerned smile. 'I would have thought that you'd be more excited about being human again. Ever since we met you made it sound as if being alive was the only thing you wanted. Seeing you today was awesome, because it was as though your days of loneliness were over. You were so happy.'

'Ice cream?' I asked remembering only vaguely the cool sensation the snack had given me. It was one of the few things I could still remember.

A loud crash of thunder erupted from the darkened sky to bring Sarah and me back to the present. I had forgotten about the storm. We had made it back to Sarah's moments before the sky became black and the rain began to pour. Sitting in her kitchen we could hear the rain as it pelted against the roof and the few remaining glass windows. Sarah's dad had removed most of the broken glass, which accounted for almost all of the windows, and replaced them with large plastic sheets that were taped shut. Each piece of plastic was violently trembling as the rain and the wind beat against them. In all of my lifetime I had never seen a storm quite this bad. In all of my lifetime I had never been in a storm that had scared me to my core like this one was doing. Something bad was in the air, and although Sarah couldn't sense it, I could. Muddled with my thoughts of being human was the feeling of dread I had only felt once before.

Quietly and alone we sat in the kitchen, the only room relatively untouched, if you ignored the massive amounts of pots, pans, plates, and cups that cluttered every available countertop. Currently it was the only room with a real window, no leaking roof, and heat. Sarah's dad was out getting some groceries and David had not yet come home from school. We both figured that he had gone home with some friends. We sat in an awkward silence for a long while waiting for the ring to recharge, testing it periodically by seeing if I could touch it. At first the ring slipped through my hand, but the latest attempt succeeded in allowing me to grasp it.

There was another loud crash of thunder followed by an intense volley of lightning that ignited the sky. Sarah and I jumped as the storm seemed to situate itself directly over top of us.

'Sarah,' I asked quietly. 'Sarah, have you ever known that something wasn't right?'

'What do you mean?' Sarah asked as her eyes showed concern, probably for David whom no one had heard from.

'Remember in your room last night when I got all weird?' I asked.

'Yeah,' Sarah remembered. 'We were talking about something and then you just froze like you had seen a ghost. Oh, sorry.'

'I had a feeling, like a tingling that goes up your spine,' I tried to explain while at the same time forgetting the words to describe touching. 'Ever since this storm started I've been getting that feeling, as though there was something out there that was causing it. Something dark and scary. Something that I should remember because I think it was what killed me.'

'What do you mean, Ben? You said that you couldn't remember dying or what killed you. And now you have a feeling that it's back. You've been around for hundreds of years. Whatever was out there must be long gone by now.'

Sarah was trying to dispel her fears that something supernatural and deadly was lurking close by. Quietly she rose from her seat by the wooden kitchen table and moved towards the window were she searched the dark evening sky in vain. The rain was coming down like pellets, clanging explosively as they hit the ground. In the distance people were being struck by the stinging raindrops without mercy as the thunder and lightning laughed. I could see that Sarah remembered the weird things that had happened since she had moved to town. She was friends with a ghost and the bearer of a magical ring. Why couldn't there be a monster thrown into the mix? I could see the lines of concern and fear crawl across Sarah's face as she painfully searched for something creeping about in the overgrown yard.

'Has it ever rained like this before?' she asked.

'Never like this, but there was one storm a few graduations ago that flooded Breaker Street. They shut down school for three days,' I answered, lying through my teeth in the hope of being some comfort. I had never seen anything like this before in my life and I hoped I would never see it again.

'This storm is unlike anything you have ever seen. A great evil has awoken and wishes to tell the world that he is back,' an unusually calm yet comforting voice with a magical echoing affect said from behind us as we gazed out the window. There was a watery reflection in the old glass, a reflection that neither of us recognised. We quickly turned to face the intruder standing on the opposite side of the door that led to the outside world. At first I thought she had wandered in to seek shelter from the storm, but she was bone dry.

Whoever she was, she was old. There were deep wrinkles and lines etched into the skin of her face. She had long white hair that contrasted sharply with her dark brown skin. The woman was wearing a long gown made of brownish suede that had been ceremoniously decorated with colourful beads and feathers. Her hair was tied into two tight braids that hung effortlessly well past her shoulders. Across her forehead was a band made out of the same material as her dress, only in the middle of it was a bright red mark. I recognised the mark immediately as one of the symbols from the ring, a circle with two lines making a tee-pee shape.

The world seemed to grow still as a result of the eerie atmosphere that surrounded the mysterious woman.

There was a long silence as we waited for the woman to do something, but she simply looked at Sarah and me with a sense of relief. Her wizened eyes were a deep chestnut brown and looked as though they belonged to a young girl, a girl I knew from somewhere. She smiled softly in our direction, and looked intently at Sarah, before shifting her gaze directly towards me. I was not even fazed that this stranger could see me; the moment I saw her I knew that there was a connection among the three of us.

'I don't know who you are, but you'd better get out of here,' Sara said. 'My dad is right upstairs and if I yell he'll be down here in a second…' She stopped to think of an appropriate threat but she couldn't find one. Her fear of this intruder was blocking her creative juices. 'Dad!' she began to shout, 'I think you should…'

'I am not here to harm you, my dear child, nor you, Ben,' the woman smiled calmly. 'I am called Moon Light Seeker and we have a great deal of work to do.'

'You can see me!' I exclaimed as my intuition was proven to be correct.

'How did you know we'd be here?' Sarah asked, as this all-knowing woman began to smile.

'I have been waiting for this day for a very long time,' the woman began. 'I am part of something much bigger than you can comprehend at this time, but soon it will all make sense. For now, all you must do is trust that I am here to help; the rest will come with time.'

'You're connected to the ring,' I said. 'Sarah, the mark on her head-band is from the ring.' Sarah looked down and noticed the same strange marking glowing brilliantly from her finger.

'Yes, but while I will answer many questions tonight, I do not come to bring news of good tidings,' the woman said as her expression grew sterner. 'There are very dangerous things coming your way. Things that are made of pure evil. Something has returned to this world with both the power, and the desire, to destroy everything it touches. He is coming for the ring you wear, Sarah Winters, and he will not rest until he has its power.'

'And you're here to help us?' I asked nervously as Sarah stood there, unusually quiet.

'No one can help you except yourselves.' The woman was being so serious it scared me. 'It is my job to see you through the first of many challenges that lie in your path. Your journey will be a long one down a very treacherous road, where you will encounter both friends and foes who will both help and hinder you. It is my sacred task to tell of the things that have been, so that they do not repeat themselves.' Moon Light Seeker was speaking with such wisdom that we had no choice but to listen. Although we both sensed that what we were about to learn would be frightening, we could not resist listening to the old woman's words.

'Ben?' Sarah asked quietly, hoping I would have some answers. My blank expression was probably not comforting. Sarah appeared scared yet thoughtful as she stared at the mysterious old woman who had appeared in her home. 'Who are you?'

'I am your guide,' the woman began. 'You see, my child, everyone has a destiny. We are all given the tools to achieve great things and with the proper encouragement we can overcome any obstacle in the way. There are those people who are naturally athletic, or are gifted with insights into the worlds of art or science that allow them to reach new heights. Some, though few in number, have destinies beyond that of normal understanding. These chosen few are gifted with the power to protect the very balance of the world, to save those who are unaware of the danger that would seek their destruction. It is those people that are connected to something greater than science can explain, yet which all can comprehend at some basic level.'

'You mean magic?' Sarah asked softly.

'Yes,' Moon Light Seeker smiled. 'All of your questions will be answered shortly, but not here.' The woman raised her arms into the air as a low whistling arose from the cracks in the walls. The air, which moments before had carried the stench of fear, was now filled with warmth. As the old woman chanted in some unknown language, the distinct beat of a drum echoed in the background. The windows and the doors leading out of the kitchen burst open as a wind carrying the smells of freshly cut grass entered the room. The wind grew in power and filled the kitchen with magical dried leaves and a sweet-smelling dust plucked from the depths of a hidden forest. The leaves danced as they traced the movement of the wind. The magical storm forced Sarah and me to shield our eyes, until suddenly everything went dark.

It was so dark that it was hard to tell if our eyes were open or shut. The air carried a sweet smell unknown in Oceanview, or anywhere else in the world. Wherever the winds had taken us was a place of pure magic. We could feel our senses heighten and our souls being cleansed by the purity of this new land.

'At the beginning of time there was no light, only darkness,' the old woman said as her voice came from all directions. 'There was no good or evil as we know it. But there were creatures that made this darkness their home. Creatures that cared for nothing other than power, until one day when all that changed.'

As if on cue, the ring around Sarah's finger burst into light as it projected its dancing symbols in golden rays. The world slowly entered into the sunlight emanating from the ring. The world around us looked like Oceanview, but it was not. The colours were more vibrant, the smells more intoxicatingly beautiful. We were in a replica of Oceanview as it would exist in a magical utopia.

Sarah and I were outside, and the rain had stopped; in fact it seemed as though there had never been a storm. As the stars began to twinkle above, the ring shed light into the far reaches of the area around us as though it were the sun. We were in the clearing where the old house had been, where my life as a ghost began, the one with the tree that the town had decided to knock down. Only, like the rest of this world, it was different. Where the old house had stood was a brand new one. Sarah and I found ourselves standing miles from Sarah's house with the old woman nowhere to be seen.

'I know this place,' I stated as Sarah looked around cautiously. 'I mean, the house here shouldn't be this nice, but I'm pretty sure I know it.'

The house hadn't been in shambles forever. At one time it must have looked like this, a large house with high spires reaching out from the rooftops and a large balcony with intricate carvings of gargoyles on each rail. There was a thick oak door with a fanged beast as a knocker. But this was not the way I had seen it. I remembered the house looking dead and decayed. The house in the real Oceanview had been literally sucked into the earth. There should have been brown, dead moss covering the railings and porch, not white polished wood.

'With the light came creatures of inherent goodness but naïve spirit,' Moon Light Seeker was saying. 'These new beings entered this world and slowly became more numerous than the prior inhabitants. The creatures of darkness feared these new beings and fled into the deepest pits to be forgotten. Yet a few remained after seeing that the new beings could be easily manipulated and exploited.'

The woman slowly appeared amidst a sudden upward wind carrying millions of brown and yellow leaves.

'Where are we?' Sarah asked. 'This isn't Oceanview. This place is different.'

'Different but the same, Sarah Winters,' Moon Light Seeker smiled as she pointed towards a circle of three stones that were the perfect size and shape to be used as seats; in the middle of the circle was a stone spire with carvings all around it and flattened top. The middle pedestal was meant for the ring, as it glimmered in the same golden light. 'This is the Dreamscape, a world of magic where time has no meaning and stories live. This is where all magic comes from and eventually returns to. Now sit with me; we have much to do.'

With a strange feeling of trust, Sarah and I followed the old woman towards the three stones and we each took a seat. Here I was real, but with all the pureness and magic flowing in the air, I hardly noticed. The ring magically floated off Sarah's finger and landed in the middle of the pedestal. The now gold ring added to the already powerful magic in the air. This mystical place was indescribably beautiful and filled me with feelings of love and hope, feelings I would not associate with the place this mystical world was replicating.

'Do you know this place, Ben?' the old woman asked.

I nodded, not wanting to say anything further for fear that the truth of my uneasiness was going to be revealed.

'This is where it all began, the journey for which the ring has sought you. The journey that was started centuries ago.' The old woman spoke with the ease of a natural storyteller, entrapping Sarah and me in the softness of her voice. 'A long time ago, this place was sacred to the Wampanoag tribe, for my people. But it was a time of great confusion and anger. My tribe and a group of people from a distant land were having great battles over the ocean and the forest. We fought bitterly, blaming each other for the misfortunes each side faced. One year, the harvests for the newcomers were terrible, and the hunting for my people had almost completely ceased. Instead of trying to determine the cause of our problems together, we fought. Our anger grew with each passing day, as though it was being fuelled by some unseen force.'

As the old woman spoke, the ring cast shadows that acted out the story as she told it. The shadows grew in shape and size and, although faceless, gave the impression of emotion and character. The shadows belonged to people from the past who were each given new life in this strange new land.

'Soon, people from both groups began to disappear. Our elders could not understand why, but they were sensing a presence unlike any they had ever felt before, an evil that was so severe that if it was not dealt with, it would eventually consume everyone and everything. My people first assumed this evil came from the newcomers who had landed and set up their homes.   Slowly a few members from my tribe discovered that the horrible things happening to us were also happening to the newcomers.'

'A demon named Omascus had travelled the world searching for ways of increasing his powers. Fate eventually led him to our shores. In the beginning he had been content manipulating the animals and nature around him, but soon he learned of the great potential within the human spirit. After watching my people and yours interact, he decided to use the hatred between our two peoples to conceal his true intentions. He stole the very souls of the people living in these woods while manipulating our mistrust to mask his deeds and very existence. Omascus was clever at covering his tracks until one fateful night.

'He had been seen stealing the soul of a newcomer by a boy who had been sent to search for his friend. No one believed the boy's fantastic tale, so he searched for help among my people, where he befriended a young girl who was determined to help.'

197

The shadows had formed a large darker shape that seemed fierce even though it lacked any expression. It was only a shadow, but Sarah and I could feel the intense power that seeped from its darkened soul. This shadow had once belonged to the demon, and still stank of trickery and deceit.

'The demon had gathered enough power to destroy the world we knew. In a desperate measure to stop him, the two children combined the ancient magic of their cultures and composed a powerful spell and talisman in hopes of stopping him. With each soul Omascus ingested he gained greater power and would soon be unstoppable, yet no one believed what the two children had to say. Unfortunately, the two youths were too weak compared to the monster's mastery of the mystical forces. Although their magic freed the souls, it was not enough to destroy the beast. Instead, it weakened Omascus and put him into a deep sleep. However there was a great cost. To attract the demon, bait was needed. The boy lost his soul to the demon, on this very spot, as Omascus tried desperately to possess the power of his soul, as the countless others were being freed.

'Through some mystic knowledge, the rescued souls knew that the struggle with Omascus was not over, and they left a piece of themselves behind. The small portion of magic each left made this talisman a powerful source of magic. The magic of the souls and the people connected to the creation of the ring breathed life into a once simple piece of workmanship.

'With the body of the creature for all to see, the people of both sides finally believed the tale and worked together to bury Omascus deep beneath the soil, and placed a magical tree on top to keep him sealed in the earth. Together, the Wampanoags and the newcomers lived for many years in peace, while the demon was left undisturbed until even the myths of his existence were forgotten.'

As the old woman spoke, the shadows cast from the ring danced around us in celebration. It made sense now; the ring was alive and its song and dancing carvings were its way of communicating with us. The shadows that danced were those that had been connected with the ring, allowing life to be added to the spoken word. Sarah and I could only sit staring at the old woman and her youthful eyes that sparkled with wisdom, while listening intently to all that she was telling us.

'What does this have to do with us?' I asked despite knowing the answer.

'The beast has been freed and is searching for the talisman. If he ever reclaims the ring he could use its energy to restore his incredible powers. He is also after the boy who deceived this great monster,' the woman replied bluntly.

'My ring,' Sarah said. 'That would mean that Omascus wants my ring and that you, Ben, you are his final victim! That's why I can see you whenever I wear it. The ring is connected to you and wants to protect you. And you, Moon Light Seeker, were the girl!' Sarah looked at the old woman and saw her smile.

'You mean this Omascus guy made me what I am and is still after me?' I muttered, thinking of the ramifications of being killed twice and the knowledge of how I came to exist as I do.

'How did I get involved in all this?' Sarah asked almost bitterly.

'The spirits guided you to it, child,' the woman told Sarah calmly. 'Nothing on this earth happens by accident. I wore the ring until my time of passing and then the ring guided itself from hand to hand until it found the person who could accomplish its final task.'

'But what can we do?' I asked, nervous about a second death. 'We're just kids...well, a kid and a ghost. If we couldn't stop him before, what chance do we have now?'

'I believe in you, and you have one of the most powerful talismans known to exist,' the woman said as she rose to her feet, followed by Sarah and then me. 'We couldn't do it before because we didn't understand what was happening. We had neither the knowledge you two will possess, the friends who will aid you on your quest, nor the power of the ring.'

'Friends?' Sarah mumbled to herself. She then turned and looked at Moon Light Seeker as she pulled Sarah and me close to her and spoke quietly into our ears.

'Omascus must not get that ring,' she whispered sternly. 'Destiny picked you to destroy him. Believe in yourselves and you will succeed. Be warned: Omascus is a demon of deception who will use whatever means necessary to regain his full power. He has already recruited the help of some poor soul from your very town. Nor is he powerless; the storm tonight was Omascus announcing that he has returned. The ring cannot be taken from you; it must be given of free will. Guard it with all your might and be very careful whom you allow to wear it, for it has great powers which are unknown even to me. I know this is a tremendous responsibility, but you are not alone; the spirits will be with you. Look for the light of the Phoenix to light the dark corners of your path.'

As the old woman spoke her final words, she faded into the air, followed by a powerful wind. The Dreamscape began to melt away, revealing the simple backyard of the Winters' home. The air seemed old and stale as the magical world was replaced with the world of Oceanview. The storm had stopped, but there was no sense of a cleansing that follows even the slightest rain.

'So now what?' I asked. 'I don't suppose the "Phoenix" is a local demon exterminator listed in the phonebook?'

Sarah laughed out loud for a second and then looked at her ring, which had returned to her finger and was silver once more. She was nervous and scared. Not that I could blame her.

'I think I liked it better when I didn't know what was going on. When I didn't know that there were demons and monsters in the world. Whatever that woman was talking about belongs in storybooks and movies, not real life. Not here,' she said as she twisted the ring around her finger. 'I never asked for this responsibility, you know.'

'Me neither, but we can do it, we've got the ring!' I said as the thoughts of confronting what had killed me centuries ago scared me to the core. I wanted to sound tough, but I had already lost everything because of this monster. What would happen if I failed again? 'I'm not afraid if you're not.'

'But *I'm* not already dead,' Sarah practically yelled, as tears of fright ran down her cheeks.

'Neither was I…' I began.

'Hey Sarah,' a young voice called from behind her making both of us jump. 'Are you talking to yourself again?'

'Look who I found walking home in the rain,' Sarah's dad laughed as he ruffled the soggy mop of brown hair on his son's head. 'Maybe I'll draw you a map next time so you don't get lost. What are you doing outside in the dark, Sarah?'

'Nothing,' Sarah said pretending to be all right. 'I thought I heard something.' She faked a smile for her dad and brother as they walked towards the house.

'Everything okay, sweetie?' Sarah's dad asked, seeing right through her smile and into the nervousness beneath. 'Why don't you come in? I don't want you to get wet if the storm starts up again. I picked up some groceries, so no more take-out for dinner. How about giving me a hand in the kitchen?'

'I'll come inside soon,' Sarah said as David and her dad walked inside, closing the door behind them to keep the cool air out.

'Well, at least you can tell your friends back in Vancouver that Oceanview isn't boring,' I mentioned, in the hope of lightening the mood. 'Look, we can't do much about this now. Why don't we go take it easy, and we'll deal with this whole Omascus thing fresh tomorrow morning?'

'I guess,' Sarah said. 'Ben, do you think we are the only people who can do this?'

'I don't know.' I shrugged.

'Do you think it's, you know, real?' Sarah asked, sounding a little confused by her own words. 'I mean, do you think it's really as serious as that woman said?'

'I wish I knew,' I said, realizing that the more Sarah thought about it, the more concerned she became. 'As I said, we can't do anything tonight. Go to sleep and think about something else. I'll see you tomorrow at school.'

Sarah agreed and said goodnight to me before walking inside. I was worried. Sarah seemed scared, and that frightened me more than Omascus or even dying for a second time.

I wished I could have been as relaxed and poised as I'd pretended to be when I told Sarah to 'take it easy'. All night long I sat thinking about what we had been told, what I had forgotten from my past life. This demon that was brought back to life could destroy everything I was, everything I knew. Unless Sarah and I could stop it. But I wasn't too sure that we could.

As Sarah and I were talking outside, neither of us noticed that we were not alone. Once David was alone he slowly peeled back an old curtain covering an upstairs window to watch carefully. He grimaced as he spied the ring around Sarah's finger, but his smile was beyond mischief. It was pure evil.

CHAPTER 11 – WITHIN THE DREAM

No force in this world is all-powerful. Magic is no different. Magic is simply a form of energy that has limitations. Where electricity cannot pass through rubber, magic through sheer force alone cannot travel into the deepest recesses of the soul, not even the magic released by Omascus. Whenever a spell interferes with a person's will, some part of that individual's soul will always remain free. Sometimes that small piece of freedom is enough to break the spell completely.

David was no different from the countless others who had been subjected to a magical incantation. Deep within his own mind, a small piece of his mischievous spirit was still free, desperately searching for a way out of the cage that had been made of his body. Unfortunately, Sarah and I had no idea what was going on until it was almost too late.

That night, as the stars tried with all their might to break through the thick layer of cloud that had once been Omascus' storm, David was asleep in his bed. His sleep was far from a peaceful one. He spent much of the night tossing and turning as a fight broke out within his dreams for possession of his soul. If someone had walked in on the young boy, they would have thought he was having a nightmare; however, the truth does not always lie on the surface.

David was involved in a full-out war where the winner would take all.

David found himself standing in the middle of a field covered by a fog which gave off an eerie glow. A darkness that could not be penetrated surrounded the field. David felt very cold and very alone. He sensed that fierce creatures of pure evil surrounded him; he could smell their vile odours. The young boy felt the cold, sharp claws of some unseen beast gripping his body, forcing him to stand firmly in place. He tried to struggle, to break free of the invisible claws, but there was no chance of release. David used all his strength to shake, squirm, kick, and yell, hoping that he would jar himself loose, or at least attract someone to his aid.

After struggling for what felt like forever, David was thrown to the ground by the invisible claws, causing him to bloody his knees as he rolled on the damp grass.

Lying face down in the cold field, the young boy had the undeniable feeling that someone was watching him from very close by. A hidden presence was drilling holes into the boy with its burning eyes. He slowly rose to his feet as the fog wrapped itself snugly around his legs. David was dressed in his old rugby uniform, black shorts and a stripped long-sleeved dark blue jersey. There were rips along his shoulders outlining where the invisible claws had been.

David watched as several large shadowy figures moved slowly towards him, veiled by the opaque mist. It did not take long for the boy to realise that the creatures he saw were identical to the one he had seen in the Fun Shoppe. They looked primitive in their movements, like beasts from a distant time. The creatures drew past the curtain of fog, allowing David to see their thick red skin, horns, and claws that could rip through a brick wall. David released a fearful gasp as he once more felt the invisible claws sink deep into his shoulders. The monsters lined the field as though they were ready to play a rugby game, a game David could not afford to lose.

David was alone and had the ball in his hands. Instinctively he ran as fast as he could in the vain hope of scoring a 'try'. He wasn't sure what was making him move, let alone run; he was being driven by an uncontrollable urge to escape this awful place. With great skill and everything to lose, the boy dodged the first creature, which filled him with the thought that he might actually have a chance. This mere moment of bliss was shattered when a huge clawed fist wrapped itself around his neck and squeezed tightly on his throat.

This monster, larger that the others, lifted David off the ground by his neck and held him at eye-level. David could smell the familiar stink of his breath and see the murderous glowing eyes of the man who had tricked him earlier, the man who had caused all of this to happen. It was the demon known as Omascus.

The giant hand squeezed tighter, suffocating David. At first David tried to call to his father for help, call to anyone who could possibly save him, but no sound louder than a whisper came from his throat. His air was being used up and no more was allowed to enter the child's body. The creature simply smiled without a care other than his own personal amusement. Soon the boy was drained of all desire to do anything but give up. The boy stopped squirming as his body went limp.

Through the darkness, David heard the scratchy voice of the demon murmuring 'The ring, boy; get me the ring!' The phrase was repeated over and over until it echoed throughout the vast emptiness surrounding the boy. The sound of the monster swirled in David's muddled thoughts until it became the only thought in his head. He had tried to fight the spell of the demon, but he was just a kid and had no power to challenge a monster of Omascus's strength. He was too tired. All

David wanted was for everything to go back to the way it was, in his old house, with his old friends, in his old school, far away from this field in Oceanview.

David had no more will left to fight.

On the verge of giving in completely to the demon, there was an eruption above his head, an explosion filled with bright colourful light that ripped through the unnatural darkness. The monster and David struggled to look into the hole ripping apart the blackened sky. It was too bright to see who was there, but David could tell it was someone on his side. The shining figure was reaching from a place opposite to this nightmare. Her soft, golden hand stretched to reach for David. All he had to do was grab it, but her fingers seemed too far away. Whoever she was, she felt warm and comforting to him, yet it was obvious she scared the demon who was holding the boy. Maybe David's calls for help had been heard and she was an angel coming to rescue him.

'Take my hand and I will protect you,' the figure said as she leaned further down from the bright hole in the sky. David tried to grasp her hand, but he could not move his arms from the side of his body. His strength and will were gone. It was a struggle simply to listen. He had never heard the wise sounding voice of the woman before, but wanted so much to reach for her, to be protected by her. For a mere moment the boy felt the warmth of her glow, the goodness of her essence.

All too soon David felt the grasp of the demon intensify and its claws sink into the flesh of his shoulder in defiance of the angel. The chant about the ring grew louder in an effort to cancel out the peaceful voice from the sky. David knew he was not alone, but the grasp of the monster was too powerful, too consuming. David let out a scream of both pain and despair, causing him to wake in a cold sweat.

Robotically, David got out of his bed and walked to his sister's room, careful not to make a sound. He cautiously opened the door and approached his sleeping sister. He searched Sarah's night-stand, her school bag, and her desk for the ring, but did not see it. There was only one other place it could be. Slowly David drew back the covers, beneath which his sister lay in a dream world all her own, and reached for her right hand, the hand that wore the ancient talisman.

The boy paused before trying to remove it. With the skill and steadiness of a surgeon's, David's steady hand reached for the ring.

Once he had made contact with the magical ring he received a large shock. Bright blue sparks erupted from the ring as a defence from being removed. David winced and quickly withdrew his hand and blew on his singed fingers. After his fingers had cooled, he tried again, only this time the shock was stronger. The boy caught his breath and, still following the chant ringing in his ears, he reached unsuccessfully for a third time and received such a tremendous jolt that he was thrown back several feet, landing in Sarah's closet. The noise caused Sarah to sit upright in her bed as she looked around for the intruder.

'David,' she said loudly. 'What are you doing in here?'

David sat dazed on the floor. For a brief time he felt his head clear, as if the demon inside him had vanished.

'I don't know,' he said. 'I was having a weird dream and I guess I was just sleep-walking. Sorry.' The moment of freedom ended as quickly as it had begun. David got to his feet and went back to his bed.

'Well, don't do that again!' Sarah called behind him.

David returned to his room and got back into his bed. He closed his eyes and entered back into his nightmare.

CHAPTER 12 – OMASCUS

From the moment I left Sarah I knew that things had changed. No longer was my life a mystery; rather it was now but a part of the larger picture. I was a part of a destiny that pitted me, and a girl I had recently met, against a demon older than time. Even after centuries of being asleep, he was still a powerful threat to my tranquil town, my friends, my life. Earlier this day I had been wondering who I was, never dreaming of what was heading my way. Now I had answers, but wished that I was still naïve about my existence. A part of me felt cursed, having met Sarah and waking up to all this, while another part yearned for revenge against the monster that had trapped me in this limbo, robbing me of a chance to live and die as a normal human being.

The only consistent emotion I could feel was the bubbling of a fierce uneasiness that forced me to fly in endless circles around Oceanview. My mind was in overload as it processed all of the information

217

Josh Sadovnick

Moon Light Seeker had given us, trying to remember what I had forgotten in those dark woods long ago. With every answer I discovered, or connection I made, new fears and questions emerged about the rest of what I had forgotten. I could imagine someone asking me what I had done today and my response being: 'Today I found out how I died and that I was destined to save the world and avenge my death.' Truth was, I'd discovered how I died, but was still clueless as to how I had lived.

As the Dreamscape had faded and Sarah and I found ourselves alone in her yard, our innocent view of our world vanished. A demon was hidden somewhere in our quiet town and he was planning something sinister that would see him reign supreme, no matter what the cost. The magic we had discovered seemed more dangerous than ever.

There was only one certainty in this whole mess, and that was that the demon could not make his move until he was restored to full strength, and to do that he needed Sarah's ring. Ignorance is bliss, but knowledge is power, and Sarah and I had been given a heads-up as to what this demon would be planning. The warning from Moon Light Seeker was an omen of the things to come. We could no longer trust anyone other than each other, and we would always need to watch our backs.

Something bad was being planned and no one would be spared if Sarah and I failed.

Trapped in this town, I was vulnerable, and Omascus knew it. As I travelled high in the sky over the beaches near Oceanview, I understood that this demon was not a fool. He knew Sarah has the ring and he knew that I existed just as we knew about him. Moon Light Seeker had said that he had some power left, and if he was notorious for trapping souls, he could probably sense their vulnerability. I had watched this community grow from its infancy and I could not stand by and watch it all end.

Then there was Sarah. Even after the short time we had known each other, I felt that I would do anything for her. If anything happened to her and I didn't try to stop it, I would be as responsible as Omascus. It was my duty to protect them all, even Axle. It was my destiny, and no matter how much I wanted to escape from it, there was no way that I could.

I circled the town as though I were a vulture looking for fresh meat, only in my case I was looking for a leathery demon. The pit of my stomach was in a knot. I wanted to do everything I could to protect the town, but at the same time I wished that I could have slept soundly in a warm bed completely unaware of the ever-growing danger that would soon violently shake my world.

By the time the sky filled with colour from the distantly rising sun, I had become confident that with Sarah by my side we could defeat Omascus and make everything all right. It was the start of a new day and although I had no idea what would head our way next, I knew that we could handle it. After all, Sarah and I had been chosen by a power greater than good and evil. We had been chosen by fate!

I worked my way over to Sarah's to see how she had been managing since the news from Moon Light Seeker, or at least to make sure she had gotten some sleep. I waited impatiently outside her door so that I could let her in on all that I had been doing. When she finally walked out of her house towards the car with her brother and dad she didn't even look up at me. The ring was not on her finger. My heart stopped. A thousand fears burnt tracks in my head. Had the battle been lost already? Sarah acted as though there was nothing out of the ordinary going on around her...no ghost, no monster, no magic. I had turned invisible again, and as far as I could tell she had no clue that I was floating inches from her.

More confused than ever, I followed Sarah to school, keeping my distance the entire time, searching for an ambush by the demon. If Omascus had the ring and the warning was right, I was his next target. When the car stopped outside of High Point, Sarah said good-bye to her dad and brother and headed towards the thick wooden doors. I quickly flew towards her in the hope that if I tried hard enough she might be able to sense me. As I got close, I heard the music from the ring and saw it sparkle beneath her shirt. Sarah had fastened the ring to a chain and wore it around her neck, keeping it safe and out of sight, but making me invisible in the process. Was this her way of ignoring me? It was as though Sarah was trying to make everything extraordinary that had happened since we met disappear.

'We need to talk,' I whispered to Sarah as she walked up the stairs towards her locker. There was no response, which was no surprise since she was not wearing the talisman.

I hung around Sarah all morning, hoping she would eventually put on the ring and speak to me, even if it was just to tell me to 'get lost'. No such luck. She literally walked right through me and acted as though we had never met. More worries shot through my head about what to do. Was I now alone in the fight against Omascus? Had Omascus somehow gotten to Sarah?

I hovered around her all day, only to learn that she was trying hard to be a normal teenager with no great magical power meant to help her save the world.

The bell rang for lunch and I had come up with a theory by this point. Maybe Sarah had taken off the ring to keep it safe. By ignoring the ring's power and me with it, she was making sure that if Omascus already controlled some of the people at school, they wouldn't suspect her of being the ring-bearer. Maybe she was waiting until she had a chance to sneak up into the attic where we could talk in private. My theory was dead in the water when, instead of trying to communicate with me about our mission, Sarah decided to go for lunch with Tayvn.

Together, the two of them parked themselves on the main field by the school. Because it was a bright and sunny Friday, they sat in the middle of the oval field surrounded by the asphalt track. Sitting on the grass, they started to eat their lunch and talk about regular teenager stuff.

For the first little while, Sarah seemed slightly distracted. Not by me, since as far as I could tell I was still invisible to her, but by some deep thought she was wrestling with in the back of her mind. She was so out of it that she missed a lot of what Tayvn was saying.

'Are you okay, Sarah? You seem kind of spaced out,' Tayvn asked after Sarah failed to reply to something he'd said for the third time.

'Huh?' she said blankly. 'I've just been thinking about some stuff. What were you saying?'

'Just asking how you things were going. You know, with the move and all,' Tayvn restated pleasantly.

'It's okay; I've just had to deal with some, uh, distractions, that's all,' Sarah said honestly piquing my interest immediately.

'What do you mean "distractions"? Is life here really that different from where you came from?' Tayvn asked, slightly defensively. 'Small-town life isn't really as lame as people think, or at least I don't think it is.'

'Nothing like that…hey, Tayvn, I have a question for you,' Sarah said, waiting for Tayvn to give the go-ahead. 'What did you hear about me before I moved here?'

'I heard the gossip that was going around; it was pretty hard to miss. It's funny what people say when they're intimidated by a new kid,' Tayvn said bluntly. Good answer. 'I don't usually listen to that stuff. I try to make my own opinions. I figure everyone has rumours going around about them for some reason or another. I try not to listen to them, because usually they are completely backwards.'

'What did they say?' Sarah was determined to find out.

'Nothing important…well, nothing that really made any sense.'

'I can take it; please tell me.'

'Are you sure?'

'Yes.'

'They said you were a witch and you burned down your old school and ate a kid,' Tayvn said this so quickly I almost missed it entirely. Sarah laughed. 'But I'm guessing that it isn't true; I mean, there is no way you could eat a kid. I'm betting people taste awful, and that you would be in jail.'

'I have another question for you.' Sarah definitely had something going through her head.

'Shoot; just don't make it anything that's going to get me in trouble, or eaten,' Tayvn laughed.

'I promise not to turn you into dinner,' Sarah smiled back. 'If someone told you that you were responsible for doing something huge, would you?'

'I don't get it,' Tayvn said, a confused look in his eyes.

'If you were, well, meant to do something important. Like you were born to do it,' Sarah said, and I was suddenly very interested in what she was trying to say.

'You mean like fate? I don't know. I guess it would depend,' Tayvn said. 'Like if I was born to make it into the NBA, I would totally go for it. But if I was destined to, I don't know, do something dangerous, I would have to think about whether it was that important to me. If it was, I would. If it wasn't, I wouldn't. That is, if I had a choice.'

Wrong answer, Tayvn. I knew at this point that this conversation was no longer going my way.

'What if this thing you had to do was something only you could do?' Sarah asked as I began to slowly float away. 'Like a secret mission.'

'Everyone has some secret or another,' Tayvn said, a little more serious than usual. 'It's all a matter of how you deal with it and who you let in on it. My understanding of fate, though, is that no matter what you do, eventually you will have to deal with the problem.'

Rather than sit around and watch Sarah get more advice on how not to deal with Omascus, I decided to do some more demon-hunting. I was determined. It no longer mattered whether Sarah was going to help me fulfil our destiny. I knew what had to be done, and I was going to do it regardless of the cost. I headed down Breaker Street at full speed, looking for the monster whose shadow had struck fear in us while in the Dreamscape. If Omascus was anywhere, someone might have seen him, or seen something unnatural that was his doing.

I floated around all the local hangouts of the town gossips, and kept both my eyes and ears peeled for information. I was hoping to hear something I could link to the demon, but after a while and still no mention of anything out of the ordinary I decided to search elsewhere.

I was flying towards the woods where the monster's house once stood when I saw something that didn't fit. David was walking down the street. By the blank look on his face I could tell that something was out of the ordinary; besides, David should have been in school. Helping me with this conclusion was the fact that there were no other children to be found.

I flew over to the boy and decided to follow him. His sister might be trying to avoid the unusual, but I wasn't about to let anything happen to her brother. Regardless of what was going through

Sarah's head, she was my friend. Maybe if Omascus tried to attack her brother, I would be able to scare the demon away…Moon Light Seeker could see me; Omascus should be able to do the same, and then Sarah would know how serious this was. If worse came to worst, I could get a huge pit-bull angry and use it to scare the demon. My imagination began to run wild with images of me saving the day and defeating the demon. Wrapped in my own fantasy, I floated right past David as he stopped in front of a peculiar store.

I quickly swung back and followed him into the store, which I had never noticed before. There were dancing lights and electric gizmos displayed in the large plate-glass window at the front of the store. The door was painted a rich purple, and above it a flashy sign said, 'Welcome to the Fun Shoppe'. I slipped through the door and saw a large selection of very cool high-tech toys. It was an amazing store, where everything seemed to be alive. I was pretty surprised that I had never seen it before; I mean, it had all the things anyone would stop in their tracks to explore. It was weird, even though I have no use for the things in the shop, I had this intoxicating feeling that I wanted to buy everything.

That feeling was quickly replaced by one of dread. The sick feeling in my stomach had returned as I began to sense the presence of Omascus, feel the death and despair he spread.

David seemed right at home in the store. He made a beeline through the displays of science, past the unattended cashier's desk, and behind a thick velvet curtain. I wasn't sure what to make of all this, other than that something really bad was about to happen and that I needed to follow the boy.

Behind the curtain was a dark room lit by candles that gave off black flames. The darkness was thick and murky, being fuelled by an evil magic, one I could taste. The room was bigger than it should have been; it appeared bigger than the building that housed it. Omascus must have recovered a great deal of his power to create this realm, his Dreamscape. There was an odd smell in the air, the scent of musty wood that you would find deep in the darkest corners of the forest where there was nothing but rot and decay. In the centre of the room was a thick iron cauldron with a purple bubbling liquid within it, in which there were floating candles.

Behind the cauldron was a hunched figure wearing a dark cloak. The closer I moved towards the shadowy figure, the worse the tingling in my spine became. I tried to hide in the far right corner near the ceiling and be inconspicuous. If that was Omascus, he would have to search for me.

'You have returned empty-handed, boy,' the figure said in a cracked voice, keeping his head down beneath the hood of the cloak.

'Whenever I tried to take it, it fought back with magic.' David sounded very robotic, possessed. The figure must have been who I sensed he was. It was Omascus in the flesh.

'Fool,' Omascus replied angrily. 'I told you that the ring cannot be taken! It must be given, which is why I chose you in the first place! She gives the ring to you and you give it to me…a simple plan even for a mortal!'

The figure stood upright and the cloak dropped off his shoulders and head, landing by his feet. I had had my own visions of what had cast that looming shadow in the Dreamscape, but Omascus's appearance was worse than anything I had expected. He was tall, with scaly red skin covering his face and hands. There were thick clumps of whitish hair parted by a sharp horn that could tear through the hardest stone. His ears were pointed to fine tips, matching the shape of his jagged teeth. His eyes were sunk deep into his head and were as black as the night sky. There was no spark of goodness anywhere within his marble-sized pupils, only destruction.

'If you remain useless to me, boy, I will exterminate you! I have no need for…hello, what is this?' The demon stopped in mid-sentence as he lifted his nose into the air and took a deep and powerful sniff. 'Perhaps you are not as empty-handed as I had assumed.'

'What is it?' David asked as he looked into the air. David was completely under the demon's control, and I was counting my blessings that it was not a family trait that allowed Sarah to see me.

I wasn't sure what Omascus was smiling about, but I had a bad feeling that if it made him happy, it was not good. Omascus waved his thick hands over the cauldron and mumbled some words. Soon a thin mist filled the room, a mist that seemed to cling to me like slime. I was frozen in fear and Omascus was somehow making me visible.

'It's the boy who robbed me of my strength and helped bury me. The vile youth who tricked me, a feat he will not have the honour of doing ever again.' Omascus moved around the room until he stopped and snarled at my encased form. He took in another loud sniff before raising a wrinkled, leathery hand and pointed directly at me. Great! Moon Light Seeker could see me, Omascus could sniff me out like a bloodhound, and make me visible and there wasn't as much as a spider handy that I could make angry and use to attack the monster. All my daydreaming had ended in me being nothing more than a scared kid. David looked confused, as he saw nothing more that a coloured blotch in the air.

'You have made hunting for you much easier, you foolish youth, but I suppose it is time to finish the job I started, and make you pay for what you did. Let this be a lesson to you, boy…if you can't finish a job, don't start it in the first place!'

I held my breath and prayed for someone to save the day.

Omascus began to speak in an ancient language, as a ball of light formed at the tip of his finger. I still could not remember about my life before I became a spirit, but the rush of fear that was going through me felt very familiar, fear about what I knew was coming and was powerless to prevent. It was a fear that was making me shiver all over, as though I had thousands of ants crawling on my skin. My heart was racing a mile a minute.

Omascus' eyes began to spark rapidly as the intensity of the light at his finger grew. Bolts of light and power lunged from the demon's finger and struck me in the chest. My head was spinning, as I felt sharp burning nails drilling into me. My body burned, as every nightmarish vision I had ever seen flashed before my eyes, a torture I knew Omascus had planned. Slowly I was being drawn closer to the demon, and the world was going black.

As quickly as Omascus's spell started, it ended with a shout of intense pain from the creature of darkness and deceit. Omascus grabbed his wrist and fell to one knee. He must not have had enough power to add my soul to his power, or maybe someone heard my prayer and decided to buy me some more time. Without the ring he couldn't steal souls, at least not yet, but I wasn't going to wait around to see what the demon could still do. I turned and flew as fast as I could through the curtain, out of the store. But now I knew the demon should have taken his own advice and not started his revenge, for his plan was now clear as day.

I was scared and in a panic. I had no idea what had just happened, but my chest still burned from where that light had struck me. I needed to go somewhere where I would be safe, so I went to my home, to the secret attic.

When I arrived, I saw that a light had been left on and a few boxes were opened, including the one with the skull and crossbones drawn on it. I called out Sarah's name, but no one answered. The thought that Omascus had been snooping around was my next thought, followed by the urgency to tell Sarah about her brother. I was about to fly to Sarah's house so I could warn her about what I had seen when I noticed a piece of paper pinned to the couch and an old dream catcher hanging from a rafter. I could tell that both of these were from Sarah.

Dear Ben,

I came up here to see you but you were gone. I wanted to apologize for the way I was acting today. There really isn't any other way to say it, but I was scared. My whole world was changing and it was too much for me. I needed to take some time to be a normal kid and figure things out. Being told that it is your destiny to destroy a monster who's after your ring and your friend is a lot of pressure and it weirded me out in a big way. I thought that maybe if I just ignored everything, it would all disappear.

I felt you leave when Tayvn said that if I thought things were too dangerous I should try to avoid them, change fate. Truth is, if I avoid this, everyone suffers, not just me or my family. What good is it being normal if it costs everyone else their souls?

I came up here to tell you all this, but you were gone and I had to get home. I hope you don't mind, but I borrowed some books from a box that I thought might be helpful and I found something for you. I left it on the trunk. The ring is next to it. I figure it will be safe with you; besides you'll need it.

Come by tonight, we have a destiny to fulfil.

— Sarah

What could she have left for me? I turned around and saw an old black leather-bound book lying on the trunk with the ring gleaming beside it. I picked up the ring and felt myself turn human once again. I then remembered my urgency to tell Sarah something. I thought hard but I could not remember what is was;

some weird music was all I could hear, a song I had never heard before, making me forget.

Carefully, I blew the dust off the old book and opened it to a page that had been marked with a faded red ribbon. There was a picture of the ring on the brown-edged page, and the same story that Moon Light Seeker had told us the previous night. I read it carefully and flipped the page. My heart skipped for a second as I saw a drawing of the demon, the pain in my chest suddenly coming back to me as the music being played on an out-of-tune fiddle intensified. I turned the page quickly and the music faded slightly. There was a picture of a boy I had seen before.

It was me.

The same boy I had seen in the mirror. I quickly looked in the dusty mirror in the attic to make sure. Right down to the freckles on my nose, the boy in the picture was me. There was a name scrawled underneath the drawing in large calligraphy: Alexander Lloyd Erikson.

This book was about me! I was so exhilarated by this discovery that nothing could have distracted me. Later I realised that this forgetfulness was aided by dark magic.

All of my questions about my life were about to be answered. I had a chance to find out exactly who I was. Did I have sisters or brothers? What were my parents like? Did I have friends? Nothing else in the world mattered except what this book had to say.

The book explained in detail about my past and expanded on the story Moon Light Seeker had told us. I didn't really expect much to change in this version of history, but the book had pictures of my family, my friends, and me. I had had two brothers and a sister who were all very young when I confronted Omascus the first time, the time I lost. I was seeing their faces on these pages, but they looked like complete strangers to me, as did the faces of my parents and my friends...as if I had never met them before.

I flipped through a few more pages and saw a detailed sketch of Alexander and a young Moon Light

Seeker fighting the demon. I read on about how I had approached the home of the demon and demanded that he face me. Moon Light Seeker was right, I had used myself as bait. The story continued by saying that I had left a note to my family, knowing I would not survive the night. I had believed that I would be making the ultimate sacrifice. In a way, I had.

I felt the effects of the ring begin to fade as a warm purple mist wrapped itself around my body and I began to feel that light feeling again. Suddenly I remembered about David and Omascus. I had to warn Sarah and tell her that her brother was under the spell of the demon. I tried to pick up the ring, but I couldn't touch it; it needed to recharge. It was up to me to warn Sarah without the ring, assuming it was even possible and that I wasn't too late.

As soon as Omascus recovered in the back room of the Fun Shoppe, moments after I had fled, he raced to the dark cauldron. He waved his hands over it and chanted a series of intricate long-forgotten words. Briefly the flames from the candles ignited as a black fiddle that looked as though it had been poured from a viscous liquid rose from the purple fluid. A rusty music that would cause shivers in any mortal began to play. The demon stepped back and listened to the sounds he considered to be beautiful.

'To undo what has been done, to forget what has been seen,' Omascus said to David who was standing motionless in the corner. 'Come, boy, we have work to do, and not a lot of time before this song ends and you no longer remain of use to me.'

The demon began the transformation into his human form of Rex Sheffer as he led the boy out of the room.

CHAPTER 13 – TAYVN

While I was seeing the true evil that was Omascus, Sarah had been dealing with our fate in her own way. She never told me what made her accept our destiny and join the fight, but I believe that Tayvn had something to do with it.

Sarah needed to talk to me once she had made up her mind. She placed the ring back onto her finger and as soon as class ended, snuck into the attic in the hope that I would be there. While she waited for me to show up, she began to explore the many sealed boxes and crates of long-forgotten artifacts and memories. When she came close to the box marked with the skull and crossbones Creepy Sweepy had drawn, the ring began to sing its song. Up until this point the ring had only responded to magical beings and Tayvn, not objects. This sparked Sarah's curiosity.

Sarah carefully peeled back the intricately-placed tape that kept the contents of the box hidden. With a mixture of fearful hesitation and excitement as to what secrets the box held, she lifted the stiff flaps of cardboard.

Had Sarah been more experienced with magic she would have sensed the immense power contained within those thin walls of cardboard. At the very least she would have seen the bright beam of light that leaped from the newly opened box like a shooting star, a beacon showing that this great power had been released. Intuitively, and by noticing the speed at which the carvings around the ring spun, Sarah was aware that the stacks of old books and the old Wampanoag dream catcher were of vast importance to our quest. She removed the dust-covered books and was astonished at how each one pulsed in her hands, as though they were alive.

Many of the books were in foreign languages, some of which Sarah did not recognise, and each book was a unique shape and size. However, there were two books that seemed to call to Sarah in a mystical and unexplainable way. The first was a thickly bound book that held a hand-written log of everything that had occurred in Oceanview around the time of Omascus, a book that focused on my life, and death. After reading it quickly where she stood, Sarah knew that she had made the right decision to face our destiny and stop the demon from causing any more damage.

The other book was a heavy scrapbook. It was about the height of an atlas and the width of an encyclopaedia volume. The cover was made of a leathery material that was smooth to Sarah's touch. The book glowed with age and wisdom; it was undoubtedly the oldest thing in the box, quite possibly the oldest thing Sarah had ever seen. She sat down on the couch and placed the book on the trunk so she could examine it closer.

A long time ago Sarah's mother had told her that books, contrary to what most people thought, chose their reader and took each one on a unique journey, teaching the reader what they needed to know through the stories it held. The intense singing of the ring told Sarah that this was one of those books that had an unbelievable journey in store for her.

Sarah blew the dust off the plain cover and braced herself for whatever the book contained. She was surprised when she discovered that the thick, hand-made pages of the book were blank. She flipped through the pages of parchment hoping for a clue as to why such an intricately crafted journal would be left empty, yet call to her in such a powerful way. The ring on her finger was going nuts; she felt the importance of this book in every nerve, yet there was not so much as a word to be found within it. Following instinct alone, Sarah opened the book and left it exposed on the trunk. She closed her eyes and placed her hand, the one with the ring on it, in the centre of the blank pages.

There was a deep silence.

Suddenly the ring gave off an intense light that made everything in the attic glow momentarily. Out of the ring poured the mystical symbols that danced gleefully across the pages, burning into the parchment words that would forever change our lives. This was the book that held the most powerful spells of the demon Omascus. This was the book that had helped a young Moon Light Seeker and Alexander Lloyd Erikson seal their fates over a century ago. This was the book that held the most primal forms of magic, the most powerful form known outside of the Dreamscape.

Sarah knew instantly that this book could be a great advantage against the demon, or a tool that would increase the power Omascus had over Oceanview. She would have to master its strength so that we would have a chance to defeat the demon. Sarah remembered her grandmother tell her that it wasn't enough to know the words of a spell; to release its true power you needed to understand the root of the spell, its higher meaning. Grams would go on to say that the study of magic was as intense as the study of science, in that if you tried something before you knew all of the facts you could unleash a major disaster. Sarah knew from the words of her grandmother that understanding what she had discovered would take time. After a moment of debate with herself, Sarah decided to take the book home, where she could study it relatively undisturbed as well as more inconspicuously than hiding in the attic all weekend.

Quickly Sarah wrote me a note, left the book about my life marked to a specific section, took off the ring, and left the room. She was hesitant to leave the ring unprotected in the attic, but she felt that it would be safe. Moon Light Seeker said that it had to be given, it could not be taken, and she was technically giving it to me, but just to ensure its safety, Sarah hung the old dream catcher in the middle of the room. If somehow Omascus discovered our secret hideaway, maybe seeing the symbol of his enemy would scare him away.

Sarah had had her back to the hall as she closed the door to the attic when she heard a voice call her name. At first she thought that it was Axle looking for trouble, because school was out for the weekend and other than the basketball practice in the gym, no one else was around. Bracing for impact, Sarah hugged the heavy book to her chest and turned around.

'Look, I don't have time for this right now...' Sarah began, annoyed as she whipped around, expecting to find Axle and her thugs. Instead she saw Tayvn dripping in sweat and no longer smiling.

'Uh, sorry I...' Tayvn stammered, shocked by Sarah's reaction; it was not what he was expecting.

'Oh, it's you. I'm so sorry, I thought you were someone else,' Sarah immediately apologized. She smiled as Tayvn leaned over to wipe his forehead on his shirt. He was breathing hard and red in the face. Dressed in a pair of blue basketball shorts and a grey basketball jersey that had 'High Point' across the chest he must have come directly from practice. Even though she was happy to see him, Sarah was worried that he had seen the entrance to the attic. If he found the attic, things would be much more complicated then they already were.

'Man, I've been looking for you everywhere. Where'd you disappear to after English?' Tayvn was still trying to catch his breath. 'The way you took off after lunch, I thought I had said something wrong; y'know, scared you off.'

Sarah smiled, momentarily relieved that he hadn't mentioned seeing the hidden doorway.

'What is it with you? Are you training for some secret Hallway Olympics? First football and now track. Back home we generally play sports in the gym or on the field.' Sarah smirked before getting serious. 'I had to check on a friend, uh, back home. I wasn't very nice to him before I left and I wanted to call to see if I could apologise, but he wasn't home.'

'What's with the book? In Oceanview we might train in the halls, but we do like to enjoy our weekends by goofing off, not reading books that look older than, well, the planet.' Tayvn asked as he pointed to the book that was still held firmly in Sarah's arms.

'It's for my dad...' Sarah said as she thought quickly to change the topic. 'What are you doing here? The basketball practice was over an hour ago and, as you say, most kids in Oceanview go and "goof off" on the weekends.'

'I'm an addicted hall runner and I can't get enough of it. My Mom says that I should join a support group,' Tayvn joked as he began to stretch. 'We had basketball practice, as you already know, and I…uh…well…I got distracted and kinda caused a head on collision between the coach and one of the other players. Coach didn't think it was funny, so after practice he decided to give me laps. It was cold outside so I decided to do them in the school. What are you still doing here? And don't tell me you were in the library, because that closes as soon as the final bell rings on Fridays.'

'I had to uh…' Sarah searched for a good excuse and then remembered about the book she was holding. 'My dad's a writer, and he's doing research for a new book. He wanted some historical stuff about Oceanview and thought that we could get some bonding time in by doing research together. Personally I think my dad has his hands full with the move and wants to keep me and my brother as far from the house as possible until he gets it organised. One of the history teachers had a stack of books for me to dig through and said that I could stay as long as I needed.' The excuse sounded good to Sarah, and she hoped Tayvn would buy it.

'Cool, I've always found the town history boring, but I hope you found what you needed. You should get your dad to sit in on one of Ms. Tarnal's Town History weeks, which never change and have no hint of excitement,' Tayvn suggested. 'You moved into the old McMiller place right?'

'How'd you know that?' Sarah asked, surprised that he would know where she lived. 'I thought you didn't pay attention to gossip.' Warning bells about who else might know where she lived were ringing loudly in her head.

'It's a pretty small town and that house has been empty for years. No one ever thought it would be bought, so when the moving truck showed up it was the front page story in the local paper.' Tayvn began to laugh as Sarah was thinking about how dull his town must have appeared to those not fighting demons.

'Sorry to break it to you, but your jokes aren't that funny,' Sarah asked confused by his sudden amusement. 'What's so funny?'

'It's nothing. Just that when I was little, I used to think monsters lived in that house. On Halloween we used to dare people to climb over the fence and knock on the door. Of course no one ever did because all my friends are wimps, so instead we would throw rocks at the windows. There's also this tradition that when you start at High Point you have to at least step onto the property, a coming-of-age thing. It's a lot of fun to watch people try to squirm out of it and then finally place one foot on the driveway before panicking and running away. We all had our turn...even me, and I'm proud to say that I went the furthest...at least three feet up the driveway before a flock of bats flew from out of nowhere and tried to land on my face. I screamed like I was meeting Frankenstein and sprinted back to my place. I didn't feel that bad though 'cause everyone else bolted as well.'

'Baby! Try sleeping there,' Sarah laughed. 'A word of advice, though: my dad is trying to fix all the windows right now, so I'd keep the part about throwing rocks at them to yourself if you are ever around him. He isn't having a lot of fun, and I think he's broken more windows trying to fix the old ones. Because of you and your friends we have these huge plastic sheets over most of our windows, making it feel like we're living in a circus tent.'

'We never thought anyone would move in,' Tayvn said as he turned red again, only this time out of embarrassment, but Tayvn was still pretty amused by his memories of the old mansion. 'I only live a few blocks up from you. If you give me a second to change and get my stuff, I'll walk home with you.'

'I'll meet you by the gym,' Sarah smiled as she watched Tayvn finish his lap through the halls. Ever since she had seen him on that first day she knew there was something different about him, something unique. There was the mystery of his tattoo having the same design as the ring, and the fact that he seemed so much different than most of the teenagers she knew. There was something deeper to Tayvn Lynch, something that made him connect with her on a different level.

It only took a couple of minutes for Tayvn to emerge from the change room dressed in his day clothes, his backpack slung over his shoulder. His hair was still wet from the thirty-second shower he took after every gym class to get rid of the sweat and attempt to look human. Sarah was waiting patiently in the hall, absently looking at the trophy case; the book from the attic was tucked securely in her bag that was strapped over both her shoulders. Every recent trophy had Tayvn's name on it, yet every team picture had him hiding in the back, as though he didn't want the recognition of being the star player.

Tayvn and Sarah smiled and greeted each other as they started their walk home. Sarah told me that for a moment she felt as though she was a normal teenager.

'So what type of stuff does your dad write?' Tayvn asked as they walked down the path to Breaker Street. 'Anything I've read?'

'No,' Sarah responded as she walked. 'Well… you might have read one of his books. He usually writes crime mysteries involving corrupt doctors or politicians, depending on his mood, as well as a few books that require "deep intellectual thought",' Sarah said in a deep 'sophisticated' voice.

'You mean the ones where you read a page four times and still have no idea what's going on? I think I had a geometry book like that once.' Tayvn laughed as he stopped to tie his shoelace. 'Way to break the rules, Tay.'

'What?' Sarah asked as she overheard Tayvn mumble to himself. 'What rules?'

'Nothing…' Tayvn said as he got up. 'Me and my buddies made up these stupid rules on how to act when you're with a girl.'

'I like stupid things... tell me about these rules.' Sarah was smirking as she watched Tayvn roll the idea in his head.

'When we were eleven there was this girl we all had a crush on, so we made up rules on how to act around her...you know like not chewing with your mouth full, don't eat garlic, and other things that would make us look "unsophisticated". Stopping to tie up your shoe was somewhere between picking your nose and slobbering.'

'That's probably the stupidest thing I've ever heard,' Sarah laughed.

'I never said that they worked,' Tayvn smirked as he continued to walk. 'Back to what we were talking about before...has your dad ever written anything that someone as lowly as me, living in the backward town of Oceanview, might have read?'

'Probably not, though he did write something once that was for little kids...but, like your rules, it was pretty dumb,' Sarah said as they walked down Breaker Street unaware of anything out of the ordinary.

'He wrote this book for me when I was little; he thought it was cute. It was a story about a talking animal that was always following this little girl so that they could be friends. If you were over the age of three you probably wouldn't have heard of it, and if you have you probably need some serious mental help.'

'*Purple Phil the Phunky Platypus*?' Tayvn guessed correctly, causing Sarah to stop in her tracks. She was in absolute shock.

'Please tell me that you've been researching me and that you didn't guess that out of thin air,' Sarah pleaded.

'My little brother used to love that book. He made me read it to him every night for months,' Tayvn said. 'I thought about burning it a few times, but I don't think my dad would have been very happy with me destroying Jesse's favourite thing in the world.' Tayvn reminisced. 'I'd say that I'm now even with your dad over the whole window thing. That book was torture…no offence.'

'So there was someone other than us who bought it,' Sarah laughed. 'Now that you know most of my family's deep hidden secrets, tell me about yours. What does your dad do?'

'He's the chief of the fire department, which is nowhere near as cool as it sounds, and my mom is a computer programmer for some company in Boston. She writes the programs down here and sends them over when she's done.' Tayvn saw that Sarah wanted to hear more, so he continued. 'Other than that, I have a little brother, Jesse, who is five, and a dog. I enjoy running through the halls of an empty school, creeping around haunted houses, and the occasional Triple-Everything World Burger. But enough about me, how's your dilemma going?'

'Which one?' Sarah asked.

'The whole destiny thing,' Tayvn replied, trying to be helpful.

'I think I have it figured out,' Sarah smiled. 'To tell you the truth, it scares me, but as you said, I'm going to have to face it sometime, so I might as well do it on my own terms.'

'Know the feeling,' Tayvn answered. 'Are you going to let me in on it? Maybe I can help.'

'It's sort of personal and a bit weird,' Sarah grinned, tempted by his offer but not sure how to truly explain what was going on in Oceanview without sounding crazy.

'Tell you what,' Tayvn said. 'I'll tell you something personal and weird about me and then, if you think it adds up, you can let me in on your big secret. If not, you can laugh at me for opening up to a practical stranger and move on your merry way without any flak from me.'

'How do you know I won't go and spread your secret all over school?' Sarah asked.

'I trust you,' Tayvn whispered. 'Besides, I haven't told anyone about your ring that plays music and makes dancing shapes.'

Tayvn quickly looked around to ensure that there was no one nearby to overhear before pulling

Sarah into a thick patch of trees where neither of them could be seen. Sarah had not blinked after hearing that Tayvn had heard the 'Remembrance Song'; rather, her eyes were stern. This could be Omascus making his move. 'You've seen my tattoo, right?'

'It's hard to miss when you're always running around in a basketball jersey,' Sarah responded bluntly, waiting to see where this was going. 'Why didn't you say something about the ring before?'

'I wanted to make sure it wasn't in my head, that what I saw was real.' Tayvn answered. 'But when I saw my star show up on the ring, I knew that you were someone I could trust. You see, I've never told anyone how I got the tattoo because I don't even believe it myself sometimes. I was waiting for someone who wouldn't think I was insane after hearing my story...someone who believed in magic,' Tayvn whispered as he opened up to the newcomer.

'I'm all ears,' Sarah said preparing for another trip to the Dreamscape.

'When I was six, my parents and I went to this park on top of Shalwell Cliff, overlooking the ocean. I don't know what it was, but something called me over to the edge of the cliff that day. I was flying this bright red kite, when I heard the sound of a bird and a voice in the distance that was telling me that my time had come…that it was time for the "joining".

'I can remember it as clearly as when I was six; a warm wind picked me up off my feet and carried me right over the edge of the cliff. No one saw me until it was too late. Now, the thing was that this cliff is over forty feet high, with a rocky beach below.

'My parents freaked and thought I was dead. My dad called for a full rescue team and raced to the bottom, where there are about ten feet of jagged rocks and sand before the waterline. He was expecting to find me dead, or at least badly injured. Imagine his surprise when I was standing there waiting for him surrounded by a perfect circle of scorched sand. It was as though I had been faster getting to the bottom and was waiting for my dad to catch up. There was no sign of fire, only me, standing by myself, completely uninjured and slightly bored.

'The only proof that that day ever happened was the tattoo of the star that somehow appeared on my shoulder and has been there ever since.'

'There wasn't a big leathery monster waiting for you when you landed was there? Something that reeked of death?' Sarah asked, still cautious about the warning from Moon Light Seeker.

'That's just it. All I remember was feeling at peace. I was warm and cared for the entire time. From that day on, I haven't ever felt alone or scared. But I know that I changed that day. I was stronger, faster, and smarter than I had been before, as though I was connected to something greater. Every night since then when I dream, I see the world from high above or through the eyes of a stranger, and I can remember things that happened hundreds of years ago in far off places I never knew existed.

'The real reason I always hide in the back of those photos, the ones you saw in the hall, is because

after that day being the centre of attention, being the
star of the team didn't seem to matter. I was content
just being me. I also wanted to hide my newfound
"gifts" so that no one would ever get wise and think
that I was a freak.' Tayvn smiled, surprised that he had
spilled his biggest secret for the first time. There was a
strange silence between Tayvn and Sarah as she
debated telling Tayvn about Omascus and me.

'Your story is a happy one,' Sarah said
breaking the silence. 'Your secret is about life, while
mine is not. I want to tell you, but I need to speak to
someone else first.'

'Then I guess we should get out of these bushes
before some new gossip starts,' Tayvn said as he led
the way back to the sidewalk. They walked in
awkward silence until the reached the old McMiller
house.

'This is my stop,' Sarah said as they passed the
gap in her fence where the gates once stood. 'How
much further are you?'

'Three blocks,' Tayvn pointed up the street. 'The big blue house with the weeping willow tree in the front.'

'I'd invite you into the disaster zone, but we haven't really got anything in there to do except build world monuments out of old Chinese and pizza boxes,' Sarah said.

'No problem; I think we've had enough adventure in each other's worlds for one day,' Tayvn said as he looked at his watch. 'I should probably get home soon, anyway. I promised my dad I would be there after the game so he can show me some new fireworks for a fund-raiser next week.'

'Well, then, I guess I'll see you later,' Sarah said, breaking a slightly awkward silence as she headed for the front door. 'Wait this isn't right...you told me your secret. I should tell you something; it's only fair.'

'You said you had to wait, and that's fine. Sarah, I trust you and I know that if it's important for you to wait, I shouldn't rush you.' Tayvn said.

'Tomorrow's Saturday; we can get together and talk or just hang out. I have soccer in the morning, but after that I'm free to do whatever. Call me; I'm the only Lynch in the phone book.'

'Sounds good, but I'll probably swing by since we don't have phones yet,' Sarah said.

'Sure,' Tayvn answered. 'Maybe by then you'll have figured out why your ring keeps singing when I'm around.'

'If I understood any of this I would have dealt with it all by now. So far the ring does what it wants and I have no choice but to follow,' Sarah explained. 'Tayvn, I want you to know that I understand what it is to feel like the freak with a secret, to have something in your life which makes no sense.'

'Somehow I knew that from the day I met you,' Tayvn smiled, the first real smile he had shown since revealing his soul. 'I guess we all have a destiny, and sometimes we are fortunate enough to know what it is ahead of time,' Tayvn said as he started to walk away.

Sarah was still confused about what he had told her on their walk home. Were their destinies somehow linked? Was he a part of their quest, one of the people Moon Light Seeker said would aid us?

After pondering everything that had happened during the day, Sarah eventually entered the house. The lights were off and no one was home. At first Sarah feared the worst, that Omascus had sent Tayvn to distract her while he did something terrible to her family, but then she saw a note on a small table near the door.

> *Sarah,*
>
> *We are having a guest for dinner, a friend of David's. I've gone out to get some groceries and I will be back soon. We'll eat around 7:30, so get all your homework done. Hope you had a good day.*
>
> *Love, Dad*

Sarah put the note in her pocket and began to wonder who this friend of David's was. He hadn't mentioned anyone earlier; in fact he'd been complaining about not having any friends ever since they'd moved here. The thought passed quickly out of her mind as she ran upstairs into her room.

She quickly closed and locked the door and placed her bag on the desk. It was time to work on something that was a little more important than her homework. Sarah unzipped her bag and pulled out the leather-bound book. The time had come to start figuring out a way to stop Omascus. As Sarah laid the book on her desk, she noticed something on the cover that had not been there earlier. The Northern Star was embossed on the cover and it was identical to the tattoo on Tayvn's shoulder.

CHAPTER 14 – DINNER WITH MR. SHEFFER

I had waited an eternity to have a place in the world and now that I had one, I had screwed up. I had seen the demon and knew who he was using to get to Sarah, but rather than warning her, I had wasted the magic of the ring. My friend's life was in danger and this ring was the only way that I could warn her. If only I hadn't put it on to read the book. If only I had gone straight to Sarah and told her what I knew. Why hadn't I remember sooner what I needed to do? There were just too many things I could have done to prevent a disaster, yet I did nothing. The ring needed to recharge because I was distracted by my need to learn about my life and that scratchy music that made it impossible for me to warn Sarah. Omascus had won. Deep down I knew the music was his, but I had ignored it. The monster had been in my head.

Not knowing what else to do, I raced to Sarah's house, leaving the ring behind. Maybe there was something I could do to protect my friend. The moment after I left the attic, I began to have nightmares of the terrible monster I had seen attacking Sarah, only I was very awake. I could clearly envision Omascus torturing Sarah as her brother searched everywhere for the ring that was sitting powerless in the attic. At least no one but Sarah knew that the room existed, making it the perfect hiding place. These waking images weren't letting up; instead they were getting worse.

I was flying faster than I knew I could. There were no more distractions, no detours, no wasting time. Nothing, not even Omascus's spells, would keep me from the McMiller house, from helping my friend and her family.

As I passed through the stone fence, it didn't look as if anyone was home. I headed straight through the front door and called out Sarah's name. I shouted for her, although I knew that she would not hear me. Without the ring I was as invisible, and as silent, to her as I was to everybody else.

No one was on the main floor, but I heard a faint noise upstairs. Was I too late? I quickly flew through the ceiling and aimed for Sarah's tower room. The room was pitch black except for a few candles that had been lit on Sarah's desk. Sarah looked deep in thought as she studied the contents of a thick leather book.

I floated over to her and tried to get her attention, but it was no use. I looked down at the pages she was reading so intently and saw delicate calligraphy on thick parchment paper. The book appeared ancient and was written in a language I had never seen, yet Sarah seemed able to understand it perfectly. As she read the foreign text, she scribbled notes on a small yellow pad. I looked at some of the notes that lined the desk, her school books acting as paper weights, and saw sketches of monsters and notes scribbled in the margins. On one sheet I saw a picture of Omascus with a description of his powers; he was able to create intricate illusions, control people's minds like puppets, and he had incredible physical strength, to name a few. Great. As if a ghost and a high-school kid could stop him. If only I could tell Sarah that her brother was under the control of the demon and that Omascus had already tried to destroy me.

The room was momentarily lit by an outside light as Sarah and I heard a car come up the driveway. It was her dad and her brother. Sarah moved to the window and then returned to her desk, blew out the candles, and left the room. I gasped as I noticed Tayvn's star in the centre of the book's cover. Something must have happened while I was searching for Omascus and I needed to know what.

Realising that Sarah was no longer in the room, I flew to find her.

'Hi, dad,' Sarah said as he handed her one of the two big bags of groceries he was carrying. She then looked at David, who was also carrying a big bag of food. 'I hear you finally found a friend.'

'Yeah,' David smirked back. 'And he's not imaginary like most of yours.'

'Enough, you two,' Sarah's dad responded. 'Mr. Sheffer will be here in an hour, and we have a lot of work to do.'

'Who's Mr. Sheffer?' Sarah asked, puzzled, as the trio emptied the groceries as best they could in the cluttered kitchen with its counters covered in a combination of fast-food boxes and home-repair tools.

'He's my friend,' David said as they attempted to separate the garbage from the tools so that the food would have room. 'He owns this really cool shop on Breaker Street that has really sweet games and toys. I met him yesterday on my way home from school. He played rugby for England when he was a kid, and said that he might be able to help me start a team at school.'

'How old is this guy?' Sarah asked her dad as she began to grow sceptical. The strange Wampanoag woman had said that Omascus had already done something to certain people in town. Was this Mr. Sheffer working for Omascus? Within the book, Sarah had discovered that Omascus also needed to be invited into a home before he could enter. If Omascus could get one of his minions to be invited in, then whomever the demon was controlling could invite whomever he wanted.

'Pretty old, I guess,' David said before his dad could respond. 'But he is really cool. He collects all these really neat things from all over the world and has them in the back of his shop. Remember that old crystal Grams had with the sparkly green stuff in the middle?'

'He has a Custos Rock?' Sarah asked. Her grandmother, she'd told me, had a rare crystal which changed colour depending on how much magic was nearby; green meant powerful and Sarah had never seen the rock turn that colour.

'Yeah, he could be friends with Grams. We should introduce them when she comes to visit.' Sarah smiled as her brother planned to introduce their grandmother to the stranger.

'Make you two a deal,' their dad said as he entered the room with another heavy bag. 'I'll cook while you clean up the dining room and set the table. I think the dishes are unpacked.'

'Dad, we've had your cooking...' Sarah smiled as she and David remembered painfully the last big dinner their dad had tried to make. 'But we'll set the table anyhow.'

This must have been Omascus' big plan, she thought. He was using David to get into Sarah's house and steal the ring, and if Sarah refused to give in to him, he could use her family to force her to give him the talisman. What she hadn't figured out yet was whether Mr. Sheffer was also under the power of Omascus, or was he Omascus. The book had said that Omascus could create powerful illusions, and he might have been able to make himself appear human. It would make sense; no one had mentioned seeing a huge red scaly monster roaming the streets.

Dinner was at seven, which gave me an hour to get help. Without wasting time I raced back to the attic, hoping maybe the ring had had enough time to recharge.

Once I was there I tried to touch the talisman, but it still slipped through my grasp. After waiting and trying again and again I flew through the ceiling to the floor below to find a clock. The small hand was almost at seven. I flew back to the attic and tried the ring again. This time I was able to lift it for a second, but before I had the chance to even think about getting to Sarah's it dropped to the floor. I was out of time. I had to get back to Sarah's and come up with a new plan.

'Moon-Light Seeker!' I yelled to the ring before I left. The native woman who had spoken to us earlier said that she was here to help stop Omascus and that she was tied to the ring. I was desperate and I was willing to try anything. 'We need you! Get to Sarah's as soon as you can!' With that I bolted through the window and raced back to Sarah.

I flew faster than I had earlier, but dinner had already started. I glided into the dining room and saw who I assumed was Mr. Sheffer at the one end of the table, opposite Mr. Winters. Sarah and David were sitting on either side of their dad.

'David has told us a lot about you,' Mr. Winters was saying.

'And he has told me much about your family,' Mr. Sheffer replied in a thick British accent. The old man didn't look all that impressive. He was pretty wrinkled and had short white hair. Mr. Sheffer was stockier than most people his age, and there was something odd about the way he smiled, almost as though he was constantly hiding his disgust with people. Then there were his teeth. Everything about Mr. Sheffer appeared human, except his teeth. They were jagged and sharp, more like an animal's teeth than a human's. There was no mistaking it, I decided; this man was Omascus. I could sense his coldness and bitterness in my core as the feelings of dread returned in full force. 'Your son tells me you're a writer, Mr. Winters.'

'Yes, and I would like to think a decent one. Please call me Matt; Mr. Winters always sounds too formal for me.' Sarah's dad smiled as he passed a bowl of vegetables to David along with the encouragement for his son to at least try some.

'What do you do?' Sarah asked rather rudely. She appeared unimpressed with their guest, and I had a feeling that she suspected his appearance a little too 'convenient'.

'I have a small shop on Breaker Street called the "Fun Shoppe". We carry gadgets and gizmos to entice all ages. Marvellous contraptions that inspire the imagination while making life a touch less dreary.' Mr. Sheffer sounded like a human advertisement.

'David says that you are interested in magic,' Sarah said bluntly causing David and her dad to suddenly look up.

'No I didn't,' David protested as though he had betrayed a secret trust he held with the old man.

'Sarah,' her dad said. 'I think that we have had enough of that nonsense.' Matt Winters didn't seem angry, but I don't think he liked the idea of Sarah's talking about magic. Who could blame him? He must have heard the rumours running around town and, after all he had experienced, he probably preferred to leave that chapter of his life in the past. In many ways his denial of the supernatural was very similar to that of his daughter's. After all, with Grams in Europe there was no magic, or so he wanted to believe.

'I have always been interested in the mystical arts,' Mr. Sheffer smiled. 'Fantastic stuff, the ancient legends of oracles and magical swords. I believe that the study of what ancient cultures thought held the secrets to life is often rewarding, in a purely anthropological sense.'

'Cool,' David muttered in awe. 'He's also really rich, and he has these awesome books, and mask, and crystals from all over the world.'

'David,' Sarah's dad said sternly. 'We don't talk about money at the table, especially other people's.'

I had heard enough. Omascus was killing time, playing with what he thought was a simple mortal family. The knots in my stomach and the burning in my chest where his magic had struck me were increasing. All I needed was a plan to expose him to Sarah.

Omascus was able to sense me when I was in his store; maybe he could still sense me here even when he was in his human form. I floated through the centre of the table and faced Omascus. I took a deep breath and yelled as loud as I could to attract the demon. Everyone else at the dinner table kept eating and talking except for Sarah and Mr. Sheffer. Rex dropped his fork and looked straight at where I hovered; his nostrils flared before he snarled in my direction. Sarah seemed to have sensed something, for her eyes were fluttering from her guest to the table.

'What's wrong?' Sarah asked suspiciously.

'Nothing; I thought I heard something,' Mr. Sheffer said. 'Matthew, this chicken is excellent.'

'Thank you,' Sarah's dad replied. 'See? It's safe to eat,' he stated under his breath to his children, neither of whom had touched their food.

'Sarah,' David said as Sarah's gaze locked on Mr. Sheffer. 'Why don't you show Mr. Sheffer the ring Grams left you? Maybe he can tell you how much it's worth. Or if it has any real magic in it like Grams said it did.'

'I can try,' Mr. Sheffer said as he smiled coyly. 'And please, call me Rex.'

'I don't think so,' Sarah said as she looked at her brother. I then got an idea that Sarah was realising what was going on and that I was nearby. I yelled again and Sheffer jumped in his seat as Sarah's face grew impatient and angry.

'I'm thirsty. Does anybody else want some water?' Sarah excused herself from the table and walked past the swinging door that connected the kitchen and the dining room.

Once on the other side, she took in a deep breath. She walked straight to the sink and turned the tap on, letting the water run into the empty sink. She looked out the window and stared at her own reflection, listening to the running water as it emptied into the drain.

'Ben, I know you are here someplace,' Sarah stated, looking out the one of the few uncovered windows in the house. 'Is Rex who I think he is?'

I tried to answer Sarah but she couldn't hear me. I looked past her out the window and noticed a large animal sitting on the grass outside. It must have wandered through the opened gate.

I had an idea.

I flew out the window and hovered over what looked like a grey wolf; it must have wandered in from the woods, maybe a sign from Moon Light Seeker. I looked back to Sarah, who was still at the window. I screamed at the wolf and circled around its head. For once I was glad animals hated me. The wolf growled and jumped in vain efforts to catch me in its teeth.

'Ben?' Sarah asked to herself as she watched the commotion. It was working. I spotted some cans of paint by the window and flew, with the wolf nipping at my feet, towards them. The wolf knocked one of the cans over, spilling white paint all over the ground. It was dark, but my plan might just work if I could act fast enough. I moved the wolf into the puddle and then made it follow me out onto the grass. Using all of my flying expertise I flew in a perfect circle and then towards the window. As the wolf chased me it wrote in white footprints the letter *O*. The wolf was still trying to bite me and I was getting dizzy, but Sarah got the message. Without a moment's hesitation she turned from the window and ran through the dining room past her surprised family and their guest, and upstairs.

By the time I had arrived in her room she was busily flipping through the large book with Tayvn's star on it. I tried to warn her that I heard someone coming, but she couldn't hear me.

'Dad's wondering where you went; he said you were being rude,' David said as he burst into his sister's room. He strode over to Sarah's desk and looked at the book.

'Listen to me,' Sarah pleaded as she looked up at her brother. 'This might sound nuts, but that guy downstairs isn't who he says he is. I want you to get out of here now. My friend Tayvn lives up the street, go find him and wait.'

David looked blankly at his sister and stood motionless.

'Are you deaf?' Sarah demanded. 'You have to go now!'

'Oh, he heard you, little girl,' Rex Sheffer said smugly as he entered the room from behind David. The old man walked calmly into the room and looked around at the scattered clothes, the sports gear, and the book on Sarah's desk. 'But you see, he is under my control and can do only what I tell him. Now be a dear and hand over the ring and that book of yours.'

'I know who you are, Omascus,' Sarah said bravely as tears filled her eyes. 'I know what will happen if you get my ring, and I will never give it to you.'

'You've been a busy little brat, haven't you? Finding the book that was stolen from me and learning its secrets, befriending the dead, and trying to save your pitiful family.' His words sounded sinister and deadly. 'I shall have to be less of a gentleman and more of a monster.'

Omascus looked at the baseball bat lying by Sarah's bed. The aluminium bat jumped into the air and twirled as though warming up to hit a homerun.

'Leave her alone!' I ordered, hoping it would distract Omascus for a minute.

'Be gone, boy,' Omascus responded with a bright flicker in his eyes. The bat levelled out and flew straight towards me. The magic moving the bat allowed it to hit me squarely in the gut. The force of the attack knocked the bat and me out the window, shattering the glass to pieces.

'Ben!' Sarah called out as she saw the bat fly through the window. She quickly flipped the pages of the book looking for something.

Violently David slammed the book close on his sister's hand.

'Sorry, Sis, but my master wants your ring,' David said, possessed, as he pushed the cover harder onto her hand. 'Give Omascus the ring.'

Sarah looked at her brother, her eyes watering from the pain and from the thought of what Omascus had done to her little brother. She looked into David's eyes and saw that someone else was in control of his actions and thoughts. Sarah closed her eyes tight as the pressure on her hand increased.

'David,' she pleaded without any change in him. 'I hope you don't remember this.' Sarah took her left hand and grabbed her math textbook, which was holding down some notes on the desk. In one single motion she swung the book and hit David on the side of the head with it. He winced in pain and fell to the ground dazed. Sarah flipped the book back open and looked at the redness of her hand. She looked at David and felt a desire to help him, but she couldn't help him the way he needed, at least not yet. With the book open in her hands, Sarah raced for the broken window in search of escape. She looked outside and saw the baseball bat lying motionless on the ground. It was too far to jump and there was nothing she could use to climb down. She was trapped.

'There is no where for you to go,' Omascus said as he began to grow larger and more menacing. His skin began to darken into a blood-red as his hair lengthened. He was changing into his true demon form. 'Now give me back the *Phoenix Book* your friends stole from me, and the ring. In exchange I will free your family and leave this god-forsaken town.'

Omascus's voice had grown fiercer. Even if she had had the ring, Sarah made a vow right then and there never to give it over to this monster.

Sarah quivered in fear as Omascus finished his transformation. He was the most hideous thing she had ever seen, or imagined. Suddenly she thought she heard growling from behind the monster as Omascus was forced to the ground. Once the bat passed through the window it had lost its power. I, on the other hand, was in a great deal of pain but able to move. I had found my faithful wolf waiting for me and managed to get him to chase me through the kitchen window and up to Sarah's room. If the wolf hated me and I was a good guy, it would absolutely despise Omascus. Maybe there wasn't much I could do, but this wolf enjoyed sinking his teeth into the demon. David jumped to his feet, still dazed and tried to help his master. Meanwhile I flew over to Sarah.

Those few seconds as Omascus knocked away the animal were all that Sarah needed to find what she was looking for. She dropped the book to the ground and pronounced clearly and crisply:

'THARNAT CONMANA ROKTAGAF UCKTAR APPROPRTAR! DEMON BE GONE!' She closed her eyes and wrapped her fingers into the shape of a triangle. Bright circles appeared where the tips of her fingers met, which began to spout out large bursts of wind. The wind moaned as it twirled around the demon, whispering strange words as it intensified. The wolf whimpered as it ran out of the room and

David backed away from his master. The wind seemed to bind Omascus, and slowly lifted him off the ground.

Bright silver sparks began to flash within the wind as Omascus was carried towards the window. Sarah kept her hands held tightly in the shape that had brought forth the powerful force. In a flash of light the wind carried the demon out of the house and into the darkness of the night. David saw the spell in action and looked at Sarah who was frozen, her eyes a brilliant white. Without a thought of his own, David raced after his master.

Soon the circles that had appeared faded away and Sarah dropped to her knees in exhaustion.

'Ben,' she sighed. 'The spell only "disinvited" him from my house. He'll be back, I…Omigod, Dad!'

Sarah forced herself to her feet and raced to the dining room. She was still weak from the spell and grabbed onto anything she could to help her stand. She felt as if she had run a marathon, but she had to see her father.

Once we got to the dining room, Sarah fell into one of the chairs and began to sob. Her dad had been sitting in his chair completely frozen. His hand held a fork near his mouth, which was wide open. He sat motionless, a human statue. She moved beside him and tried to make him move, but it was to no avail; he was under a powerful magical spell.

'We'll cure him and help your brother, I promise,' I said to help calm my friend. I didn't care if she could hear me or not.

'Ben…I mean Alexander. I don't know if you are still here, but I guess it doesn't really matter.' Tears began to form in Sarah's eyes at the prospect of losing the rest of her family. As the tears rolled down her cheeks, her voice became stern and determined, she was done waiting. 'Omascus stole my brother, invaded my home, did this to my father, and hurt my friend. I don't care how evil or scary he is. I don't care what type of magic he can do. All I know is that he is messing with my family, and no one is going to do that. He's never getting my ring and he's going down in a big way.'

Sarah took a moment to look at her dining room for possibly the last time and then shakily rose to her feet. 'Omascus made a huge mistake tonight, and now it's his turn to be afraid. I'm through playing.'

CHAPTER 15 – THE PLAN

By the time we approached the school, the stars were out in full force. After everything that I had experienced over the past few days, I no longer found darkness comforting. The peaceful solitude I used to find at night was replaced by a turbulent uneasiness as an unseen monster lurked in every corner. The streets were quiet for a Friday, as though people could feel the coming evil in the air. If Omascus got what he wanted, everything in the world would change for the worse.

Sarah was determined to end this fight. She could not afford to be afraid; there were too many lives at stake. We both knew the first victims would be her family, and that was simply not an option. As we ran in utter silence, Sarah and I stopped being children.

Before leaving her house, Sarah had changed into dark clothing and slapped a black baseball cap on her head. In the next few hours we would begin an offensive and she was going to be ready. Strapped securely to her back was her bag holding the *Phoenix*

Book, the latest mystery to surface in the past few days.

Trying to be as discreet as possible, Sarah manoeuvred the back streets until she reached the school. There was no telling where Omascus had landed or who else he had under his control. One thing we were certain of was that our secret hideout was now the only safe place in all of Oceanview. More important, though, was that the object of Omascus's obsession, the most powerful talisman in the world, was sitting inside completely unprotected.

Luck was on our side when we reached the school because the doors were still unlocked. The Theatre Club had recently finished a performance and the janitors were in the process of closing down the school for the weekend. This made life much easier, as all we had to do was get to the attic without being noticed, rather than first having to break in. The coast was clear for Sarah as she slipped in through one of the side entrances and made her way to the top floor.

A young janitor was polishing the floor right outside of the attic door as Sarah rounded the corner. His back was towards her and his headphones were on so he didn't notice that a student was still in the building. Sarah crouched down low in the alcove that was part of the stairwell to stay out of sight while keeping the janitor in view. She waited patiently and watched as the young polisher worked, oblivious to the fact that he was being observed. Finally he moved down the hall connecting the sides of the square building and vanished. Sarah waited a little longer to be safe and then ran without making a noise to the attic door. In a single action she pried it open with a thin metallic ruler she had brought from home, entered the hidden staircase and closed the door behind her. She took a moment to lock the door before she ran up the steep stairs.

The lights were on, since I couldn't exactly turn them off when I left earlier. Sarah muttered to herself as she looked for the ring in the dim lamplight. I hovered over where the ring had last fallen and yelled to get Sarah's attention, even though I knew it would make no difference.

'You had to drop the ring on the floor didn't you?' Sarah muttered. 'This place is disgusting!'

She crept along the floor on her hands and knees while I worried that she would discover something really gross under the couch.

'It's over by the right leg of the couch,' I tried to inform her, but without the ring on her finger she couldn't hear me and these directions were useless. Eventually she found the talisman and sighed a breath of relief, for as she searched she wondered if someone had found it before her, someone who should not be wearing the ring. Without hesitation Sarah slipped the ring onto her finger and looked for me to appear somewhere in the room. She was hoping her intuition was right and that any second she would see a purple mist appear out of thin air surrounding my body as I faded into clear sight. Finally, after being invisible for so long, I appeared to my friend.

'You have no idea how good it is to see you,' Sarah said as she attempted to give me hug and then discovered the challenge of hugging someone who was basically made up of air. 'It's weird, even without the ring I knew that you were with me at the house. That stunt with the wolf was quick thinking.'

'Yeah,' I said still rubbing the spot where the bat had nailed me. 'Could you do me one favour...in the future, only keep soft teddy bears and pillows in your room. That bat of yours hurts. Oh, and sorry about the glass.'

Sarah cracked a slight smile, the first one I had seen since she first suspected that Omascus was sitting in her dining room.

'So my dad has one more to fix; at least we know that magic can affect you,' Sarah said before stopping to worry about whether her dad would ever be able to fix it.

'I already knew that,' I muttered to myself.

Sarah sat down on the couch ignoring the clouds of dust that rose from it. She flopped her backpack onto the ground by her feet and pulled out the old book. Carefully, she placed the *Phoenix Book* on the trunk and flipped it open to a page that was marked with a colourful slip of paper.

'By the way, that was an awesome spell you did; guess you really are a witch,' I said as Sarah looked for something. I floated down towards her and looked over her shoulder, but the words were still foreign to me.

'Funny, but right now we have bigger things to deal with,' Sarah said in a serious voice. 'I found that spell earlier and thought that it might help. It's supposed to take away any invitation given to a supernatural being to enter a home. I figured since you always run into a wall when you enter a place you're not invited to, if someone was already inside, some force might be able to kick someone out.'

'It sure looked cool,' I said, causing Sarah to think about a response.

'It was weird,' she started to say as she remembered the spell. 'I had this surge of power flowing through me which I guess was always there. It made me feel stronger than ever during the spell, but exhausted once it was done. I guess I have to get some practice in before I'll be able to control the magic.'

'Where do you think the spell sent him?' I asked, hoping it would be far away from here.

'He can't leave Oceanview without the ring. All I did was buy us time,' Sarah said as she went back to the book.

'Where'd you learn to read this stuff?' I asked as I stared at the blank pages of the book.

'I started to read when I was about five,' Sarah smirked. 'I'd like to think that I've mastered the art of reading English a long time ago.'

'But the page is empty!' I retorted, causing Sarah to look puzzled before she remembered the magic she had seen earlier when she placed the ring onto the pages of the book. Sarah explained to me how all the symbols jumbled around and reformed into English. She had assumed that the book itself had changed, but now she realized that only her understanding had been magically altered. The magic of the ring allowed Sarah to read what no one else could see.

'Now we have to figure out how to stop him and free my brother and dad.' Sarah suddenly stopped as a new thought formed. 'I don't think it was a coincidence that you found this place. It was too easy to find this book and learn about who you were...are. I think the people who have been having so much fun playing with our lives have been working at making our job as easy as possible. I think the woman from the woods has been planning this whole thing for a really long time.'

'Her name is Moon Light Seeker,' I said quietly as I began to feel the pressing need to tell Sarah about what I had seen earlier at the Fun Shoppe. 'There's something I have to tell you, Sarah.'

'You remember the spell you and Moon Light Seeker used?' she interrupted as if she hadn't heard what I had just said. 'I was thinking that if we find it we could use it to stop Omascus and bury him back in his hole.'

'Are you nuts?' I asked, momentarily side-tracked. 'Have you forgotten that the last time we used the spell I ended up like this?'

'No,' she said refusing to look up from the book. 'But have you got a better idea? I need to get my family back, and so far I can't think of a better plan.'

'What if it…'

'Right now I don't care,' Sarah looked towards me and I could see the frustration and determination in her eyes. There was nothing I could possibly say that would deter her search, unless of course I could think of something better. 'Now what was it that you wanted to tell me?'

'I saw something today while you were at school…I tried to find you, but then…' I said slowly knowing that the moment I told Sarah what I had seen our relationship was going to drastically change. 'Your brother…'

'What about my brother?' Sarah said as she drilled me with her eyes.

'I followed him and found out that he was possessed by Omascus. I tried to do something, but I was scared…' The look of shock on Sarah's face was something I would never forget. I can't remember how long the silence between us lasted, but every moment was more painful than the one before it. I felt lower than I ever thought possible. I could see from her eyes that she was blaming me, that she held me responsible for what had happened tonight.

'Tell me exactly what happened,' she said, trying to hide her anger and bitter disappointment.

'While you were with Tayvn on the field I decided to look for Omascus on my own. I ran into your brother and wondered why he wasn't at school. I followed him, you know, to make sure everything was all right. He went into this shop, the one Sheffer was talking about, and I saw Omascus and your brother together. David has been under his power for a while. Omascus picked him because he knew he had the best chance of getting to you. Your brother had had already tried to take the ring while you were asleep.'

I was pleading for forgiveness, yet afraid my plea was falling on deaf ears. I knew I should have found a way to tell Sarah sooner; I should have remembered.

'I can't believe you,' Sarah said with anger, unsure what to do, who to trust.

'It's not as if I could have done anything,' I tried to defend myself, make her see that I was as helpless as she must have felt. 'Omascus attacked me and somehow made me forget what happened. I heard this weird music whenever I thought about what I had seen, and it made me forget what was important. I know that Omascus was in my head and I wasn't able to fight him. Besides, even if I did remember, you weren't exactly in a helpful mood...you were pretending I didn't exist.'

'What are you talking about?' Sarah said, trying to act as though she hadn't been acting strange and uncertain all day.

'You were too freaked to do anything. At least I tried to do something. I saw your brother, and he was with Omascus, and then I was attacked. If you hadn't been so creeped out and flirting with Tayvn, we could have stopped Omascus then and there.'

I was spitting fire in the hope that I could shift some of the blame onto Sarah. It didn't take long before I realised I was being nothing more than a jerk.

'Maybe you haven't noticed, Ben…or Alexander…or whatever your name is,' Sarah said as she approached me. 'But you've already lost everything. You are dead and I am not. I have to live my life *and* deal with a demon who wants this stupid ring. He has my brother and my dad under some spell. Sorry if it has taken a little getting used to. I'm a teenage girl who wants nothing more than to live a normal life, and so far I haven't even come close to doing that. Everywhere I go there is one big mess after another.

'I know what it's like to see someone you love die, and now because of this stupid ring I might never

303

see the rest of my family ever again. This is what I was afraid of, and this is exactly what happened, no thanks to you. I wish I could be like you and forget everything, but I can't. I have to deal with it every single day.'

'You're right,' I said as I floated towards Sarah. 'When I put the ring on I should have come to you as quickly as I could and told you. Instead the book and the music distracted me. I should have realised sooner that something was wrong. All I can say is that I'm sorry, and if I could change what has happened I would in a heartbeat.'

'But you can't; no one can,' Sarah said sternly, looking at her hands. 'Ben, Alexander, you know what you are and what happened to you. You could go around with nothing to fear because you have existed for centuries and no one can really hurt you. My job is only beginning and, to be honest, I have no idea what I'm doing.'

'Alexander Lloyd Erikson is dead,' I said bluntly. 'My name is Ben, and I am very much a part of this. If anything were to happen to you or anyone else in this town I would feel as hurt as you. Maybe I'm not like the rest of the world and maybe losing my memories is a good thing, but I am your friend and I will always be. More than that, I am the partner whom destiny has given you to defeat Omascus.'

'Ben,' Sarah said a little choked up, I could tell that she was fighting back the tears. 'I thought we were a team and that we would look after each other, but now…this is too much for me…I have to go…I have to get out of here.'

'You are a team,' a voice said from a dark corner of the room. 'A very good one.'

Slowly, out of the darkness, Moon Light Seeker appeared, along with the smell of cedar. Sarah and I both turned and stared at the old woman who stood under the swinging dream catcher Sarah had hung. There was a warm breeze emanating from the Native woman, a breeze that carried with it soothing voices of people long forgotten.

'I didn't ask for this,' Sarah said to the woman now standing patiently gazing at us. 'I moved here expecting things to be normal, and instead I find out that I can see a ghost and I have to fight a demon. When do I get to be a teenager and live a normal life with my family? All I want is to close my eyes and pretend that none of this is happening.'

'Then your world is doomed and your family will be the first victims of Omascus,' Moon Light Seeker said plainly, but without even a touch of judgment.

'I'm sorry I let you down,' I repeated. 'If you want to get rid of the ring and me I'll understand, but what about everyone else who has no idea what is coming? The people like David, who have no chance at protecting themselves from Omascus. Or Tayvn, who will wake up one day to find the world he knows gone. I know this isn't what you were expecting; it's not exactly what I'm used to either. Everything I know has changed. Your life has been rough and I'm sorry that I complicate it...but you need to know that you are and will always be my best friend, regardless of what you choose.'

'Ben,' Sarah smiled, trying to hide her confusion as she spoke to the two supernatural beings in her presence. 'It's not that you let me down. It's something I can't explain. The responsibility for saving the world is huge, and it rests on the shoulders of someone who can't even drive yet. I don't like being forced to carry this burden and I wish I could hand it off to someone else and walk away. I can pretend to be strong, but it's just an act.'

'You always have a choice, and you are not alone,' Moon Light Seeker said, as though she knew more than she let on. 'The test is living with the consequences of the choices we make. The symbol on the book belongs to a creature that has seen the evolution of humans as well as that of mystical beasts. Where there is the choice of death there is also the choice of life. The boy, Tayvn, who wears this symbol holds the key to what Omascus fears, for he is the one the Phoenix has chosen to represent his strength in the human world. A creature that breeds death and despair is trapped in the same town as the boy who is connected to a force of life and happiness. Tell him your secret and he will be the missing piece.' With that, Moon Light Seeker gave a warm smile and the wind picked up around her. She held her hand over the *Phoenix Book*.

The book responded by giving off a dim orange glow as the pages began to magically flip themselves as though guided by an invisible hand. There was a flash of bright light and Moon Light Seeker was gone.

Sarah and I both looked at the book as she read the page left opened.

'Sarah,' I said quietly. 'I'm pretty scared about all this, too.'

'You're dead, Ben,' Sarah said, a little confused by my confession. 'What can anybody do to you?'

'Everyone I care about is alive; I guess that makes me vulnerable to more than magic,' I stated pretty clearly.

'I guess we're alike in some ways,' Sarah said pausing from what she was reading for a second. 'We are both different from everyone else in the world; neither of us really knows what we're doing here in this town, or where we belong. Omascus can affect both of our lives and he already has. I'm sorry, Ben.'

'So everything is okay?' I said, trying to sound accepting.

'I think it will be,' Sarah said as she continued to read. 'Tell me what you know about Omascus.'

'Um, okay,' I said as we switched topics. 'He has some of his powers but not all, he has a shop on Breaker Street, he can make things come to life, he's really ugly…'

'How strong do you think his magic is?' Sarah asked as though she was planning things in her head. 'And he looks physical…unlike you, he can be touched.'

'Yeah, that wolf could touch him and Omascus was able to touch things and be seen by normal people.' I was catching on. 'As soon as the bat and I were out the window the bat stopped being alive. He must only have a short range for his powers.'

'Right,' Sarah said as she pieced things together. 'And Moon Light Seeker says that he's scared of Tayvn.'

'Wait a second,' I said as something struck me. 'If I were Omascus, why would I waste my time controlling your brother and attacking me when I could have used my magic to get you to give me the ring?'

'Maybe the ring gives me some shielding against his magic,' Sarah said excitedly. 'And with the spell Moon Light Seeker left us, I think that we might have a chance at stopping him.'

'But we'll need to find him first, not to mention get David to safety,' I pointed out, trying to stop Sarah from rushing into things.

'The Fun Shoppe sounds like a good place to look for him, and I think I might have a plan,' Sarah said confidently. 'Do you remember where the store is?'

'I don't think I could forget,' I said, hoping Sarah would fill me in on what was going through her mind. Carefully she placed the thick book into her bag and looked at her watch; it was almost eleven at night.

'I have a plan that might work,' she said, 'but first we have to find Tayvn. As Moon Light Seeker says, we have a secret to tell him. One I should have trusted him with a lot earlier.'

Sarah rushed down the stairs towards the exit. She wasn't certain we could pull off the plan that was slowly coming together, or even if it would work. We could only hope that whatever we ended up doing would be enough.

CHAPTER 16 – THE CHALLENGE

The first rock missed its target.

The second rock hit the window dead centre and made a faint 'ping' sound. A third and fourth stone followed this, but there was no answer from within. Sarah and I needed to get in touch with Tayvn, to learn his part in the defeat of Omascus. Sarah and I alone would be unable to fulfil her plan, a plan that could as easily be described as pure genius as it could utter insanity. Tayvn was a crucial player and we needed him now.

After leaving the attic, we found ourselves in the pitch black night. The night air was still and crisp, foreshadowing the danger ahead. The school had been deserted; every light had been extinguished and every door locked. After several failed attempts, we were able to open a ground floor window and exit the school. We realised instantly how late it had become. The stars and moon had retreated behind a layer of cloud, cloaking the town of Oceanview in a complete blanket of darkness; no cars or people seemed to be on the streets. Sarah and I were alone.

Without a word, Sarah and I rushed to Tayvn's, following the back streets that Sarah had used to get to the school. We had been busy in the attic and there was no way of telling what Omascus had been up to, so we figured it would be safest to remain unseen. There was no telling where the town's loyalties might lie, with us or with him. Quickly we moved up the dark roads in the hopes that when we reached Tayvn's house he would be able to help as much as Moon Light Seeker believed.

Finally we arrived on the sidewalk in front of Tayvn's house. It was dark and we could not see much of the landscape, never mind the house. All that was visible, illuminated by a small outside light, was the front porch. I had Sarah follow me around the back of the house, where I pointed out the two windows that marked Tayvn's room. I tried to look through the glass to see if he was home but it was no use; it was too dark, and if I moved any closer I would have been smacked by the brick wall barrier that kept me from where I was not invited.

Sarah removed her backpack and dug out the flashlight. She shone it on the ground to look for stones to throw at the window in an attempt to wake her friend. It was too late to ring the doorbell and we really had no other means of getting his attention. Sarah had decided that the games being played by Omascus had gone on for long enough, and that it was time for him to be stopped. Tonight was the night that our destiny would unfold.

After two handfuls of stones, Tayvn had not responded. I assured Sarah that that was Tayvn's room, but even I was feeling a little doubt. I feared that he was staying at friends' for the night or, worse, that Omascus had found him and done something terrible. After all, Moon Light Seeker did say that he was connected to something that Omascus feared.

'Maybe the book has some sort of locating spell,' I suggested, not really sure if that was even something that made sense. 'Or maybe it has a spell that would let you teleport into his room and get him?'

'I told you I don't have much control over the magic,' Sarah said, frustrated, as she threw another stone against the glass. 'For all I know I'll teleport to some other town or the bottom of the ocean.'

Sarah continued to pitch the stones against the glass as I flew around the house looking for some sign of movement before returning to her. As I flew around the corner, I noticed a figure approach Sarah from behind, a figure holding onto some large animal by a leash. At first I feared that it was danger, but then I recognised the familiar movement and I kept my distance. It was time for Sarah to be alone.

'Okay I get it,' the figure said to Sarah causing her to jump. 'I was a jerk kid who trashed some windows. I'm really sorry, and if it means that much to you and your dad I'll help pay to fix them. There's no reason to start throwing things at my house.'

Sarah turned and hugged Tayvn, as she sighed in relief that something was going her way. As she did this I could have sworn that a tear was forming in her eye.

'You have no idea what I've been through tonight!' Sarah said, anxious to finally tell Tayvn her secret. As she hugged the slightly confused boy, Sarah's ring began to sing its song as the symbols reformed to show Tayvn's star. I kept my distance up near the top branches of a tree so that I could hear what was going on, but far enough away from Tayvn's large golden dog, Arrow. If the dog started going nuts, the whole idea of being unseen would be down the drain.

'What's up?' Tayvn asked as he knelt down to pat his dog. 'Do you want to come in?'

'I think that it's time that I told you the whole story,' Sarah said as she followed Tayvn to the front of the house. Tayvn turned on the rest of the porch lights from an outside switch as he and his friend sat on a swinging bench to talk. Arrow rested at his owner's feet and began to doze. I followed them to the front of the house while keeping my distance, fearful of the noise the seemingly peaceful dog could make.

'Are you sure?' Tayvn asked as he sat uneasily on the rickety old bench-swing his dad had built years ago. 'What about your friend? I thought you wanted someone to be here when you told me.'

'He is,' Sarah smiled as she looked up at me in my hiding place. 'Do you believe in monsters?'

'A bit,' Tayvn answered as though something was rattling in his head.

'I saw one tonight,' Sarah continued. 'He tried to take my ring by attacking my family. I managed to get away from him, but my dad and brother weren't so lucky. He has them under his power, and I think that if I don't do what he says he will hurt them. It's this monster that I am destined to stop, and if I fail the whole world could be destroyed. This monster can control anyone and he can do almost anything.'

'That's heavy,' Tayvn said with serious concern on his face. 'If this monster is so powerful and can be anywhere, why do you trust me? How do you know that I'm not possessed?'

'I trust you because you are like me, Tayvn,' Sarah said as though she had been practising. 'We both have secrets that connect us to something most other people wish to ignore. You have your star and I have my monsters to fight. The world we are a part of is something everyone else has managed to forget or ignore, but we know better. We know the monsters that are lurking under the beds...I know this sounds crazy, but since I met you I knew that you were different, and so did my ring. I think that is why it sang to you...to tell you and me that you were a part of my destiny.'

'Is that why you're here at two in the morning? You're going to confront your destiny tonight?'

'Two in the morning...I didn't know it was that late,' Sarah said as she looked at her watch. 'I have a plan, and I need you and Ben to help.'

'Who's Ben?' Tayvn asked, guessing at something. 'He's not really your cousin, is he?'

'It's sort of complicated. Ben is a ghost who has been in Oceanview since the beginning,' Sarah said as though it was common knowledge that ghosts exist. 'He was the one who made me freak out that first day in Tarnal's class.'

'And to think that just last night my brother was having a nightmare so I told him that there were no such thing as ghosts,' Tayvn said ironically.

'And people who fall off cliffs don't normally end up alive and wearing strange tattoos, monsters don't creep around small towns, and rings don't sing and make different shapes,' Sarah responded before making a connection in her head. 'What are you doing up this late? And don't tell me it's because your dog wanted to play; he looks exhausted.'

'I had a dream,' Tayvn said as he looked down at Arrow. 'Or more like a nightmare. I saw this thing, something that was not quite human. He was hunting in a big dark place, maybe a cave, searching for prey. Then I saw him leap upon another figure in the darkness; I thought it was a bear, but it was a person. The monster sucked the soul right out of the body of its victim. I sensed pure evil coming from the demon; I

319

could smell his burning flesh and see his blood-red eyes. When I woke up, my tattoo was on fire, burning hot to the touch. When I looked at the bed sheets, I saw charred marks in the form of my star, and it was then I realised it was more than a dream. Something was out there. My skin was soaked in sweat and burning…I needed to get some air, and I ended up here.'

'I found something that I think might belong to you, or to whatever gave you the tattoo,' Sarah said as she removed the powerful book from her bag. 'This book used to belong to the demon, but I think he stole it from whatever force you are connected to. I found it in an old box at school and thought it might be useful, and so far it has been.'

'You found it that day I walked you home,' Tayvn said as he pieced the puzzle together. 'When I got distracted during basketball, it was because I heard a flood of voices and I could see millions of pictures flashing before my eyes. I was seeing memories of all the people ever connected to this star on my arm, memories from people from all over the world, from all different times, past, present and future. It was as though I was watching a million movies overlapping on the same screen at once, but somehow it all made sense. Through all the noise, though, I became aware of the monster in Oceanview, the demon Omascus.'

'I can feel him,' Sarah said as she felt the embossed star on the cover of the book. 'It's like having spiders crawling on your skin all the time and not being able to scrape them off.'

'Until tonight,' Tayvn smiled optimistically. 'Where is this ghost friend of yours?'

'He's been here the whole time,' Sarah said as she pointed to the tree that I was hovering in. 'You can only see him when you are wearing the ring.'

'I see,' Tayvn grinned. 'So it's really the equivalent of having an imaginary friend.'

'You've been talking to my brother,' Sarah replied before her face grew pale.

I realised that now might be a good time to give Sarah a break from explaining everything. It was my turn to make an appearance. I flew from the tree to where Tayvn and Sarah were sitting. Immediately Arrow shot to his feet and began barking and nipping. He got a surge of energy as he sensed something supernatural. Tayvn quickly tried to comfort his dog so the entire neighbourhood wouldn't be woken. Sarah simply sat back and watched.

'Tayvn, I'd like you to meet my invisible friend Ben,' she said finally. 'Maybe this will make things a little easier.'

Sarah took off the ring and tossed it in my direction. Tayvn's mouth dropped as he saw the ring spin in the air until I caught it and placed it on my finger. He was even more surprised when a purple mist swarmed around a human shape that gave off a brilliant light. In a matter of moments I had once again become human.

'I know you,' Tayvn said as he watched the purple blur around my body fade and I gently lowered myself to the ground. 'But not as Sarah's Cousin'

'My name is Ben,' I said as I reached out my hand to the person I always wanted to meet.

'Your real name was Alexander,' Tayvn corrected me as he remembered one of the images he had seen. 'I saw you in one of those memories…for a moment. It's hard to explain, but I have seen you before.'

'That was a different life. My name is Ben,' I said as I patted Arrow, who had grown silent as soon as I had become human. I had never touched an animal before, but it seemed to calm Arrow immediately.

Sarah quickly explained about my existence in Oceanview and her plan in detail. Tayvn seemed intrigued by all of it. We talked in depth about all that had been happening in Oceanview since Sarah's arrival.

'So where is this demon?' Tayvn asked. 'And how do we stop him?'

Sarah smiled at his eagerness to join in our fight. 'You don't have to help if you don't want to.

What we are planning will be dangerous, and there is no telling what could happen,' she said, but Tayvn stood up and looked ready for action.

'I know,' he said taking on the pose of a soldier ready for action. 'But I want to help. Besides, if the visions that I saw were true, I know what will happen if we fail. I couldn't sleep after what I saw, and that was in a dream. Anyhow, what is the point of being mystical and not getting to do exciting other-worldly things?'

'That's how they explain it in all the comic books,' I said as Tayvn, a kid who had been my hero, was now becoming my ally.

'Does your dad still have those fireworks?' Sarah asked.

With Tayvn on our side, Sarah and I felt true confidence for the first time. Knowing that I might need to be human again, we decided that I should give Sarah back her ring. I said good-bye to Tayvn, slipped the ring off my finger, and handed it back to its rightful owner as I faded from sight. It was strange speaking to Tayvn through Sarah but we got the hang of it, even though Tayvn kept speaking to me while facing in the completely wrong direction.

The first thing he did was to change into dark clothing when he put Arrow inside for the night. It was time for the most difficult part of the plan to take place. It was time to find Omascus and end this once and for all.

The Fun Shoppe was where we would start our search. We were sure that Omascus would not be there after exposing himself to Sarah, but he might have left a clue behind. After all, Sarah still had the ring, and Omascus wanted it more than ever. If worse came to worse, Tayvn suggested, we would leave him a note in a place where he would not be able to miss it. It was at that suggestion that he pulled a can of spray paint from the backpack he'd brought with him. Sarah smiled at his ingenuity, and was pleased at being able to share both her secret and her burden.

Along the way to Breaker Street Sarah, Tayvn and I spoke very little. Each one of us had a thousand thoughts running through our minds. What if we won? What if we failed? Every now and then one of us would make a joke or see something funny which helped lighten the mood, but equally often we heard a noise that made us cautious and fearful. Tayvn was brought up to speed on everything except about the attic; Sarah had decided to wait until we were a hundred percent sure that Tayvn was on our side and could not be easily corrupted by Omascus. That was one secret that gave Sarah and me an advantage, because it was a place where we were untouchable.

We reached Breaker Street and walked towards the store I had seen David enter. The street was empty. It was now three o'clock in the morning, and anyone with any sense was either in bed or at home thinking about going to bed. Together, like a crime-fighting trio from a comic book, we marched up the street focused completely on our target. About a block away we saw another familiar trio hanging around a street lamp.

The comic book had turned into an old Western where the good guys were about to confront the outlaws or, in this case, Axle, T, and Brock. Sarah and Tayvn both looked at each other, unsure of what to do next. Run and avoid them as best they could or continue towards the Fun Shoppe? One thing we knew for sure was that they were here because of Omascus; coincidence could only go so far.

Sarah looked at her ring and thought hard about what she had to do, and laughed at the thought of worrying about human bullies when we were about to wage a war against a monster.

Axle, wearing her black leather jacket, walked towards Sarah and Tayvn, massaging her fist in her opposite hand. T and Brock were following a few steps behind, preparing for their battle. Apparently they weren't ready to forget what Sarah had done to them, and Omascus had found a way to use their desire for revenge to manipulate them into being here. We could all smell the stench of his magic.

'If you want to run, I'd do it now,' Sarah whispered to Tayvn.

'Are you running?' Tayvn replied already knowing the answer. 'Then I guess I'm sticking around.'

'And to think we were just about to head home,' Axle said as she stood face to face with Tayvn and Sarah.   T and Brock flanked my friends, preventing them from escaping. 'We had a feeling that you would be showing up tonight. Guess some dreams really do come true. What to guess how it ends?'

'If dreams come true, how come you haven't been tossed out of town yet? Half the school dreams it every day,' Sarah said as she tried to squeeze her way past Axle. 'I don't really care why you're here, and I don't care what you think you can do to me...I have stuff to do and right now you are in my way.'

'She thinks we care?' T asked. 'She really is a new kid. C'mon, Tayvn, haven't you explained to her how things work around here?'

'Guess those Canadians aren't that bright, huh?' Brock laughed.

'No, Brock, it's you guys who are the dummies,' Tayvn retorted. 'If you had a brain you'd have figured out a long time ago that you were being used to make Axle feel cool. Can you even dress yourselves without her approval?' Tayvn was unafraid of the bullies as he always had been. Brock laughed sarcastically and then slapped him on the side of the head.

'I have something important to do tonight, and dealing with you is not it,' Sarah snarled. 'Get out of our way!'

'You don't get it yet, do you, witch-girl?' Axle said. 'You have no say in the matter. After what you did, we are going to pound you, and your little boyfriend here. We're gonna teach you that it's not safe to be out this late…there's no telling what might happen.'

'You mean I might run into a possessed teenager who can't count to ten without help,' Sarah heckled her. 'Did Omascus get to you through a dream or did he actually convince you to do this? I guess he figured it would probably be easier to tell you to go pick a fight than waste energy doing it himself.'

'You'd think a demon would have more classy henchmen, or at least scarier ones,' Tayvn smirked, causing Axle's face and ears to go hot pink.

Axle had been dreaming of this moment since the incident in the hall the other day. The vengeful feeling that had been bubbling inside her, the feelings of hate towards Sarah, must have called to Omascus the way a lighthouse calls to ships. Omascus had somehow managed to pry these three from their homes this late to buy him time, but Sarah had other plans.

'You're dead,' Axle said as she swung a fist at Sarah. Instinctively Sarah ducked out of the way, causing Axle to miss and lose her balance. I'd have hated to see what would have happened had the bully connected with Sarah's face. By the time Axle recovered, Sarah was standing firmly and glaring into the bully's eyes with a fierceness unknown to those but the very desperate.

'If you beat me up, what will that prove?' Sarah asked confidently. 'I know I made you look bad, but I'll make it up to you because I have no time to fight you.' Sarah was using Axle's greed to her advantage. 'I'll make a deal with you Axle...if you have the guts.'

'Oh,' Axle said, shoving Sarah but this time without much force. 'What do you have to offer me, a dolly? Maybe one of those crying ones that wet themselves? Wait, that's going to be you every time you see me walking down the hall at school once we are done.'

Brock and T started to laugh as they made fun of my friend. I felt helpless, but without the ring I was nothing more than a spectator.

'How about all the stuff you can carry from the Fun Shoppe?' Sarah said manipulatively. 'A friend of the family owns the store, and we were heading there to drop some stuff off. If you let me go you can have

331

whatever you want, and I promise you'll find something worthwhile. I'll even publicly apologise to you three at school on Monday.'

'They have some awesome things,' Tayvn piped up. Axle stopped for a minute to think, and then called over her goons to discuss this new development. Sarah figured she could use the bullies as pawns, the way Omascus had planned to use them on us.

'All right,' Axle said, followed by T and Brock. 'But if this is some kind of set-up, you're going to pay like never before.'

'Trust me,' Sarah said with a hidden smirk. 'You are not going to believe what is inside.'

Sarah gave me a quick glance and, half pulled and half pushed, we were escorted by the unlikely trio towards the store. Sarah knew that the store was probably enchanted; how else would everyone find exactly what they'd always wanted? How she was going to use these bullies to our advantage, however, was still a mystery to Tayvn and me.

We reached the shop and glanced through the large plate-glass window that allowed for an excellent view of what treasures were within. Axle and her buddies peered through the window and drooled at seeing the things that they had always craved to own and figured they would soon get for sparing Sarah's face. There would be plenty of time to beat her up later.

'What are you waiting for? Open it up!' Axle demanded as she pushed Sarah towards the large purple door. I'd been confused when Sarah said nothing and acted as if a family friend really did own the shop. I was half expecting to see her pull a key out and unlock the door when she stopped with a hand deep inside her pocket. She turned around and took a deep breath.

'Hold on a second,' Sarah said, pretending to have had a sudden inspiration. 'If we go into the shop through the front door and I let you help yourselves, the owner will know that I gave the stuff away. I'll be grounded for a month and he'll track the stuff to you three and get it back.'

'Does that mean we get to pound her?' Brock asked his fearless leader.

'We have to make this look like a robbery. That way we all win,' Sarah quickly explained.

'What if we broke the window with one of those huge rocks I saw in the alley down the road?' T asked, taking the bait as Sarah expected he would.

Sarah smiled and nodded as T ran around the corner to grab a large rock in the hope that his idea would impress Axle. I was surprised at how dumb the kid was. He was oblivious to the fact that he was being manipulated to do something that could get him arrested, again. T returned quickly with a heavy rock in hand. He checked behind him to make sure the coast was clear, and then wound up to break the glass. Tayvn and I couldn't help but smirk at how easily Sarah had turned the tables.

'Wait a minute,' Axle said, causing T to stop in mid-motion. 'How do we know that there aren't video cameras or alarms? This could be a trap by the new girl to get us arrested.'

Sarah grew pale as her plan reached a major hurdle. She looked at me and then at Tayvn for advice, but we had none to give. Sarah was on her own.

'You're right, Axle, this could be a trap,' Sarah said slowly. 'But there are no cameras and there are no alarms. I should have known that you'd chicken out. You are just like the rest, all talk and very little action. You want the power, but are too scared to do anything with it.'

Sarah must have hit a nerve, because Axle nodded for T to throw the rock.

The rock burst through the middle of the glass, causing it to shatter into a thousand small sparkling pieces. The sound echoed through the empty streets, unnoticed by anyone other than the six of us. I watched each piece of glass land on the floor amidst the display of lava lamps and electric balls as everyone stood with baited breathe for what was to come next.

No alarms sounded.

Carefully the five of them climbed through the broken window, making sure not to cut themselves. I, of course, could slip in through the walls without a problem. As Axle, T and Brock sifted through the merchandise, Sarah, Tayvn, and I approached the back curtain where I had first seen the monster. Slowly Sarah pulled the thick velvet curtain aside and braced herself for whatever hideous things lurked on the other side. I held my breath, but deep down I felt that something was missing.

The space was completely empty. Omascus had moved his cauldron of purple ooze and all traces of the candles. The magic that had made the room seem so big had been replaced with the regular emptiness of a broom closet. What had been missing was the feeling of dread Omascus always made me feel when he was close by. Now what?

Sarah and I walked out of the back room with our heads hung low because of our failure. We didn't even realise that Tayvn wasn't with us; he had remained motionless behind the curtain. As we pushed past the thick curtain we saw Axle, T, and Brock standing frozen in fear. Their eyes were bulging and their skin was whiter than snow, as if all of the blood in their body was pooling down by their feet. Sarah and I turned to see what was causing them such fear, and were not surprised to see Omascus in his natural form — red leathery skin, sharp pointed teeth, and powerful claws. It was weird, but by now the two of us were getting so used to the ugliness of Omascus that the sight of him barely fazed us; only the fact that he wanted to destroy us caused the fright. It was as though we had watched the same part in a horror movie so many times that it no longer bothered us, and in some ways it even seemed funny.

There was something different about Omascus this time. He looked as though he wasn't completely there. He was more like a projection on glass; you could see him, but you could also see right through him, as though he was made of air. He was completely transparent, but he was still enough to scare the daylights out of the three goons; in fact, I think Brock was beginning to cry.

Omascus began to release a deep growl, his trademark noise, and that was enough to send Axle and her lackeys over the edge. The three of them screamed as they ran out of the store window in an almost comical way and tore down the street, too scared to look back. Omascus chuckled at the feebleness of the three bullies who had terrorised Oceanview before his return.

Meanwhile Sarah and I bravely stood our ground.

'I've always loved bullies,' Omascus chuckled as though Sarah and I were old friends and not his enemies. 'They never cease to entertain me. Their souls are weak, yet I always feel tremendous gratification in having them do my dirty work and then sucking out their very life forces.' Omascus grinned, showing his teeth as though he was savouring his next meal.

'I want my brother and dad back to normal, Omascus!' Sarah demanded of the beast.

'What? You break into my shop and then make demands? I had no idea you modern children were so rude!' Omascus snickered as he passed a partially see-through hand towards Sarah's face. 'I know what you are thinking, my dear.'

'You have no idea,' Sarah muttered under her breath.

'If I were you I would be thinking of a spell to get rid of me, but as you can see I am not really here.' Omascus floated around the store and looked at the shards of glass that were once his storefront window. 'Masters of magic such as myself have mastered the art of spiritual communication…what you see is nothing more than a projection being sent directly into your head.'

'Yeah, because that sounds so much easier than picking up a phone,' I said unheard and unnoticed by the demon. I then flew towards him to get a closer look at the apparition he was projecting. In a moment he spun around and swatted at the air, as though I was a bug.

'I can sense you even as I sense this boy,' the demon snarled as he looked directly at where I was floating. 'Haven't you figured it out yet boy? You are powerless to stop me. If I must kill you again, I am more than ready.'

The demon was laughing as he turned his attention back to Sarah. His deep-set eyes looked as though they were reading deep into her mind.

'I guess after all those years of sleep you've forgotten that he and Moon Light Seeker stopped you once before,' Sarah fired back at the beast. One could only guess what was going through his mind as he crumpled his face as though ready to lash out in revenge. 'Good will always beat evil, and in this situation we will always beat you.'

'You simply do not understand that I am beyond such petty things,' Omascus replied carelessly. 'I do not care about what you believe any more than I care about those broken bits of glass or this town. I am no more a monster than most human beings are when it comes to the things they value. I have seen what has happened on this planet while I have been buried, and I am surprised that it was all the work of humans. You really are simple creatures, easy to anger and even easier to control.'

'Save it, Omascus!' Sarah snapped, red with anger. 'We know all about you and your lies. Now give me back my brother and dad!'

Sarah and I were both frightened by the direction this conversation was going. Omascus was up to something, all right, but neither of us knew what. It was only then that I realised that Tayvn was missing.

'You have no power here, witch,' Omascus said, barely hiding his annoyance. 'You are a bug, and so is your ghost. This is my town and I will decide what happens in it. Now give me my ring or suffer pains like you have never before imagined.'

Omascus raised his hands and lightning extended from his fingers, hitting the ceiling. The room began to spin, causing Sarah and me to grow nauseous. Next, amidst the spinning, the ground began to shake as pillars of stone burst from beneath us, forming spires of rock. The demon was causing the whole store to crumble around us and we could not move.

'Shadows and illusions will not scare us, demon!' a voice said, strong and stern from behind us. It was Tayvn. His eyes were burning red as his tattoo flamed right through his shirt. 'It is time for you to leave this place and go back to the pit you crawled out of.'

As quickly as the destruction around us began, it stopped and faded from sight as though it had never occurred. It had all been a magician's trick, smoke and mirrors to scare Sarah and me. The scariest part was that it had almost worked.

'A new twist,' Omascus said as he looked into Tayvn's eyes for a moment, before he recoiled in what could have only been fear. 'Your soul... its... it can't be. You cannot be here.'

'It is time for you to go,' Tayvn repeated, causing Omascus to growl. Tayvn was not showing any fear to the creature as he refused to turn away from him. His eyes never blinked as they burned brightly. By the sound of his voice it was clear that whatever he was a part of was in charge and Tayvn and Omascus knew it.

'You cannot be here...I don't understand,' Omascus muttered, barely loud enough for us to hear.

'What's he mean by that?' I whispered to Sarah as she was still recovering from the spinning Omascus had caused.

'We are always where we need to be, and right now I need to be with Sarah Winters and Ben,' Tayvn said, his voice growing deeper and his eyes burning brighter.

'Free my family or face what you have coming!' Sarah said as she once more stood strong next to Tayvn.

'Brave words for a little girl dealing with powers she cannot comprehend,' Omascus snarled as he turned his attention to Sarah, almost thankful to be free of Tayvn. 'I will depart, but before I leave you, children, I have a final offer, a trade, if you will.'

'He's going to ask for the ring...you can't give it to him,' I pleaded. 'If you do he'll destroy the whole world and who knows what else?'

'Talk,' she said loudly.

'Excellent,' Omascus roared, pronouncing each syllable with a thick English accent. 'Meet me in the woods alone tomorrow night at midnight and I will consider a trade; the ghost will lead you, he knows where I will be. However, do not try anything foolish, because your father's and brother's lives are in my hands, and I will not have any trouble ending them of their miserable mortal existence. I may not be able to take their souls, but I can rip the flesh from their bones. And as for your new friend, he may not be involved in our arrangement, for I still have the *agrestis* and he knows it.'

In a blast of red light, the transparent figure of Omascus was gone.

There was a deep silence as we stood looking at the spot where Omascus had stood. Seconds after he vanished, the fire coming from Tayvn's shoulder died down, leaving the singed remains of a northern star imprinted on his shirt. Tayvn blinked and his eyes returned to normal as he briefly stumbled.

'What was that, Tayvn?' Sarah asked, showing confusion for the first time.

'It was weird; it was like I could hear thousands of voices inside my head and they were speaking through me,' Tayvn said uncertainly. 'I can't really explain it, but there was something inside me that was incredibly powerful, and Omascus was scared of it. When we went into the back room it was triggered, and I know it sounds weird, but I knew everything. I was everywhere at once, a part of every living object in the world. I was a part of every blade of grass, animal, human... Then it was all gone.' Tayvn said as he slowly remembered the sensations that had come over him. 'When Omascus vanished, so did the voices. It all feels like a dream, kind of hazy and not real.'

'I think there is more to you than we thought,' Sarah stated.

'Now there is an understatement,' I said.

'What did he mean by *agrestis?*' Sarah asked, concerned by the demon's confidence with this term.

'I have no idea, but I have a feeling we'll find out soon,' Tayvn replied. 'Where are we meeting him tomorrow? Does Ben really know?'

'The old house in the woods,' I said softly. There was another moment of silence as we stood there in thought. This moment was shattered by the sound of a police car and its blaring sirens coming closer. The three of us quickly climbed through the window and raced to Tayvn's house. We would not be sleeping much that night, nor were we going to let each other out of sight. Without saying much, we disappeared into the darkness of the night.

'No matter what else happens,' Sarah laughed for the last time that night. 'It was great seeing Axle, T, and Brock freak out like that.'

We found out later that as soon as we passed through the broken window, the shattered glass magically lifted up off the floor and recreated the original clean smooth surface of the window. It was as though it had never been broken. No one would ever know that anything unusual had ever happened in the shop owned by a powerful monster.

CHAPTER 17 – CONFRONTATION

The final countdown had begun, and by this time tomorrow we would either stand victorious or lie broken. Neither Sarah nor Tayvn fell asleep until after sunrise. Sarah was doing her best to put on a brave act, but we were not fooled. It was obvious that she was scared and worried, perhaps more so than we could understand. It was *her* family that was being held for ransom, it was *her* family that would suffer regardless of whether we won or lost, it was *her* family that had already been cursed by Omascus. Still, she acted bravely and fearlessly, as though this was nothing more than a test of wills.

Personally, I was hoping that Moon Light Seeker would appear in her unexpected way and tell us that this was all a horrible dream and we would be waking up any minute. If only this could have been some big mistake that the powers that be had corrected and we could all go back to our old lives. Unfortunately, I knew the truth. Soon I would have the opportunity to get revenge on the beast that had killed me, or suffer the consequences of having my soul devoured.

Tayvn remained cautiously silent throughout the night. Since leaving the Fun Shoppe, he had barely spoken. He had glimpsed something Omascus would kill for…ultimate knowledge. Tonight for a few short moments Tayvn had been a part of every living thing on the planet, a part of his true nature, and it was not surprising that he was a little shook up. He could never return to the state of blissful ignorance that he had previously enjoyed now that he had seen what he was a part of, something bigger than he could ever have imagined. Every time he closed his eyes and began to fall asleep he would startle himself awake for fear of what dreams he might have. Tayvn was connected to a powerful force that had made a pact with a demon, and deep down I knew that he was scared to learn which side he was on. Was he a force of good or of evil?

Josh Sadovnick

There were monsters out in the world. Our parents had been wrong; the boogieman did exist. Sarah and Tayvn needed the comfort of checking under the bed and in the closet several times before they could even pretend to relax. Eventually out of pure exhaustion they both drifted away into a light sleep. Tayvn tossed and turned in a sleeping bag on the floor, and Sarah slept uneasily in the bed.

Once I was certain my friends were safe in their dreams, I decided to check on Sarah's father, to make sure his motionless body was safe. I knew that Sarah had not stopped thinking of her family, but it was too hard for her to even approach her new home. I also knew that my friend would rest easier knowing that her dad was safe, away from Omascus's reach. Effortlessly I flew through the walls of Tayvn's house and sprinted through the pink rays of sunlight towards the McMiller place.

The house was motionless as I entered through the front door, which was still slightly ajar. As I entered, I felt the sensation that the house was trying to

350

help heal the wounds that had been caused by Omascus. I drifted into the dining room and saw Matthew Winters frozen in his seat, the table still set from the fateful dinner. I floated in front of Sarah's father in awe of the man who had raised Sarah, a man who cared more for his children than for anything else in the world, a man who, like his children, had been through too much.

'I want to thank you, sir,' I said to Matthew, frozen in time with a fork still inches away from his mouth. 'Thank you for coming to Oceanview and bringing Sarah into my life. I promise that I will protect her, no matter what it takes. We will make things right. She is a brave girl who loves you and David with all her heart, and no monster, no matter how strong, will change that. Your family will be put back together…I swear it.'

After I was satisfied with Mr. Winter's safety, I flew over to the edge of the woods. I had resisted going to that place for my entire existence. It was the place where I had faced true evil and lost my life.

Tonight my friends and I would have to venture back to the place where all this began, into the woods where the final fight over good and evil would ensue, the place in the woods where no other living thing dared to go.

It was Saturday, so school was closed and the town was slow to awaken. I returned to Tayvn's house and stood guard over my sleeping friends. Tayvn left his parents a note on his bedroom door saying that he had had a friend stay overnight, and that they would take care of themselves. It was his polite way of saying 'DO NOT ENTER,' and his parents respected his wishes.

Around noon Tayvn and Sarah awoke, slightly refreshed yet bearing the weight of the world on their shoulders. They quietly made their way downstairs and found the house deserted. I told Sarah that Tayvn's parents and brother had gone out to do errands and had left a note on the kitchen table. I also told her that her father was still safe at her house.

Sarah and Tayvn ate quietly, knowing that if they spoke it would be about the monster in the woods, and that was something they did not want to think about. It was the eerie beginning of a fateful day and it was gnawing away at all of us. As I hovered over my friends, I couldn't help fear the night that was approaching. The clock ticked in the background, giving a steady countdown to midnight.

'We can't sit around her all day,' I said to Sarah, unable to take the silence any more. 'We need to go somewhere. We need to get out of this house and away from all our worries for a while.'

Sarah looked at me with eyes that hid the depth of her soul, the fears that she dared not speak, the hopes and dreams she was prepared to give up for the safe return of her family. She turned to Tayvn and their eyes locked, as though he understood what I was saying to her without a word being spoken. We were synchronised. We were united for one mission, one task that would determine the fate of the world.

Quietly Tayvn and Sarah cleared the dishes and left the house. We could all smell the crispness of the air as the leaves turned from green to red. It was a beautiful day to all who did not know the truth about what would occur when the clocks struck midnight. Sarah, Tayvn, and I stepped from his porch and onto the path that led out of his yard. Once we had all passed the threshold of his home, a warm wind surrounded us and the world turned misty, as though we were looking at it through a waterfall. The colours blended and glistened as the sweet smells and sounds of the Dreamscape filled our senses. Once the wind had cleared we were in the woods facing Moon Light Seeker. She smiled warmly at us and motioned for us to step forward.

'The time has come for you all to find the courage to do what you know must be done,' the ancient spirit said softly. 'The spirits of the ring wish to give you each our strength to guide you through this darkest of nights. Together you will be powerful and you will be safe. Trust yourselves and let your instincts protect you. We will never be far away.'

As Moon Light Speaker spoke, the three of us stood in the middle of a golden wood, warmed by the sun that shone brightly overhead. Each tree seemed to have a face, a personality of its own...the spirit of someone who had been trapped by Omascus. From the corners of our eyes we could see the sparkling faces of the spirits who empowered the ring, but when we looked directly at one of these nameless spirits all we could see was the bark of a magnificent tree.

'Tell us, Moon Light Seeker,' Sarah said as Tayvn became accustomed to the surroundings he recognised although he had never seen them before. 'Will we defeat Omascus?'

'Only time will tell, child,' Moon Light Seeker said in a way that was comforting though rather uninformative. 'For now, rest...you have been through much, and the adventure has yet to begin.'

With those words, Moon Light Seeker faded from our sight in a gust of wind and leaves. We were alone in the Dreamscape, the one place Omascus could not enter, and surrounded by spirits who were depending on us.

Hours passed in the Dreamscape as we slept beneath the warm sun. Suddenly there was a chime, the ringing of a great grandfather clock somewhere in the distance. With each gong of the clock the Dreamscape seemed to fade. One…two…three…four…the woods grew darker and the sun began to sink into the distance. Five…six…seven…eight…the wind began to gather the leaves off the ground. Nine…ten…eleven…the three of us saw the peace of the Dreamscape wash away and be replaced with Tayvn's room. The time had come to prepare for what was waiting for us in the woods. Flashlights in hand, Tayvn, Sarah and I bravely entered into the darkened forest that had once protected Oceanview, but now hid something that could destroy our small town. We had one chance for our plan to work. Our supplies were ready and our objective was clear.

It was showtime.

Even on the nicest of days, the forest that bordered Oceanview was a dark and mysterious place. There were rumours of monstrous creatures and dangerous beings lurking beneath the thick foliage of green. Every tale involving monsters, ghosts, goblins or evil witches always ended in these woods. This was where I was born. This was where Omascus lay buried for centuries. This was where Creepy Sweepy had vanished graduations ago. This was where my life ended.

Tonight I would be leading my friends into the world of Omascus, a world created out of fear.

The woods were darker than I remembered. Sarah, a newcomer into the wilderness that surrounded Oceanview, was not used to seeing such a vast undisturbed forest so close to the heart of a growing town. Tayvn had been in these woods countless times, but never at night and never to battle a demon. The old tree marking where Omascus was buried lay in the centre of the woods…a place that reeked of something impure. All we had to do to find the spot was to follow the tracks left by the bulldozer that had released the beast.

Omascus had been beneath the forest for so long that his evil had seeped into the roots of the trees, making them grow crooked and hateful-looking as they reached for the sky. The trees were a shade darker than most; even the leaves seemed to be a more sinister shade of green. Maybe it was only my imagination and the pounding of our hearts that amplified the unnatural darkness and loneliness of the woods. Our destination was clear; we needed to go to the remains of the old house that had been decayed and run down even when I had first opened my eyes as a ghost. It was located in a clearing in the centre of the forest where animals feared to go and all but one tree refused to grow. If we had to describe to someone what death was, it would be that part of the woods.

According to the book that Sarah had found, Moon Light Seeker and Alexander had had a similar plan to the one we were about to try. They had forged a ring of pure silver and carved the symbols representing the four corners of the earth, and the symbolic representations of creatures of goodness, around the outside surface. They then placed it in a pure blue fire for a day to bind all of the symbols magically to the ring. Once that was done, they had each smeared the ring with their blood.

The book described how the symbols of the ring at that moment began to dance and sing. Next Moon Light Seeker and Alexander lured the demon out into the open. The spell that would release the spirits needed to be performed at exactly midnight under the night stars. After several days of searching, the two had discovered Omascus's home in the woods and, that night, attacked.

Alexander had tricked the demon out into the open by offering his own soul on the doorstep of the monster. He distracted the demon by fighting for his life as Moon Light Seeker performed the spell. As Omascus removed Alexander's soul, the countless others he held captive were leached from his body and siphoned through the ring as they raced towards freedom.

Tonight that door would open again and there was no telling what would be on the other side.

Whenever a cool breeze passed us we shivered, unsure of whether it was nature coaxing us along or Omascus breathing down our necks. It was dark, cold and scary, and with each step it got worse. Tayvn's and Sarah's backpacks were filled with whatever we thought might be useful, as well as a book of magic, and a magical ring. Even these few items felt heavier to them as we drew closer to the house of Omascus. No one wanted to admit the fear they were feeling, not because we wanted to be brave, but because there was no need. The intense feelings of insecurity and uneasiness were the same within each of us. We were terrified.

We worked through the thick foliage of the woods that had unnaturally crept along the recently made tracks of the bulldozer. Our hearts pounded harder and our breath became harder to catch with each step. As the leaves crunched beneath our feet we could feel the death that lay before us.

The stars had grown mysteriously cold and all of the animals moved in silence. The world knew what was coming and it was planning to stay as far away as possible. Maybe the animals could sense the evil, or maybe they were gathering somewhere so that they could watch three teenagers as the waged the ultimate battle. Either way, the utter silence was deafening.

The flashlights that Tayvn and Sarah carried started to flicker as the batteries magically lost their strength to the evil force in the woods. It had been an hour since we'd entered this nightmarish land and it was only now that the trees began to thin to reveal a clearing, our destination, the scariest place I could picture. We were stepping into the world of a demon that was bent on destroying the world.

We stood on the edge of the large clearing and silently stared. Things were not as I remembered. The moon and stars were hidden behind a thick blanket of black cloud. The one living thing in the entire clearing, the tree that had marked the place of Omascus's slumber, was no longer there. Where it had stood was a gaping hole, around which were scattered the charred remains of the once spectacular tree. It was as though the tree had been the first to experience the vengeance of Omascus.

More magic was at work.

Tayvn and Sarah shone their dimming flashlights across the large empty space and rested it on the house that stood in the centre. It too had changed.

The house was supposed to be a rundown old building deemed unsuitable for living. This was not the house that I had seen. It was as though all the stories I had heard and all the things I had remembered were completely wrong. This house looked brand new, although it was built in a very old style. The house stood high against the motionless sky in the centre of the treeless area. There were large wooden steps that led from the barren ground up to the front door. It was a large, thick door made of a blood-red wood. Around eye level was an old gargoyle knocker which, even from far away, seemed to be sneering at us.

The house was three storeys high, with intricate carvings of strange shapes around each of its many borders, especially those around the stained glass windows on either side of the door. There were large metal spires coming out of the roof, which were sharpened to a point, and large hanging spires made of wood dripping from the small overhang covering the door. In order to enter the house, one would have to go through a doorway that resembled a mouth.

Omascus had made his house truly resemble his soul, a gothic and frightful looking home that bred vile creatures of the night. Thin tower-like structures, topped with slim metallic spikes, stood on either side of the house. A small balcony jutted near the top of these towers and held twin stone gargoyles which squatted as though they were ready to leap to life and protect the house.

There was a strange aura around the house that made it seem ancient and, without knowing that a demon lived inside, you could sense the magical energy seeping from the structure. All three of us could feel the evil that had created this house. We could taste the bitterness of Omascus that dwelled within it.

'What are we doing?' Sarah asked as she began to question herself. 'I performed my first magic spell only a day ago, and now I'm going up against Omascus? I'm not ready for this...I should have been practising. We should go back!'

'I don't even know magic,' Tayvn said, his voice shaky. 'All I've got is some voice that takes over when it feels like it. But you heard Omascus; if we don't do this, your family is toast.'

'Omascus took away the choice to ignore him the minute he took over your brother,' I reminded Sarah. 'And now the only hope David has of getting his life back is if you go in there and get it.'

Sarah's face grew stern. I'm not sure if she believed she could do it, but I wasn't going to let her quit.

'Then I guess we should get started,' Sarah said, as she took a deep breath to steady her nerves. 'Here goes nothing! You guys remember the plan?'

We both nodded our heads as Sarah reached into her backpack and removed the thickly bound book. Following our leader, we emerged from the protection of the forest and stepped into the clearing.

The moment we stepped on the rotten land, a thick white mist rose from the ground and swarmed around Sarah and Tayvn's feet. In unison Tayvn, Sarah, and I made our way towards the front door. The mist was cool and damp and never rose above their shins; if this was Omascus's way of scaring us off, it wasn't going to work. About halfway to the front door, the voices started. At first we thought that they were coming from the wind and our imagination but soon they cleared and became more like echoes from the past.

Each voice came from a tree or the ground, and each voice begged for help. Some were in English, while others were in languages we had never heard before. The voices cried in horror, for they were the sounds of Omascus's victims. There was a piece of every soul the demon had stolen living in the mist. The sounds we were hearing were the memories of the last moment of fright before the demon accomplished his dark deed. We tried to ignore the voices, but the closer we got to the house, the louder and clearer they became. Tayvn looked down into the mist and saw the imprints of faces looking for salvation in their final moments of despair.

The chorus of souls suddenly went silent as one single voice echoed through the mist. It was the voice of David, Sarah's brother, calling to his sister weakly, begging her to save him.

'Could this be another one of Omascus's tricks?' Sarah asked as she turned to face Tayvn. He had stopped a few paces behind her and his eyes had gone bright red; his tattoo was burning the star emblem right through his shirt. The red fiery light was shining like a beacon.

'These are the voices of the stolen souls at the moment of their capture,' Tayvn said in a voice that was not his own. 'They will destroy...they are the sign of the *agrestis*. We can go no further.'

'What are you talking about?' Sarah said, concerned.

She got no response from Tayvn. Rather he raised his hands above his head and stretched upwards to the concealed night sky. There was a bright flash high in the darkness as a single red feather fell to the ground. It drifted down through the clearing and landed in the space between Sarah and Tayvn. Instantly the feather ignited, causing the mist to burn a brilliant orange, only there was no heat. Omascus's first spell of the evening had been broken and neither Sarah nor I had any idea how Tayvn had done it.

'The *agrestis* was a deal made with the demon and those who are a part of,' Tayvn said about himself, his eyes still glowing. 'Tayvn cannot enter that house and he cannot battle the demon. He is a part of an oath that cannot be broken. He cannot use his power to defeat the monster.'

'Then he will wait out here,' Sarah said with authority and the understanding that it was not Tayvn with whom she was speaking. 'Stopping Omascus is my responsibility, not his. He has a part to play and he will do it…out here. I will not ask him to fight the demon, but I need him here tonight.'

'For tonight he will be released,' Tayvn said as his eyes returned to normal and his tattoo's light faded. Tayvn blinked and was confused as he felt his burning shoulder and examined yet another star emblem burnt into his shirt. 'I have to stop doing that!' he muttered.

'Here goes nothing…You both ready?' Sarah asked receiving nods from us both. With the mist gone she felt herself confident and powerful; the mist was made of our fears and we had defeated it. She quickly walked to the wide stairs leading to the door to the monster's world. Sarah turned her back to the house and placed her bag and flashlight on the ground. She was ready to start the battle. She gave one last smile to Tayvn and me before turning and walking up the stairs towards the front door with only the *Phoenix Book* in hand.

'Good luck,' I whispered to my friend as she took each step one at a time.

Sarah stood in front of the large knocker and took in a breath. She looked at her watch and read the time; it was exactly midnight. Carefully, expecting Omascus to do something underhanded, she reached for the knocker. When her hand was about to seize the brass ring that hung from the gargoyle-knocker's nose, the ornament sprung to life. It snapped furiously at Sarah's hand as though there was a miniature body on the other side struggling to break free from the door so that it could attack. Sarah screamed as she withdrew her hand, the sharp teeth of the gargoyle narrowly missing her flesh.

After the shock of the knocker going berserk, Sarah took a few more breaths and reached for the handle. She ignored the growling and snapping of the tiny head and opened the door. It was unlocked. Sarah pushed open the heavy door, keeping her distance from the violent knocker that was biting at the air. Once the door was opened, Sarah slid inside and took my position by the window.

'I'm here for you, Omascus!' Sarah said, as the door slammed shut behind her.

It was even darker inside than outside the house, and Sarah wished she had brought her flashlight with her rather than leaving it behind. She looked around and could barely see her hand in front of her face.

Still holding the magic book in her arms, Sarah reached into the sky. She closed her eyes and whispered words into the still air. Sparks emerged at her fingers as large bubbles appeared above her. Each bubble contained a brightly coloured light of red, blue, or green. The lights from each bubble shone brightly, allowing Sarah to look at the inside of the house clearly. As the bubbles rose towards the ceiling they grew more brilliant.

Sarah found herself in a large entry hall. There was a pale marble floor beneath her feet and cave-like walls that rose from the ground all the way up to the top floor. There was a spiral staircase that extended from the ground to the third floor, which seemed exceptionally far away from where Sarah was standing. At each floor the stairs led to a small landing that was railed in by thin wooden bars. Large tapestries hung from the ceiling of the high room and ran all the way down to the marble floor. Along the walls stood suits of armour which were cleanly polished, no doubt a collection from many of the far places Omascus had travelled and peoples he had tortured.

Other than the entrance behind Sarah there were no other doors in the room, just the stairs. In fact, the room she found herself in seemed too big for the house she had seen from outside; there was definitely magic being used. Was she still in the woods or was this an elaborate illusion?

'I'm here, Omascus, and I am through playing games. If you want the ring, come and get it!' Sarah cried out into the echoing darkness, feeling a bravery she had never felt before. *'Animi Aconitae Lumen Meus Semita!'*

With the pronouncement of the magical words, the bubbles exploded in brilliant flashes of blinding light. Again Sarah found herself in darkness. Suddenly the chandelier high above her head sparked to life, along with candles that stood in claw-shaped holders all around the room. It was dim, but Sarah could see everything, including Omascus, who was perched in his demon form on the second floor balcony.

'Are you trying to impress me with simple parlour tricks?' Omascus sneered. 'I have destroyed witches who learned that trick while they were still in diapers. Face it, child, what chance do you really have? You have no real skill, even less than the fools who attempted to destroy me before. Like them, you too will simply fail.'

With a powerful thrust of his legs, Omascus leaped off the platform and floated slowly down to the main level. Sarah stepped quickly backwards and rested against the smooth surface of the stained glass to the right of the door, still clutching the magical book of spells. She could smell the evil of the crimson-coloured monster and it made her feel sick.

'I won't let you win,' Sarah said as the demon stepped towards her, making an awful scratching sound with his toenails as he moved closer to her. His smile showed off razor sharp teeth, and his horn gleamed from some unknown source of light. Omascus seemed much bigger in person and much more dangerous. He clicked his teeth as each step brought him nearer to Sarah. The frightened girl was within his grasp when he stopped his movement.

'Have you realized the pointlessness of your ways and come to give me the talisman? A very cowardly thing to do, but I suppose that it is natural for a weak human girl. Avoid personal pain even though it will cost the world dearly.' Omascus grinned as he opened up his hand and stretched his thick, leathery, red palm towards Sarah.

'You are evil, Omascus, and I will find a way to stop you,' Sarah sneered.

'Do you not understand, child?' Omascus replied. 'I am not about evil anymore than you are about good. That ring on your finger is the key to power, a key to knowledge. That is all I have ever been after. Ultimate power to be used in any way I choose. I am no different than the monsters of the human species…I crave the taste of knowledge, the power to decide who lives and who dies, to determine what is wrong and what is right. This whole ordeal is about power and I will have it. Now give me the ring!'

'You know the deal,' Sarah gulped as her voice cracked. 'You have to free my brother and my dad to get the ring.'

Omascus released a deep laughter and then looked directly into Sarah's eyes; she could see the true darkness of his soul and knew that he needed to be stopped.

'No family, no ring. I'm not an idiot, and I know that you are a liar and a cheat, so free them first.' Sarah could feel her heart pounding as the nervousness she had been experienced earlier multiplied in the pit of her stomach.

'Ah yes, the deal,' Omascus snapped his fingers and a light shone on the railing of the third floor balcony. The light revealed David standing steadily on the ledge hanging over the railing. 'I have a new deal: the ring, or your brother jumps off the third floor and lands on nice hard marble floor. It will be rather messy don't you think?'

Sarah gasped as her eyes focused on her brother leaning against the thin wooden beams, the only thing stopping him from tumbling to his death. He had no control over himself and no idea of what he was being forced to do.

'David!' Sarah cried. 'Get him down or I'll…' she ordered as the demon laughed even more heartily. 'This wasn't what you promised!'

'I thought you knew that I was a liar and a cheat,' the demon laughed before his face grew determined. 'The ring!'

'I'm warning you,' Sarah threatened. 'I may not be a full witch like Grams or Moon Light Seeker or even Alexander, but I have tricks of my own.'

She leaned against the stained glass window with her arms stretched towards the ceiling. The fear she had felt was replaced by a determination to end this nightmare.

'What are you going to do, scare me off with clenched fists? I believe I could beat you if we arm-wrestled, little girl,' Omascus mocked.

'As you said, Omascus, it's all about power, but you forgot something,' Sarah said confidently. 'Right now the power is mine!'

Sarah dropped her arms and dove between the demon's legs. She quickly jumped to her feet and ran towards the stairs, still holding onto the book. The demon stood confused by Sarah's bravery, moments before a barrage of various fireworks burst through the stained glass windows and circled around the inside of the demon's house-like fortress.

When Sarah left her bag outside, she had also left the ring. As soon as she entered the house, I placed the ring on and became human. Together Tayvn and I quickly set up the fireworks we had borrowed from his dad so that we could send them rocketing into the house when Sarah gave us the signal which I could see from my vantage point near the stained glass window.

So far this was all according to plan. We lit off tons of different fireworks, which blasted into the house, catching the demon off-guard as they shrieked and exploded within his home. The windows of the mansion were being ripped apart as the multi-coloured rockets tore around the interior, setting ablaze the tapestries and rugs as they exploded into various shapes and colours. Through the darkness we could see the bright greens, blues, reds, oranges, purples, and yellows, and knew that we were doing a good job.

Meanwhile, Omascus was diving for cover to avoid the exploding rockets. He knew that in his weakened state fire could hurt him just as much as anybody else in the world. While the demon was distracted, Sarah raced up the stairs towards her brother, who remained motionless in spite of all the commotion happening around him.

The first part of the plan was working beautifully as Omascus ran for cover. Sarah reached the third floor railing and pulled her brother away from it. The boy fought to hold his ground, but Sarah was more determined to move him and had little trouble. Unfortunately now she was trapped. Omascus had recovered from the attack and leaped all the way to the third floor to face Sarah who, without the ring, was powerless against the demon's magic.

Tayvn and I, having run out of fireworks, rushed towards the front door. Tayvn pulled out the can of spray paint he had packed the night before and aimed it at the gargoyle knocker that was biting at us with all its might. In one hand, Tayvn held the aerosol can of spray paint and in the other, a barbecue lighter we had been using to set off the fireworks. He clicked the ignition of the lighter, revealing a small flame as the knocker continued to try to rip itself off the door and bite us.

Tayvn grinned as he pressed down on the cap of the spray paint. The paint erupted into a pillow of fire as it passed the open flame and hit the knocker. The knocker winced in pain and began to whimper as the door swung open. I ran inside, but Tayvn seemed trapped at the doorway. The force that he was connected to would not let him enter...he could not come inside. Once the door was open, we saw the damage we had caused as we watched the tapestries go up in flames and the suits of armour char and topple. We looked up and saw Omascus land with a crash on the third floor balcony.

'Sarah, we're coming!' Tayvn shouted as he tried to force himself through the invisible barrier that refused to let him enter. I looked at Tayvn and told him to wait outside. I removed the ring from my hand but held onto it firmly. Since the ring had not run out of power yet I could change back into my ghost form and still touch the ring. Not even waiting for the full transformation, I jumped off the ground and charged up to Sarah, ignoring the queasiness of the change. I flew right past the demon and slid the ring onto Sarah's finger. She didn't even look up as she began to flip through the pages of the book to the one that she had marked.

'I thought I said to come alone!' Omascus bellowed as he recovered from his landing.

'Yeah, well just 'cause I'm the good guy doesn't mean I always do as I'm told,' Sarah sneered back without even looking towards the monster, whose eyes were flashing madly.

'You could learn a lot from me!' the demon said as he struck the railing, causing it to plummet into the flames below. 'My powers may not work against your ring, but my strength does and so does the fire below which you caused. Face it, dear, you are trapped between a demon and a hard place.'

He was right; the fire had spread very quickly and if we didn't move the fire would destroy Sarah and David.

'Stay away from her, Omascus!' I shouted at the demon as I floated right up to him. 'We couldn't stop you before, but this time we've had help and you don't stand a chance!'

Omascus laughed at me and twisted his wrist, releasing a beam of green energy that held me firmly in place.

'My magic is stronger here than anywhere else, boy,' he said as the string of energy that held me was still attached to his wrist. 'Not only can I see and hear you, I can destroy you!'

With that the energy string snapped off Omascus's hand and pushed me over the edge of the balcony, causing me to fall heavily towards the marble floor. I crashed into it and felt enormous pain all over my body, as though every bone was broken and my skin was on fire. Rather than falling through the enchanted marble I was held tightly in place, as the green energy that swarmed around my body grew heavier, making it impossible to move. I was stuck. All I could feel was the throbbing pain in my body and the warmth of the flames that flickered right through me. There was nothing I could do to escape. Sarah was now truly on her own.

Sarah quickly began to flip through the book while Omascus was distracted attacking me, until she found the marked page Moon Light Seeker had shown us in the attic. She looked up and smiled at Omascus in the way the demon had once smiled at her, as though she knew something that he didn't, something that would cost him dearly.

'They were wrong before,' Sarah said smugly. 'They tried to destroy you, but you are way too powerful for that. But not for this: '*Errabundus Animus Coniungere Tuus Potestas Prep Metallum! In the name of the souls of those you have tortured I call for redemption!*'

As she spoke those words, the magical book began to shimmer in a silver light and floated in front of Sarah. The young witch raised her hands into the air and was surrounded by a similar outline of light. A strong vortex of wind erupted from Sarah and the book that circled Omascus, binding him as though an invisible rope had wrapped around him. Red and yellow sparks appeared in the air around Sarah.

'*By the powers of the beyond I summon the spirit of the earth, the water, the wind, and the fire to make you pay for what you have done!*' Sarah's hair stood on end, as a funnel of glowing energy erupted from beneath her feet and enveloped her body. Even from where I was trapped in the floor, I could see the whitish light that was surrounding my friend, a light that was so bright I could barely look directly at it. She had become completely engulfed by a magical flame which, rather than burning her, was invigorating her, increasing her natural and supernatural powers.

Stripes of blue light raced from Sarah to Omascus as the demon screamed in agony at the magic being performed. Voices could be heard from the light of the energy around Sarah, repeating in unison every word Sarah had spoken. They were the same ones we had heard in the mist. The spirits of the ring were joining Sarah in her fight.

'*For what you have done, I strip you of all your powers and sentence you to humanity from now until the end of your natural days!*' Sarah said, followed by the medley of voices that now accompanied her. The bright light and sparks increased all around her until their glow filled the house, while the blue electric stripes that connected her to the brilliant red aura around Omascus became thicker and more powerful. The wind that held the monster was almost suffocating him.

Sarah's eyes began to glow a brilliant gold as the spell reached its climax. She could feel the energy exploding from her toes to her out-stretched fingertips. She made a fist with the hand that wore the magical talisman and pointed it towards the monster. Sarah then grasped the wrist of that hand firmly and aimed it at the demon. The emblems engraved on the ring began to spin rapidly as a purple stream of pure energy erupted from the ring and struck Omascus in the chest.

Slowly his horn began to sink back into his scalp and his skin began to lose its reddish colour. Omascus was turning permanently into Rex Sheffer; he was becoming human. His entire body began to shrink into the proper proportions of the elderly man who had dined at Sarah's table. The creature screamed in pain as he tried to fight the powerful magic, but he did so in vain. In one last attempt, he yelled and released a large cloud of flame as he opened his mouth. The fire sailed through the air towards Sarah, charring the air itself.

It was a last-ditch effort by the demon to save himself, and it took all his remaining strength. The thick orange and red fire ripped through the air, guided by pure hatred and anger. Sarah either ignored the fire or was too wrapped up in the spell to be affected by the oncoming counter-magic. The heat struck the magical aura around her and diverged on either side of her body. While she could feel the heat, she was totally unaffected by the fire and smoke, thanks to the magic of the ring.

However, the talisman did not protect the *Phoenix Book* that contained the spell. The glow that surrounded the book disappeared as it fell to the ground, consumed by the fire. At Sarah's feet was a miniature inferno that consumed all the pages of the book as though it had been doused in gasoline, leaving nothing but white ash.

As soon as the ancient book was destroyed, all the light and power that had surrounded both Sarah and the demon disappeared as though they had never existed. Both beings were exhausted, and Omascus was reduced to his human form. Sarah tumbled to the ground as her fragile legs could no longer support her. The wall behind her back was engulfed in flame, but she could barely move. The spell had taken all her strength to perform, and now there was nothing left to save her. Luckily Omascus was no better as he lay in a heap on the floor.

'Jump, boy, jump!' Omascus weakly instructed David as he propped himself up against the wall. He then crossed his arms and let out a deep growl. In a burst of green light and smoke, Omascus vanished from sight. 'This is far from over!' he promised as the smoke cleared.

David stood up from the corner his sister had moved him to and walked to the edge of the balcony where fragments of the railing remained. David did not blink or even stop to look at his sister as he walked to the ledge.

'No!' Sarah cried with the last of her energy as her brother walked past her. She made eye-contact with David, but saw nothing other than the power of Omascus controlling him; the spell must not have worked. Sarah took off her ring and closed her eyes before tossing it over the ledge of the balcony. Shortly after the ring dropped, David stepped off the terrace and fell towards the ground.

Sarah tried to scream, but everything went dark as she watched her brother tumble over the edge towards his doom.

CHAPTER 18 – START OF A NEW DAY

I watched as the reddish sun poked through the remainder of Omascus's clouds, marking the beginning of a new day. The events of last night were slowly melting away under the rays of light, signalling the long-awaited end of the nightmare, only this nightmare was not quite finished. My friends were gathered around me, unconscious, one from pure exhaustion and two due to the work of magical forces that had sought to destroy the world.

I hovered helplessly around the three sleeping bodies afraid to leave their side. Omascus was gone, but his memory would never be forgotten.

Lying near the foot of a tree on the outskirts of the vast clearing lay Tayvn, Sarah, and David, my friends who had risked everything to stop an evil demon. Across from their motionless bodies were the remains of a once magnificently crafted medieval house, which was now little more than ash and rubble. The structure had exploded within itself, as the flames that still flickered on the once impressive wooden remains destroyed what was left of the evil that had once dwelled inside it. No one would have known that until last night this house had been magically restored by a demon with unspeakable powers who was bent on taking over the world, a demon who had made the past few days seem like forever.

I glanced at Sarah and hoped that she would soon awaken; only after she opened her eyes would the fear that she might never return to me go away. Until a week ago, Sarah had led a relatively normal life. Then she moved to Oceanview and, with the aid of a magical talisman, she was able to see and hear a ghost. Shortly afterward, she learned about her destiny and performed an intense magic spell against a monster.

To her right lay Tayvn who, until yesterday, had no idea that there were such things as magic and monsters, but quickly learnt that he was a part of the mystery that surrounded Oceanview.

To Sarah's left lay her brother David, who had spent the majority of his time in Oceanview under the influence of Omascus and had been forced to do his bidding, even if it meant hurting himself and his family. Together the three humans lay slumped against one another, with me floating diligently above as their protector.

I let out a huge sigh of relief when finally Sarah's eyes flickered as she slowly came back to the land of the living. She yawned and slowly opened her eyes. She was still weak from the magic she had performed and was feeling aches all over. Carefully she pulled herself up into a sitting position against the tree, making sure that she did not move the still-sleeping bodies on either side of her. She looked towards the burning rubble and then down towards her finger at the talisman, the small silver ring that had started this whole adventure.

'What happened? How did I get the ring back?' Sarah asked weakly amidst coughs from the lingering smoke. The last thing that she remembered was watching her brother walk off the balcony while she remained sprawled on the floor, surrounded by flames, unable to move. She was confused and a little dazed as the smell of burnt timber filled her nostrils.

'As soon as Omascus vanished, the magic he put on me disappeared,' I explained slowly, knowing that my friend was not ready for a complex explanation, not that I had one to give. 'I caught the ring and put it on to become human. I saw David tumble towards the ground and jumped to catch him before the change was completed. For a moment I was human and flying towards your brother. I caught him and together we tumbled to the ground, where I broke his fall and, I think, my arm.'

I remembered the pain that had surged through my arm as the two of us hit the marble floor.

'David?' Sarah said in a panic. 'Is he okay? I mean, is he free from Omascus?'

'I don't know,' I replied honestly. 'He was unconscious when I got to him.'

'I felt them, Ben,' Sarah said as she remembered the spell she had performed. 'I felt all of them, every spirit that Omascus stole. They were inside me, giving me the strength to beat the demon. Moon Light Seeker was right...we are not alone in this.'

'You were never alone, Sarah,' I smiled back to her.

'How did we get outside?' Sarah said as she tried to pull together the pieces of what had happened so that she could find out the end of the story.

'Tayvn was able to enter the house after Omascus left, but he was different. The tattoo was burning and his eyes were glowing as if they were on fire. There was a weird glow around him as he raced over to me and your brother,' I explained while Sarah looked at Tayvn as he slept peacefully. 'The fire literally moved out of his way as he helped me get your brother out of the house. We then rushed back in to find you.

'There was a lot of fire everywhere, but Tayvn did not seem to care. It was as though he was the fire and it obeyed his command. He told me to tear some cloth from my shirt and put it around my face so I would not get sick from the smoke. He then grabbed onto my shoulder and led me up to the third floor, where we saw you lying unconscious. Together we carried you down the stairs and out the door.

'Moments before the ring lost its charge, Tayvn and I brought you and your brother over to the tree, where we thought you would be safe. I then put the ring back on your finger and faded from sight. Tayvn turned to watch the house burn and smiled; he then lay down beside you and the fire vanished from his eyes as he passed out.'

'How's your arm?' Sarah asked as Tayvn began to cough and sputter as though he was bringing up a lung. Slowly, he too gained consciousness and worked his way up to a sitting position against the tree.

'As soon as I became a ghost again the pain stopped,' I explained to Sarah as Tayvn rubbed his eyes to jump-start his brain. 'Welcome back, Tayvn.'

'Thanks,' he said groggily as he shook the cobwebs from the inside of his head; he had no memory of what the force within him had done. He fingered the burnt star on his shirt for a few moments in an attempt to figure out what had happened. 'Did we win?'

'No,' Sarah gulped as she looked at her brother, who was still not moving. 'Omascus destroyed the book before I could finish the spell. I don't think we did anything but get him mad. We failed.'

We all had surprised looks on our faces as Sarah explained our failure. How could all that we had gone through been for nothing?

The emblems carved into the magical ring around Sarah's finger began to dance slowly as a ray of light bounced off it. With each pass around the silver band the dance picked up speed and fluidity, while emitting a purple glow. A warm wind rushed around us, picking up stray leaves and branches. After a few moments the wind started to spin in a small cylinder-like shape before us as red and white sparks snapped within the tight formation. There was a warm purple glow in the centre of the vortex that looked almost human. Within moments the wind died away, leaving behind the Wampanoag woman who had explained our destiny, Moon Light Seeker.

'Nonsense, child,' Moon Light Seeker said as she smiled warmly. She took a few steps towards us and squatted down on the ground in her long animal-skin dress. 'You should not think about what you did not do, but rather about what you have accomplished.'

She spoke as a mother comforting a young child. There was a warmth in the air around her that was almost infectious. Although we had only met a few days ago, our first encounter seemed ages ago.

'You were here the whole time weren't you?' Tayvn asked as he connected the pieces of the story which we had told him and what he had seen. 'You are the ring.'

'Yes, Tayvn, I am,' she said as she looked at each of us with those young yet all-knowing eyes. 'It is very nice to see you all again; you should be proud.'

'But the spell I didn't finish it, and Omascus still had the power to disappear,' Sarah explained as tears began to well in her eyes. 'And he was still able to order David off the ledge. We failed everyone.'

'Wrong,' Moon Light Seeker said bluntly, though she continued to smile. 'The spell might not have been completed, but you did many other wonderful things. Without any help from me, you found a powerful ally, you have found your brother, and you have trapped Omascus in human form. The spell was not completed, but enough of it was finished to make Omascus human whenever the sun is in the sky overhead. At night he will be restored to his demon state but, for now, he is half-human and no stronger or more dangerous than any other human on the planet. You have done extremely well, and have made a great leap towards ridding the world of Omascus.'

'So we really won?' Tayvn asked in excitement. 'That's awesome!'

Tayvn and I were ecstatic at the news but Sarah was still concerned.

'What about my family?' she asked as tears rolled down the sides of her face. 'Are they still under his power?'

'Don't cry, child,' Moon Light Seeker said as she reached into a small pouch strapped to her waist and pulled out a handful of sparkling powder, which she sprinkled over David. 'You did not free your family because it was not your destiny. There are many spirits connected to the ring you wear, each with their own task to accomplish. Only after the job is complete will the spirit leave the ring and return to where it belongs. It was my mission to guide you on these first steps and to protect you and your family, the same way it was Alexander's role to be your friend and protector.'

'We still have to face Omascus again? It's not over?' I asked praying that it would not have to happen until far into the future. One night of demon-fighting was more than enough for me.

'Ben,' Moon Light Seeker said as she reached into her pouch for more dust to sprinkle on David. 'Do not worry. You have the knowledge and the heart to help fulfill your destiny. Sarah, you have the strength and very powerful magic to assist you. Tayvn, you possess a force that you will one day understand and use to do great things. Omascus may be only half-demon, but he is still dangerous. Do not forget that and all will be well.'

Moon Light Seeker got to her feet and smiled as the wind she had emerged from returned to her. The warm purple glow returned as the old Wampanoag woman began to change into another form, a large black German shepherd, the same one we had seen outside of Sarah's house, the wolf-dog who had helped me warn my friend! The glow grew brighter as the light slowly enveloped the dog. It was so bright that we had to protect our eyes as the light formed the shape of a floating circle.

The ball of energy floated through the air and landed on David's chest. It then exploded into hundreds of little lights, which danced all around David, going in and out through the pores of his skin.

The beads of magic grew faster and faster in their movements and seemed to revitalise the motionless body of the young boy. Quickly and without warning all of the smaller dots of light joined back into the larger single form and shot up into the air, leaving behind a thin purple streak. Tayvn, Sarah, and I watched the purple light as it disappeared into the sky. We could tell that it was going to be a good day.

There was a cough and we all turned to David. The boy had regained consciousness and was slowly sitting up. He was holding his head as if it throbbed while he looked around, very dazed. The last thing he remembered was walking into the back room of a store on his way home from school days ago. Sarah stumbled over to her brother and was hugging him as though she had not seen him in years.

'I just had the weirdest dream,' David said as his sister squeezed him tight. 'Uh…could you let go of me? This is sort of embarrassing.'

Sarah let go of her brother, allowing him to look around. He was sitting under a tree, in a clearing in the middle of a forest, facing the remains of a large house that had recently been destroyed. It was no wonder he had no idea what was going on.

'I missed you, Elf,' Sarah said as she beamed at him. 'It's good to have you back.'

'Hey,' Tayvn smiled at Sarah's brother.

'You know, in my dream there was this monster and a house that...well, looked like it might have been part of that mess over there,' David said as the confusion and the headache made things a difficult to put together. 'How did I get here?'

'C'mon,' Sarah said, as both Tayvn and I looked to her to see how she was going to explain this. 'I'll explain everything to you one day when you are old enough to deal with it. For right now, I want to take a really long shower, eat, and go to bed.'

Sarah slowly got to her feet and, with Tayvn's help, got her brother up as well. Together, with their arms around each other for support, the three humans entered the woods that were now alive with the noise of the animals going about whatever it is they do. The

401

battle had been won and we had earned ourselves a little rest and relaxation. I watched as my friends entered the now-friendly forest and smiled. I looked over at the burned wood and brick behind me and thought hard about the days that had passed and the things we had done. Everything would be different now, but I had confidence that we were ready. The town of Oceanview had become much more complicated, but with Sarah, Tayvn, and me looking out for it, things would turn out for the best. I turned away from the pile of wreckage and caught up to my friends.

Today was definitely going to be a good day.

CHAPTER 19 – A FINAL WORD

Over the next few days life slowly returned to normal, at least as normal as it could be. Sarah went back to school, where she and Tayvn became even closer friends and where she made many new friends as well. Sure, she had the odd encounter with a now-terrified Axle, but life was gradually becoming a little less weird. With the help of her two best friends, one of whom was a ghost, she was responsible for guarding Oceanview and the world from an evil demon named Omascus. Nevertheless, during the day, she could be a teenager and I could be a free spirit watching over whomever I wanted, although it was usually Sarah and Tayvn.

Sarah's father didn't remember anything about his encounter with the demon, other than thinking it was all a bad dream. David on the other hand whined for days to find out what had gone on, but Sarah kept ignoring his questions until he finally gave it a rest and settled for a promise that she would tell him when he was older. The fact that both David and Mr. Winters were okay and had no idea what had happened was probably thanks to Moon Light Seeker, who was now far from Oceanview with her family and friends.

Meanwhile, the Fun Shoppe kept its doors closed tight, a constant reminder that Omascus was still out there somewhere.

Sarah began to dig through some of the old books from the school's attic and boxes her Grams had left behind when she moved to England. She started to learn more about magic and the unknown, while Tayvn tried to figure out what he was. We all knew that Omascus was not gone for good; he was just not here right now. He would be back. All we could do for now was get on with our lives and stay prepared. Our lives on the surface seemed to have returned to normal, but the truth is, they would never be normal again.

In the dead of the night, a large dark figure stood in the woods next to a pile of ashes. It slowly raised its arms and shot a steady stream of bright red light into the rubble. Ashes began to move as they jumped to life. There was a bright flash of red light. The wreckage on the ground no longer existed. In its place stood a house complete with a gothic knocker and gargoyles. A small pile of ash stayed on the ground and slowly started to spark. Out of the burnt mess rose an old leather-bound book with a strange crest printed into its cover. The ancient book floated right into the hands of the figure as he entered the house, laughing maliciously.

Omascus began to plot his revenge on those responsible for his misfortunes — a girl, a boy and a ghost! Next time the outcome would be very different.

ABOUT THE AUTHOR

Josh Sadovnick, the middle of three children, has been working with kids for the past eight years at a summer camp in British Columbia where he developed the skill of telling stories. One year, a camper was very upset because he kept falling asleep during one of Josh's stories so Josh told him that one day he would write a ghost story just for him and that was the beginning of *Oceanview*. Finally, five years later that story has been finished and it represents pieces of the best stories Josh has ever told. Although he is now in his final year of law school, Josh still tells stories to children from around the country.

Printed in the United States
1479100001B/10-15